TIME FOR HOME

THE LONG ROAD HOME

CROSSOVER NOVEL WITH LIGHTHOUSE SECURITY INVESTIGATIONS WEST COAST

MARYANN JORDAN

USA TODAY BESTSELLING AUTHOR

Time for Home (The Long Road Home / Lighthouse Security Investigation West Coast) Copyright 2024

All rights reserved. No part of this book may be reproduced or transmitted in any form or by any means, electronic or mechanical, including photocopying, recording, or by any information storage and retrieval system without the written permission of the author, except where permitted by law.

If you are reading this book and did not purchase it, then you are reading an illegal pirated copy. If you would be concerned about working for no pay, then please respect the author's work! Make sure that you are only reading a copy that has been officially released by the author.

This book is a work of fiction. Names, characters, places, and incidents are either products of the author's imagination or are used fictitiously. Any resemblance to actual persons, living or dead, events, or locales is entirely coincidental.

Cover by: Cat Johnson

ISBN ebook: 978-1-956588-64-4

ISBN print: 978-1-956588-65-1

❦ Created with Vellum

ABOUT THE AUTHOR

I am an avid reader of romance novels, often joking that I cut my teeth on historical romances. I have been reading and reviewing for years. In 2013, I finally gave in to the characters in my head, screaming for their story to be told. From these musings, my first novel, Emma's Home, The Fairfield Series, was born.

I was a high school counselor, having worked in education for thirty years. I live in Virginia, having also lived in four states and two foreign countries. I have been married to a wonderfully patient man for forty-two years. When writing, my dog or one of my cats can generally be found in the same room if not on my lap.

Please take the time to leave a review of this book. Feel free to contact me, especially if you enjoyed my book. I love to hear from readers!

Facebook

Join my Facebook group: Maryann Jordan's Protector Fans

Sign up for my emails by visiting my Website!

Website

Author's Note

Oliver was first introduced as Leo's brother in <u>Leo</u>, <u>Lighthouse Security Investigations West Coast</u>. You can enjoy this book without having read my LSI-WC series. I hope that after reading Oliver's story, you will want to try my other books. A listing and links are in the back of this book.

Please remember that this is a work of fiction. I have lived in numerous states and overseas, but for the last thirty years, I have called Virginia my home. I often choose to use fictional city names with some geographical accuracy.

These fictionally named cities allow me to use my creativity and not feel constricted by attempting to portray the areas accurately.

I hope my readers will allow me this creative license and understand my fictional world.

I complete research for my books and try to write accurately about subjects. However, there will always be points where creative license is used to create scenes or plots.

1

As Oliver Parker raced down the street and neared the corner, the fast-approaching footsteps coming from the alley heightened his senses. The injury to his knee was a reminder of why he left the Army and hoped it wouldn't give out now.

He rounded the end of the building and was suddenly struck from the side by a flying figure hurtling toward him. A high-pitched squeal hit his ears, and his arms instinctively wrapped around the person. Unable to keep them from falling, he twisted his body midair to cushion the fall, landing on the sidewalk with the other person on top. He continued to roll to pin them underneath him, so he pressed their slight weight to the ground.

Straightening his elbows, he looked down, stunned to see that he recognized the woman. His body was prone on top of hers, and even though he'd taken the brunt of the blow from the fall, her delicate curves were now trapped underneath him on the hard pavement.

Well, fuck... what the hell is she doing here?

2

SEVERAL WEEKS EARLIER

"No, Mom, it's fine. The woman needed to catch the flight to see her grandkids, and I didn't mind taking a later flight. Anyway, I got an upgrade to first class. The new flight will leave in five hours." Oliver Parker walked along with the crowds of the Atlanta International Airport with his carry-on bag slung over one shoulder and his phone clapped to his ear. He had just left the gate of his arranged flight to California but was now headed to the USO to kill time, get food, and maybe take a nap. "Yeah, I'll see you all tomorrow."

"Are you going to come straight here?" his mother asked.

"Leo is picking me up, and he'll drop me off at your place before he heads home to Natalie." As he talked, he looked up to see he had arrived at his destination, and the USO's sliding doors opened. Inside was a woman with a USO volunteer badge pinned to her red apron. She turned to him with a smile that seemed to light her whole face. He didn't want to appear rude, so he held up his forefinger. "Mom, listen, I'm at the USO now, so I'll see you tomorrow. Love you."

"Okay, sweetheart. Dad and I can't wait to see you. Safe travels."

He met the USO volunteer's smile with one of his own as he disconnected and shoved his phone into his pocket. "Sorry about that. I needed to let my—"

"No apology necessary! Mothers always worry, don't they? How sweet of you to let her know of your change in flight plans."

He nodded and followed her to the check-in counter, wondering how she knew about his flight change status. "Yes, ma'am."

"I'm Blessing," she said, waving her hand toward the sign-in sheet. "If you sign here, Captain Parker, then I'll take you back to where you can rest."

He leaned over to sign his name and flight information, then jerked slightly as he twisted his neck to look at her. "How did you know my name?"

"It's on your carry-on," she explained smoothly.

He glanced down at the bag he'd had slung over his shoulder. While it was true that Cpt. Parker was on the tag, her eyesight must have been better than his to have read the small print.

"Now, for someone as kind as you to give up your spot on your flight to volunteer to take a later one, I have just the place for you to rest comfortably."

He followed her around the counter, heading deeper into the USO. The hall was painted red, white, and blue. A large shelving unit overflowed with bags, duffels, suitcases, and even the occasional stroller. Another exposed room contained comfortable chairs filled with men and women in uniforms, wives and husbands, and even children.

"I take it you're heading home?"

"Yes, ma'am. Well, not exactly my home. My parents' home." He didn't owe her an explanation but somehow felt he needed to continue. "Either there or I'll stay with my brother and sister-in-law."

"You're leaving the service?"

He couldn't imagine what made her think that other than the slightly rigid manner in which he walked. The extensive rehabilitation had almost rid him of the barely-there limp.

"Yes, ma'am."

"California is nice this time of year," she continued, her ever-present smile still on her face. "Such a lovely time to be heading home."

A chuckle slipped out as he thought of heading to his parents' home. Staying there would involve sleeping in his old bedroom. While his parents had taken down the posters from the walls from when he was a teenager, he would still be sleeping in his childhood bedroom.

Blessing stopped in the hall and clasped her hands in front of her, smiling up at him. "I assume that as close as you are to your parents, staying in your old room will feel a little strange, won't it?" She chuckled and added, "Ernest Hemingway once said, 'I regarded home as a place I left behind in order to come back to it afterward.' Of course, I doubt he was talking about returning to an adolescent bedroom."

His brow lowered, wondering how she seemed to

know what he was thinking. He almost answered with his requisite "Yes, ma'am," but instead felt prompted to explain. "When you've been in the service as long as I have, the world has seemed like home."

She nodded. Tilting her head to the side, she said, "Good food and warmth, the touch of a friendly hand, and a talk beside the fire. It is the time for home." She sighed and patted his arm. "I'm sure you must agree with Edith Sidwell. I'm sure you feel it's time to find your home."

He opened his mouth, then snapped it shut because he had no idea how to respond. He honestly hadn't thought that far ahead. He'd stay with his parents for a week or so until he started his new job at the same security company where his brother and sister-in-law worked. Then he figured he'd take Leo up on his offer and crash at their place. But now, the idea of finding his own place seemed to settle in his chest.

"You might be right, ma'am. Perhaps by the end of this year, I will have my own home."

If Blessing's smile could brighten even more, it did. She inclined her head to the side and continued her tour.

"I think you'll be very pleased with our facility. I've volunteered here for a number of years and find that most service members have everything they need." As they continued, she waved to the left. "Showers and toilets are there." She lifted her right hand and waved in the other direction. "Our food is in this room. We keep the dining area well stocked, and if you want something we don't have, we'll try to accommodate."

He thought she would leave him to find a seat with the others in the large room, but she continued down another short hall.

"I'm taking you somewhere special. We call it the library. Sometimes I sense that some need... well, let's just say you'll be very comfortable there."

"Thank you, ma'am," he said, now curious as to where she was leading him.

She ushered him through a doorway into a small lounge. He was surprised because the room appeared so different from the others he'd seen as they passed along the hall—plush leather sofas faced each other, with a recliner against the far wall. The room was empty, and he turned back to look at her.

"Make yourself at home, Captain Parker. Enjoy the room."

"I feel rather foolish having this room all to myself," he protested.

"Don't worry. You'll have a chance to enjoy a little peace, then I'm sure you'll have some company." With that, she dipped her chin and turned to walk out the door.

He stared at her retreating figure, shaking his head slowly. Then he settled down in the soft but supportive cushions of the chair. Leaning back, he felt his body relax.

A few minutes later, a woman walked in, and he took to his feet, moving so fast that he leaned slightly as he regained his balance.

"Hey," she said, smiling.

"Hey, yourself." He extended his hand. "I'm Oliver. Oliver Parker."

"Nice to meet you. I'm Kate Johnson. You en route to a new duty station?"

"Actually, I've punched my ticket." They both sat down, getting comfortable on the leather chairs. "I was injured in an accident and, after rehabbing, decided I could get paid more with safer conditions as a civilian."

She laughed and nodded. "I've punched, too. Heading home to help out the family." She talked about setting up her business as a veterinarian and her home in South Dakota. "Where's home for you?"

"California." He told her he'd also head home to family and had a security job with Lighthouse Security Investigations.

They quickly discovered how easy it was to talk about home, family, and getting out of the service. Oliver never had a problem talking to someone he'd just met, and it was nice not to have to force conversation.

Kate continued, "I want a house. A big one with a white picket fence." Laughing easily, she continued, "I'm such a dork."

"I've also been thinking about buying my first house. I'll stay with my brother and sister-in-law until I find what I'm looking for. Right now, I have no idea!"

Blessing walked back in, her arm looped through a man with copper hair. She made the introductions, and Oliver stood to greet the newcomer, Matt O'Connell. Blessing smiled up at Matt, then said, "I'll leave you three to get acquainted."

Kate was chewing on candy and offered a piece to

them. It appeared to be sour if her puckered expression was anything to go by.

Matt shook his head. "By the look on your face, I made the right decision."

Oliver couldn't help but laugh. She reminded him of his sister-in-law. "That's what I thought, too."

Kate asked Matt where he was heading, and Oliver noted Matt's smile seemed to droop slightly. "Home. To Pine Ridge, Pennsylvania. You?"

"Home also. Hollister, South Dakota."

As Matt's gaze landed on him, Oliver replied, "Also home. California."

They settled on the seats when Matt looked back toward the door and asked about Blessing.

Kate immediately spoke up. "She's awesome in the most amazing way. Whatever she told you, take it to heart." When Oliver just looked at her, she explained that she had met Blessing before. "She's always right. Don't fight it. Just take the advice and run with it."

Oliver thought of her quote about home and nodded.

"How did you know she gave me advice?" Matt asked, his eyes narrowing in what looked like suspicion.

"She did, didn't she?" Kate asked Matt, then looked over at Oliver. "To you, too?"

"Something like that."

Matt mumbled about Blessing being odd, but Kate just laughed. "Maybe, but in the best way possible."

Blessing walked in again, this time with a man whose gait was stiff and slow. "Well, Corey, this is the best place for you to rest a bit." She made the introductions and mentioned that everyone was heading home after leaving the military.

Oliver rubbed his knee absentmindedly as Corey sat down carefully. They eyed each other, both silently acknowledging their injuries.

When asked about home, Corey replied, "Some place no one has ever heard of in Upstate New York."

"What happened?" he asked, nodding to Corey's leg.

Corey pulled out a bottle of medication. "My FOB blew up."

Corey didn't elaborate, so Oliver simply nodded. He went out to get some water, and when he came back into the room, Blessing was returning with another man.

"Oh, I'm glad Kate told you where the refreshments are." Blessing smiled widely. "Anyway, this is Kai." She ushered him to the recliner, saying it would be good for his back.

Kai frowned. "I didn't say I had a back injury."

"Didn't you? How else would I have known?" She patted him on the arm before leaving.

Kate offered Kai a piece of her sour candy, but Oliver warned him. "That shit is a silent killer."

Kai shook his head, then replied when asked where he was heading. "Tennessee. I have some things to do there." He leaned back and sighed.

Corey tossed back his medicine. "Anti-inflammatory pills only go so far."

"Truth," Kai mumbled.

"God, I hear you," Oliver agreed.

The five talked for a while, exchanging information,

but soon Kai fell asleep, and Corey pulled up a movie on his phone. Matt pulled out a pack of cards and invited Oliver to a game of spades. Matt relaxed, and the two laughed over their pitiful attempts to one-up each other.

He lost track of time when suddenly, Kate stood and grabbed her backpack. Before goodbyes, she reminded them to listen to Blessing, and he offered a chin lift in agreement. He had no idea what she'd said to the others, but considering he was ready for home, he had every intention of finding what he was looking for.

3

Oliver emerged from the bustling terminal of the San Jose airport. His grip was firm on the handle of his luggage, reclaimed from the chaotic carousel scene. As he walked out of the airport, he was greeted with bright lights breaking through the shroud of the dark night. Having taken the later flight, he didn't land until the wee hours of the morning but was surprised he slept for a few hours since he enjoyed the spacious comfort of first class.

In the airport's hive of activity, people milled around. Some called out greetings of joyous reunions to those they met. Some stumbled sleepily with heavy steps as they made their way to the parking lot. Young families wrangled children caught between curiosity and fatigue as they blinked in the bright streetlights. Taxi drivers lined up in anticipation, ready to receive their charges.

Amid the nighttime arrivals, Oliver's gaze locked onto a figure that stood out from the crowd. Leo was an easily recognizable beacon, considering he was taller than anyone else around. Oliver was six feet two inches, but Leo had been their high school basketball star at two inches taller.

"Bro!" Leo called out, his long legs eating up the distance between the two men. Their arms wrapped around each other, and hardy back slaps ensued. It was more than just a familiar greeting between siblings. Oliver felt the warm hug deep into his bones.

"Is this it?" Leo asked when they finally released each other and stared down at the luggage behind Oliver.

"That's it for now. The Army is moving some other boxes, and I'm having them shipped to Mom and Dad's place."

Leo leaned over to grab one suitcase, and Oliver carried his duffel as they headed into the parking garage. Seeing Leo's new SUV reminded Oliver that purchasing a vehicle was at the top of his list of things to accomplish this week.

"Are your plans still the same?" Leo asked as they stowed the luggage and climbed into his SUV.

He stretched his legs comfortably in the passenger seat. "Yeah. I'll stay with Mom and Dad this week, and that will give me a chance to check on them, get some of Mom's good home cooking, and buy a set of wheels. Then I'll head down to your place this weekend if the invite still stands."

Leo nodded as he pulled smoothly into the line of traffic leaving the airport, and they were soon on the highway. The airport lights faded into the distance, and the night wrapped around them. His brother glanced at him, and a mischievous grin spread across his face. "Are you implying that Natalie's cooking doesn't measure up to your high standards?"

Oliver chuckled and shook his head. "You married a great woman, bro. And the fact that she can put up with you and bake like she's competing on a gourmet show is even better. But let's be honest—Natalie can't cook worth a damn!"

Their laughter filled the vehicle. "She can't wait till you're home with us. She's already planning on what to bake since she knows you've got a sweet tooth. Your sweet tooth is legendary in the family."

His brother had served on a Delta team, and his wife, also in the Army, was support on the same team. She left the Army a few months after Leo had, and while they had been friends for ten years, they hadn't acted on their mutual attraction until they were both out of the military. Then it didn't take long for her to get a job with LSIWC, working alongside her husband. Soon, Oliver would also be working with them. It was well known that Natalie couldn't cook, didn't plan on learning, and didn't care. But when it came to deserts, she could bake.

"It'll be good to crash with you and Natalie for a little while as I get used to the new job. And give me a chance to check out the real estate."

"Are you planning on buying soon? I thought you were just going to rent a place to live."

Oliver shrugged but couldn't get Blessing's quote out of his mind. *It is time for home.* "I'm not sure exactly what I need to do, but if I'm staying in the area, I don't want my money to flood into rent if I can find a good place to buy."

"Real estate isn't too bad right now. I can give you the name of the real estate agent who Natalie and I used. Plus, you can do a lot of preliminary research on the internet."

"Sounds good."

They settled into easy conversations about work, sports, Oliver's continued PT, and a few of the cases Leo was working on. Their parents didn't live too far out of the city, and soon Leo pulled into their driveway. Despite the late hour, he wasn't surprised to see the front door open and his dad standing behind the screen door. Filled with a profound sense of homecoming, Oliver waved as he climbed out.

"Go on. I'll get your bags," Leo offered, heading to the back of the SUV.

As soon as Oliver stepped onto the front porch, his dad threw open the door and offered him a hug. Looking beyond his dad's shoulder, he spied his mother. Her trim body was wrapped in the thick, fluffy robe he bought her last Christmas. Her smile was bright as she stood with her arms stretched wide. Leaving his dad's embrace, he entered the house and hugged his mom, lifting her off her feet.

She laughed and clutched his jaws as her motherly gaze intently peered over him as though to assure herself that he was whole.

Leo stepped inside the house just long enough to greet his parents and hug Oliver goodbye. "I'm gonna head home to Natalie, but we'll see you next weekend."

"Thanks for picking me up, Leo."

"No problem, bro." The two siblings hugged once more, and then Leo headed outside.

Once the front door was shut and secured, Oliver was enveloped in the familiar comfort of his childhood home. Turning to his parents, he said, "You two need to get to bed. It's the middle of the night."

"Are you hinting that I need my beauty rest?" his mom quipped, her smile warm but showing signs of fatigue.

Grinning, he shook his head. "Nope, Mom. You're beautiful just as you are." Jerking his head toward his dad, he lifted his brows. "But this old man…"

His dad laughed and gripped Oliver's shoulder. "I'm not as young as my handsome boys are, but then, I wasn't too bad back in my day."

"All my men are handsome!" his mom declared. She stepped over to Oliver and reached up to pat his cheek. "Your room is ready, sweetheart. If you need anything, just—"

"Don't worry about me, Mom. Just being home is good enough, and I know where everything is if I need something." He bent to kiss her cheek, the delicate scent of her lotion filling his senses.

She smiled, and then his dad reached out to her. Oliver watched his parents walk hand in hand, disappearing into their first-floor bedroom.

He hoisted his luggage and ascended the stairs, realizing with each step that he was more tired than he'd thought. The stairs creaked, and he remembered times when he and Leo tried to sneak downstairs for midnight snacks without getting caught. He chuckled as the familiar creaks and groans of the old house were like whispers of welcome.

While he'd love to flop onto the bed, lured by the comfortable mattress and soft sheets, he needed to wash off the travel grime that clung to his skin. Finding the fully-stocked bathroom, he quickly scrubbed his body and washed his hair, allowing the water to sluice away the day's event. Pulling on boxers and a clean T-shirt, he brushed his teeth and headed across the hall. He wondered if it would take long to fall asleep, but just like every time he visited his parents' home, sweet memories of good times filled his mind, and he quickly dropped off.

As morning light crept through the slit of the curtains, his eyes blinked open, and he immediately recognized where he was. It didn't matter that for years his nights had been in college dorms, Army bases, on missions in huts or out in the open, in helicopters, and anywhere else imaginable. Something about waking up in his childhood room was always familiar.

He rolled over in the double bed, his gaze moving around the room. The transformation from a teenager's sanctuary to a guest room was tasteful, with floral curtains, a matching bedspread, and a multi-patterned rug in various colors of blue on the floor. A comfortable, padded chair replaced his old desk with a floor lamp next to it. Gone were the posters from his walls of sports, military, and even whichever big-breasted actress had been the muse of his teenage wet dreams. A more adult aesthetic with framed family photographs had replaced the remnants of his teenage years. He grinned, grateful his parents hadn't tried to make a shrine out of his or Leo's bedrooms. The space had evolved, much like him. He chuckled, remembering Blessing's comment about Ernest Hemingway. "Yeah, no way old Ernest was talking about this room."

He stretched his arms over his head, his hands hitting the headboard. As his fingers felt the solid wood above him, his feet dangled over the end of the bed. He wasn't about to complain about the accommodations, but he'd stayed in a hotel for the past week as he completed everything for out-processing and his final physical therapy appointment. The hotel was not extravagant, but he'd enjoyed the luxury of a king-size bed. It underscored the newfound realization that he needed to buy furniture of his own and placed a king-size bed on his list of necessities.

He walked across the hall into the bathroom and soon stood underneath the shower's hot spray. Invigorated when he returned to his room, he dressed casually in jeans and a T-shirt. His mind cast back to the four service members he'd met the day before at the USO. Hoping they'd arrived at their destinations, he grabbed his phone from the nightstand and fired off a quick group text. While it might seem strange to send a text to new acquaintances, his mother used to say that he could make friends quicker than anyone she'd ever known.

As he descended the stairs, the comforting aroma of bacon and coffee propelled him toward the kitchen faster. His parents were early risers, and even with his late-night arrival, his mother was at the stove, and his dad was pouring coffee. Greeting both, they were soon sitting at the table, where he filled his parents in on the last of his rehabilitation. He could tell from the expression on his mom's face that the subject distressed her. Hell, it distressed him. Not that he had to get out of the Army, but the idea that he could've been killed in the helicopter crash. He navigated the conversation, focusing on the future.

"Do you still want to buy an SUV?" his dad asked.

Swallowing, he nodded. "Yeah. If I can borrow your truck to get to the car dealership, I think I'll go ahead and buy one today."

"Do you want any company?"

He looked up to see a smile on his mom's face before turning to his dad and grinning. "Absolutely." Turning back to his mom, he asked, "Is there anything you need me to get while we're out today?"

"No, you two go take care of your vehicle purchase. I need to run errands, but I'll be home long before you. If you want to grab some lunch while you're out, then I won't worry about fixing anything until dinnertime."

With the day's plans in place, Oliver finished his breakfast, then helped his mom clean the kitchen.

By that evening, he had a brand-new black SUV sitting in his parents' driveway, and he was filled with pride as he stared at his purchase. When he'd left the Army Rangers, he was anxious for the transition into civilian life. This truck was a symbol toward defining his new normal.

The ensuing days were a blend of helping his dad in the yard, accomplishing a few items off his mom's to-do list, and enjoying laid-back evenings with his parents. Near the end of the week, he drove a few hours to the nearest Veterans Administration hospital. Leo and Natalie had told him that one of the newer Keepers had a wife who worked at the hospital. While there, he met Vicki, who helped him cut through some of the red tape before he went to see the physical therapist. Her husband, Ian, met him at the end of the day, and the three of them had dinner before he headed back to his parents' house.

He wasn't nervous about starting his new job, but it was nice to have already met another one of his coworkers besides his brother, sister-in-law, and boss.

The week passed quickly, and they prepared for Leo and Natalie to come for dinner. As soon as he heard their vehicle pull into the driveway, he bounded out the front door. Bypassing his brother, he raced around to the passenger side, throwing out a playful greeting. As soon as Natalie alighted, he picked up his much smaller sister-in-law and twirled her around. He was glad to see her, plus driving his brother nuts was a bonus.

"Oliver! We are so excited that you're coming to work with us!" Natalie enthused, her smile bright and her cheeks flushed.

"You know I'm glad to see you, Nat," he said, grinning. "But your hands are empty. Please tell me you brought some homemade goodies!"

"Put her down, asshole," Leo grumbled, walking around to them and gently pulling his wife from Oliver's arms. "Hell, you've been here with Mom all week long. You can't tell me you haven't been eating everything in the house!"

"Yeah, but it's so much fun to dick you around by hugging your wife," he said, throwing Natalie a wink.

"You're certainly gonna liven things up around here," Natalie said, playfully slapping him on the arm before she snuggled against Leo's side. She jerked her head to the side. "There are goodies in the back. Just don't shake them, or you'll be eating crumbs."

Oliver's smile widened as he leaned into the back seat to gather several plastic containers filled with what he hoped were her specialties.

The evening passed like so many he knew and remembered… good food, conversation, and a lot of laughs. Oliver had already packed his bags since he would be moving in with Leo and Natalie to start work at LSIWC the following week. Just when he was ready to get his luggage, Leo and Natalie shared a look—one he couldn't define. "What's going on with you two?"

His parents looked over with curiosity on their faces.

"Well, we had something we wanted to share with everyone," Natalie said as she looked at Leo and nudged him in the stomach with her elbow. "Go on, tell them."

Leo wrapped his arm around Natalie's waist, and a pride-filled smile spread over his face. "Natalie is pregnant. You're going to be grandparents," he announced, then looked toward Oliver and proclaimed, "And you get to be an uncle."

The entire family whooped and fell into hugs, kisses, back slaps, and congratulations. Oliver made his way to

Natalie and gently hugged her. Leaning down, he whispered, "Damn, woman. I wouldn't have picked you up and held you so tight earlier if I'd known."

Natalie threw her head back and laughed. "I hardly think a hug is going to break me."

"I promise to be the best uncle I can."

"I'm gonna hold you to that," Natalie said, lifting her brow. "With me being an only child, you will be the only uncle they have. And when you finally settle down, then your wife will be their only aunt."

He snorted. "Let's not get ahead of ourselves. I can hardly provide a woman to be the aunt when I have no prospects— nor have I looked!"

"You'll find her when you least expect it," Natalie proclaimed. "It happens to all the Keepers."

Scoffing, he kissed her head, then turned and grabbed Leo. "Congratulations, bro."

Soon, the family gathering ended, and he hugged and thanked his parents and promised to see them soon. Leo helped place Oliver's luggage into his new SUV and followed them down the road. The drive to Leo and Natalie's house was spent in reflection as he let his mind wander. Their house was the next place he would crash, but it suddenly dawned on him that it wouldn't be long before Leo and Natalie would want to get their home ready for the new baby. He wanted to help but didn't want to be underfoot while they made plans.

Maybe this is just the push I need to find my own home.

4

Oliver lingered in the comfort of his SUV for a moment, gazing upward at the majestic decommissioned lighthouse that stood as a sentinel over the rugged coastline. Adjacent to it was a building he imagined had once held the lighthouse keeper's family. The building had been modernized into the facade of the LSIWC building, which continued underneath the ground.

Old and new blended. Sort of like me.

He had followed Leo and Natalie on the drive to work. He interrupted his gazing at the buildings to hustle so he could enter with them. With as many missions as he'd accomplished, the usual adrenaline wasn't rushing through his body. Instead, a ribbon of anxiety wrapped around his gut, a stark contrast to the confidence he usually embodied. Shaking his head to dislodge the disconcerting emotion, he walked quickly around the path leading to the front of the building.

Natalie had gone inside, but Leo paused on the

expansive stone and walled patio that overlooked the rocks leading to the ocean crashing below. The site offered an appreciative view of the untamed beauty of this location. For a silent moment, he and Leo stood side by side, overlooking the water. He recognized that as amazing as the view was, the work behind him, within the walls of the LSIWC building, was even more awe-inspiring. And the anxiety that accompanied his first day on a new job slowly morphed into excitement.

Leo's voice broke the silence. "You ready?"

Looking to the side toward his brother, he nodded. They turned in unison, and just before they approached the door, Oliver said, "I appreciate this, Leo." He felt Leo's intense gaze burning into the side of his head and turned to confirm that Leo stared at him. Before he could speak again, Leo nodded.

"This isn't the kind of career I would recommend for just anyone," Leo said. "For that matter, I wouldn't recommend just anyone for the Keepers, brother or not. While a Delta, I worked with a lot of good men and women. A lot of talent, a lot of dedication, a lot of heart. But even so, it takes someone special to be a Keeper." Leo clapped his hand on Oliver's shoulder. "It was my honor to recommend you to Carson."

Oliver swallowed past the lump in his throat and dipped his chin. His stoic brother had surprised him with his pronouncement. Clearing his throat, he said, "Okay, then. Let's get started."

They entered the building, and as his eyes adjusted from the bright sunlight to the indoors, he spied Natalie standing next to a desk, talking to the woman who Leo had inferred ran the place.

"Oliver, it's nice to see you," the woman said, her smile welcoming as her hand extended toward him. "I know we've talked on the phone and through email, but it's nice to meet you in person. I'm Rachel. I know you've completed most of the work I need for your employment record, so I'll let Leo take you on back. Just stop by later today, and I'll have a few more things for you to sign."

He shook her hand, nodding. "It's a pleasure to meet you too, Rachel. I'm glad to be here, and I'll be sure to stop by."

Following Leo, they passed Rachel's desk and moved to a door, where Leo tapped onto the keypad, entered the passcode, placed his hand on the scanner, and then leaned forward for a retinal scan. The door opened, and the two men walked through.

"The retinal scan is new," Leo explained. "LSI in Maine has used one since the beginning, but we've just added it to our security."

"I assume I'll get set up with all the security today?"

"Carson will take care of everything, and Rachel will ensure you're good to go with your employment and security."

Oliver's introduction to the inner sanctum of LSIWC under Leo's guidance was a revelation. They navigated through corridors and stepped into the munitions and equipment room. A barrel-chested man with steel-gray hair and a military presence about him was cleaning guns. The man turned and looked at him, then grinned widely. Oliver recognized warmth blended with the security persona.

"This is Teddy Bearski," Leo introduced.

It was all Oliver could do to keep from chuckling at the teddy bear name that went with everything the man exhibited. But with a firm handshake and a welcome, he could see how the LSIWC equipment and compound manager was perfect for his job. As Teddy detailed the various equipment and inventory, it was evident the former military man was knowledgeable and held affection for the Keepers.

The rest of the tour included locker rooms, a gym, a break room, several conference rooms, and the main work compound area. Stepping into the room that captured the essence of the organization, Oliver's excitement spiked again. He observed the men and women who he knew were not only Leo and Natalie's coworkers, but the tight group was also their friends.

Oliver had learned the importance of camaraderie in the military, and that feeling came to the forefront now.

"Everybody, this is my brother-in-law," Natalie said as she stood with a mischievous grin on her face. "He likes my baking and puts up with my grumpy ass! And… he's single!"

Chuckles were heard throughout the room as the other men and women stood and welcomed him with handshakes. Now, he could put names to faces for them all. First to approach was his new boss and founder of LSIWC, Carson Dyer. He was formerly Army Special Forces, and Leo had told him that Carson's wife, Jeannie, was a nurse, also formerly in the Army. He had already met Ian Ridgeway, also Army Special Forces. Now, he met Jonathan Dolby, Adam Calvin, and Terrence Bennett, former Army Rangers like himself. Chris Andrews, Rick Rankin, Jeb Torres, and Frederick Poole were former SEALs. Frank Hopkins had been an Air Force Special Ops pilot and now used his pilot license for LSIWC.

Besides Natalie, he met Poole's wife, Tricia, and discovered she was an electrician who now specialized in security installments. Rank's wife, Abbie, had been a CIA Special Operator. Her brother worked with the original LSI in Maine.

Once the introductions were over, he spent the rest of the day with Carson, as his boss highlighted the vast and varied work ahead. Oliver navigated through the files of their open investigative cases, the security installments they were designing and supervising, and the upcoming security missions already on the books.

It was one thing to have been told the scope of his new job, but as he finished the day, he had to admit, it was as daunting as it was exhilarating.

"I'm sure you have many questions," Carson said. "Never be afraid to ask any of us questions. You know from your brother that we emphasize working together. And don't worry if something personal occurs and you need our help. It could be moving furniture into a new place or coming to the rescue when your girlfriend needs help."

At the last statement, he chortled and shook his head. "I don't think we have to worry about that," he said. "I don't have any furniture yet, and no girlfriend is on the horizon."

"Well," Abbie began with a twinkle in her eye and a smile. "That has a way of changing on the job."

Natalie had given him the rundown on how most of the Keepers had met the women in their lives during missions. At the time, he thought she was exaggerating, but after hearing Abbie's comment, he was no longer sure. Deciding he'd ask Leo later, he turned his attention back to Carson.

As the Keepers looked down at their tablets or the screen on the wall, Carson asked for reports on current assignments, then gave updates on previous missions they'd completed. Several new assignments were to be undertaken, and they discussed which Keepers would take the various missions.

Turning to Oliver, Carson said, "You'll spend this week learning the ropes as well as getting up to speed on current and upcoming missions. I anticipate you'll work with Poole and Tricia next week on a security installation project for a pro bono case. In fact, by Friday, they can give you their information so you can look it over and be ready for next Monday morning. Also, you'll pull an overnight security here in the compound. I'll have you work Thursday night with Jeb."

Nodding his eager agreement, he was ready to jump in. Ian and Chris walked out with him at the end of the day.

"Leo mentioned you came through the Atlanta airport."

"Yeah," he nodded. "Spent time at the USO since I took a later flight."

Chris grinned. "Did you get to meet a woman who worked there named Blessing?"

Oliver jerked slightly. "Yeah… um, sweet lady with an… um… unusual manner about her?"

Ian chuckled. "You can say that again. When I met her, she quoted some poet I'd never heard of. Said that it was all about timing. I thought she was just weird, but the timing worked out for me. Met my wife here, but we'd just missed each other at the USO and had known each other a few years before that. Anyway, Blessing seems squirrelly, but she was right about me."

"Same here," Chris added as they got to their vehicles. "She told me I had a journey in front of me, and she wasn't wrong. Met my wife on that trip back to California. The crazy-ass journey we found ourselves on was definitely more than the destination."

Oliver shook his head. "She told me it was time for home. I believe her, but I'm not sure that was too hard for her to figure out."

"Don't take her words lightly," Chris said. "I still keep in contact with her occasionally."

Ian nodded. "Me and Vicki do, too. In fact, Vicki said that she got a text from Blessing to expect you."

The three men said their goodbyes, and Oliver thought of Blessing during the drive home. He'd wished he would have a home by the holidays. *Maybe she'll also be right about me.*

He spent the rest of the first week doing what could've seemed by many to be mundane new employment tasks. Signing multiple forms for Rachel. Teddy had given him tours of the equipment and munitions rooms, ensuring he understood what was available to the Keepers for their various assignments. The rest of the time, he had been in the main compound workroom, becoming familiar with the various computer systems, security monitoring, and digital tools the Keepers used in the field and in investigations. He'd spent time with Abbie and Natalie to see what their specialties brought to the LSIWC missions. He had worked with members of the support Ranger team, performing the duties Natalie had with her Delta team. And while he'd appreciated their efforts and their work as part of the military missions, he was blown away by what she could add to the ongoing missions to the Keepers.

Abbie had a background in geospatial photogrammetry, and when he reviewed the past several missions where her information was invaluable, he was even more excited to begin in earnest.

On Thursday, Poole handed him a set of blueprints and security schematics. "Look over these. Become familiar with the building, and we'll go there on Monday for a final walkthrough."

He looked down at the title on the file—Bright Futures Home.

Carson looked over and explained. "At times, we become aware of a situation and take it on as a pro bono case. It might not be through official channels, but it's usually something or someone who needs help, especially in the surrounding community. We believe in making sure our corner of the world is safe. Those missions are just as important as something the FBI brings to us."

As Carson underscored their commitment to making a difference, he nodded his understanding of the blend of global assignments as well as community care. When he met Ian and Vicki at the Veterans Hospital, he heard their story, and LSIWC jumped in to assist with the threat to the hospital and the elderly patients. He wasn't just joining a team but was becoming part of a family of Keepers dedicated to a cause greater than themselves.

By the end of the week, he was ready for a few days off. Driving away from the lighthouse, he stared at it through his rearview mirror and grinned. One week down, and he was sure he'd made the right decision... it was definitely time to come home.

5

The aroma of freshly baked pizza emanating from inside the restaurant enveloped Oliver, and his mouth watered.

It was a Sunday evening, and he'd spent the day with his parents, taking advantage of being back in the same state as they were. Now, wanting to give Natalie and Leo more privacy, he'd stopped in the town where an upcoming security installation assignment would take him. Natalie had recommended a pizza joint, and he figured it was as good a time as any to check it out.

As soon as he opened the door, he knew he'd made the right decision. The pizzeria was bustling, but several tables were empty. He had almost got the pizza to go, but with the urge to enjoy the slices while hot and straight from the oven, he decided to eat in. A long opening in the wall between the kitchen and seating area allowed the patrons to see the pizzas moving in and out of the brick oven in the kitchen. The flames cast a warm glow over the chef, a man with an apron over a

T-shirt with rolled-up sleeves exposing his arm tattoos. He called out the pizza orders as soon as they were boxed for takeout or slid onto the servers' metal trays. Behind the hostess stand was a table with boxes of takeout orders stacked with their receipts taped to the side.

The man in front of him gave his name to the hostess, saying he had called in a takeout order. She turned, checked to make sure she had the correct box, ensured that he had paid online, and then handed him the pizza box.

As the man moved past Oliver to the door, Oliver stepped up to the stand. The perky hostess eyed him as hungrily as he was eyeing the pizzas being placed on a nearby table. "Are you eating in or carrying out?" she asked, a coy smile curving her lips.

"Eating in."

"Mmm," she cooed under her breath. "Will you be meeting anyone... um... special?"

His gaze swung back to her. "No. Just me." He wondered if her question was in irritation of using a table for a single diner, but disappointment was not the expression on her face. Hunger would have more accurately described her appraising smile.

"Follow me, please," she said, grabbing a menu and sashaying toward a table in the back. Leaning forward, she placed the menu on the table and tapped it with a long fingernail. "Let me know if you can't find what you want on the menu. I get off in a couple of hours."

"I'm sure I have everything I need here," he said,

taking a seat and picking up the menu, hoping she would leave him alone.

"Well, if you change your mind, here's my number," she said, biting her lip as her chin dipped while she kept her eyes on his. She slid a napkin toward him, and he glanced to see a phone number and her name written on it. She'd drawn a heart underneath, and it was all he could do to keep from rolling his eyes.

A shout from the window that led into the kitchen had the hostess glaring toward the cook before hurrying back to her station.

A soft chuckle met his ears through the vibrant hum of the restaurant noise. Looking up at the table in front of him, he observed a woman seeming to fight a smile. Her eyes met his before immediately dropping, and even from a distance, he could see a blush creep over her face illuminated by the light of the candle on her table. She captured his attention, but a server appeared, standing in his line of vision.

"Hey," she greeted with enthusiasm. "Can I get you something to drink?"

He ordered a beer, but instead of moving to fill his order, she lingered. Her T-shirt wasn't low-cut, but she bent forward, placing her chest in front of his face, saying, "Sorry, it's so loud in here I need to get close."

Even though he'd barely looked at the menu, he knew what he wanted. He ordered his meat-loaded pizza and pushed the menu across the table to her.

"Ooh, that's a good one. Everyone likes a lot of meat," she said, winking. "I'll be right back with your beer."

He scrubbed his hand over his face until a soft chuckle met his ears again. His gaze darted back to the attractive woman sitting alone, and her head jerked down. Even though her phone was in front of her, he could almost swear that she was laughing every time one of the servers flirted with him. He kept staring, but she didn't lift her head again. Just as he decided he needed to get over himself, the server returned with his beer.

With another wink and a tap of her fingernail on the cocktail napkin set underneath the beer, he glanced down to see her phone number.

"Here's my number if you're interested. I get off at eight."

Christ, that's two phone numbers in five minutes from two women who I have no interest in and haven't encouraged. Not to mention, they're about a decade younger than me. Keeping his gaze steady, he said, "Thanks for the beer, but this and the pizza will be all I need."

Unfettered, she kept her smile on her face. "Keep it. You never know when you might decide you want more than pizza from here." She walked away with an extra swing in her step. The hostess passed the server, slamming her shoulder into her.

He sat back and took a long pull of his beer, crumpling the napkin underneath and moving it to the side. There was a time, many years ago, when he'd be all over that. Now, the numbers on a napkin only served to make him tired. He doubted he'd ever find a true relationship that started with an unsolicited number on a napkin.

He cast his gaze around the restaurant again. The other tables were filled with couples or families, except for her—the woman who appeared to find amusement in the numbers handed to him. Like him, she was at a table alone. She sipped water and appeared to be waiting for her dinner.

Thick blond hair was pulled back in a braid that fell over one shoulder. It was the color of wheat, and he wondered if it was as soft as it looked. She glanced up, but her gaze did not appear to land on him. The softness of her features painted a picture of someone appreciating the moment.

Her eyes widened, and a delicate smile slipped over her face as a server placed a small pizza and salad in front of the woman. Her pensive expression morphed into anticipation. She cut a bite, then blew her breath across the hot pizza before nibbling an edge. When she decided it must have been cool enough, she took a bite and chewed.

Oliver wasn't sure he'd ever seen anyone with pure ecstasy written on their face. His cock stirred, and he strangely felt jealous of the cause. He'd had a number of sexual partners over the years, but in truth, he couldn't say he'd ever witnessed a truer sense of delight.

Her eyes were closed as she continued to chew and then take another bite. He couldn't help but wonder what she would look like, giving herself over to passion. His musings were interrupted when his pizza was placed before him. Sniffing the baked crust, tomato sauce, and the multiple toppings he always asked for, he could now understand the woman's look of pleasure.

Taking a bite, he also reveled in the taste that matched the look and scent of his dinner. He groaned, then snapped his eyes open, glancing around to make sure no one had heard him. The nearest tables were busy with their conversations, but when his gaze drifted back over to the woman, he found her light brown eyes staring back at him, her lips curved upward. He'd never blushed when gaining a woman's attention before but could swear the tips of his ears heated as she smiled before dropping her gaze.

Her expression wasn't one of lust but more of recognition that he seemed to enjoy his dinner as much as she did. He was tempted to pick up his plate and walk over to ask if she was dining alone and would like to have company. In his younger days, that would've been a common occurrence. But he was reticent to make that move… he didn't want to make an erroneous assumption that a woman eating alone wanted to be with someone.

A large group walked up to the hostess stand, and as he glanced around, he realized the place was full. He was sitting at a table meant for four. Looking over, the woman who captured his attention was doing the same. And just like him, her gaze was dancing around the room, her lips now pulled down in a little frown, creating a crinkle between her brows.

As her gaze landed on him, he lifted his eyes and tipped his head in her direction. It was a silent movement, indicating a question if he could join her. It was also a self-serving gesture—if she ignored him, he wouldn't be publicly shot down.

She lifted a brow, and her lips softened into a gentle smile. Emboldened, he stood and walked toward her with his plate in his hand. As she watched him approach, her lips continued to curve upward, and she nodded. The air seemed charged with a new energy, and anticipation flowed between them.

"I know this is presumptuous, but it appears they need table space. I was eating alone, but I didn't know if you had others coming or if you, like me, wouldn't mind a little company while we enjoyed this delicious pizza. Please don't feel obligated."

With a smile, she inclined her head toward the chair across from her. He set down his plate and drink, then turned to catch the eye of the server.

The server's gaze shot from him to the woman and back to him, a scowl now replacing the smile she'd given him.

"She doesn't appear to be very happy with you."

As he sat down, he looked up at the woman across from him. "I'd ensure she received the tip even if this wasn't her table. But since she's also the server for this table, she'll get everything due to her."

The woman raised her brows and appeared to fight a grin. "I'm not sure she'll get everything she wants. After all, she's probably assuming that now she wasted a phone number on you."

Unable to keep from laughing, he tried to play off the embarrassment even though his face felt hot. "I assure you the napkin she left me is crumpled and left behind to go into the trash."

She shook her head as she laughed. "I'm sorry. It's

certainly none of my business, but I couldn't help but notice that you'd barely sat down and already had two women's phone numbers. That's rather impressive."

He winced and shook his head, having no idea what to say to that. She looked down as she took another bite of her salad, once again chewing as though she thoroughly enjoyed the simple fare. A drop of dressing hung tenaciously on her bottom lip until her pink tongue slipped out to catch it. The breath caught in his lungs as he watched, his cock stirring at the innocent movement.

Desperate not to seem like a creeper, he blurted, "To be honest, I got the feeling it was more of a competition between those two women than anything to do with me." Wanting to move the subject on, he waved his hand toward the pizza. "I couldn't help but notice how much you enjoyed the dinner. I've never been here before."

"It's incredibly good."

They ate silently for a few minutes while the pizza was still hot and the flavors were at their peak. He hadn't learned her name, and since she hadn't asked for his, he hesitated to do so. If this had been a date, even a blind date, he would have asked the typical questions: Where do you work? What do you do? How long have you been in the city?

When his companion was nothing more than a bar hookup, the only questions usually asked were even more simple: What is your name, and do you want to get out of here?

But since this was neither a date nor a bar hookup, he floundered, wanting to know more yet uncertain about the propriety of asking too many questions. Considering the insecurity a woman might feel at having just been forced to share a table with a man she didn't know made the situation even more tenuous. *How the fuck do I show interest without making her uncomfortable? And does she feel the same?* The ease he always felt when around women was now steeped in uncertainty.

Her gaze lifted from her plate, and she dabbed the corners of her mouth with her napkin. "So what do you think?"

He blinked at her question, having been sneaking looks at her as she continued to enjoy her food. Now, having caught him off guard, he had no idea what she was talking about.

"Um...?" He covered his confusion by taking a sip of drink and wiping his mouth.

She laughed and was even more beautiful while obliterating any possibility that he might discern what her question was about.

"The pizza?" she prompted. "What do you think about it?"

Recovering quickly, he nodded. "It's great. I can see why this place gets crowded." Relaxing, he decided to throw out one of his lines to compliment her appearance. "Sorry to have spaced out on you. It's just that you—"

"Oh, it's okay." She waved her hand dismissively. "Believe me, I get it. The pizza really is delicious. I'm hardly a pizza connoisseur, but I've been here a few times. Well, I should say that I've gotten their takeout several times. This was the first time I decided I would eat in."

"Yeah... uh... I thought about doing takeout also, then decided I wanted to sit down and eat instead of shoving pizza in my face as I drove."

She laughed, shaking her head. "Driving while operating a phone is illegal, but driving and eating can be just as difficult! I've seen some people driving dangerously while shoving in a hamburger."

"Oh, guilty of that many times!"

"I was once on my way to a job interview. I craved a hot apple pie turnover from a fast food place and ignored the warning about it being hot. I bit into it, burned my mouth, and a big blob of apple pie filling landed on my blouse! I was so angry with myself."

Laughing, he asked, "Did you skip your interview?"

Her eyes widened. "Of course not! I had a sweater in the back seat. I pulled it over the blouse and went in." She sighed and added, "It was about a hundred degrees outside, and I looked like a fool. But I needed the job!"

It was on the tip of his tongue to ask what kind of work she did, but she still hadn't offered anything specific nor asked him personal questions. Wanting to keep her talking, he said, "I was once so hungry when I was driving, I started eating a piece of fried fish from a takeout fish joint."

"Weren't your fingers a greasy mess?"

"Yes, but I was going home. And I was too hungry to care."

They laughed together, and the moment stretched

between them as the evening light filtered through the restaurant window and the flicker of the candlelight.

The people from the table behind her were leaving, and as they stood, one of the men bumped into her chair without apologizing. A flash of protectiveness hit Oliver, and he rose from his seat to ensure the man didn't bump her again.

She shook her head and made a slight motion with her hand as she whispered, "I'm fine. They have the tables rather squished in here to get more people inside. I think the next time I'm craving pizza, I might opt for the takeout again. It's getting so loud in here I can barely hear myself think!"

Suddenly, her attention was diverted to the window next to her, and when his gaze followed her line of vision, he could see a couple of teenagers across the street. One appeared much smaller than the other, both dressed in blue jeans with oversized hoodies and knit caps. They were lost in their animated exchange, arms gesticulating.

When he glanced back to his table companion, her reaction to the scenario across the street captivated him. She was still staring out the window, a crinkle now marring the smooth skin of her forehead.

He decided to take the plunge and ask her name when the server interrupted as she plopped the checks on the table. His table partner swung her head around, looked up, and said, "I'm ready to pay. And I'll need a to-go box, please."

Taking the credit card, the server huffed as though getting a to-go box was a huge task. Oliver frowned, having wanted to offer to pay for the woman's meal. By the time he pulled his card out, the server returned with the woman's card and set a box on the table. She then took his card and flounced away.

He watched while the woman quickly scooped her pizza into one box and the leftover breadsticks into another before placing them in the tote she produced from the seat next to her.

He glanced around to see the server talking animatedly at another table and growled, wanting his card back so he could leave at the same time as the woman sitting across from him. Glancing back at her, he realized her attention was once again diverted out the window. The two teenagers were still across the street. She didn't appear afraid of them, but there was definitely recognition in her eyes.

Grappling with a sense of urgency, he blurted, "By the way, my name is—"

Before he could finish, a large group of people came into the restaurant, boisterous as they approached the hostess stand, interrupting his comment.

The woman across from him stood quickly and tossed a small smile his way as she nodded. "Thank you for the dinner conversation." She grabbed her coat, purse, and tote with the leftovers, quickly darted through the crowd, and slipped outside.

Frustration spread through him as he hurried but was thwarted by the large group. He could not push past them in the small area without appearing rude. He stood to the side as the hostess gathered the menus and called for one of the servers to push two tables together.

Waiting, he thought of the woman and hoped he would be able to see her again. He had no idea what it was about the pretty woman who captured his imagination. She was beautiful in a girl-next-door way. He'd had his share of bar hookups over the years with attractive women in teeny dresses who understood the score– one night of horizontal fun, and that was all. He'd seen enough marriages fail while in the Army to figure love wasn't in the cards for him as a Ranger. But now? He was kicking himself that the woman who'd held his attention had slipped outside before he'd worked up the courage to find out her name.

Still waiting to reach the door, it dawned on him that she'd mentioned coming here before. He decided this pizza shop might become his newest place to visit. Suddenly, a scream jarred him from his thoughts, and shuffling feet met his ears.

6

At the sound of a scream, Oliver jerked around to see several nearby people losing their balance as though pushed, and his arms snapped out to catch an older woman who teetered near him. In the chaos, he steadied her even as he jerked his head around to see the cause of the problem.

Movement outside the now-open door caught his eye, and he watched as the two teenagers raced down the street, clutching three boxes of carry-out pizza in their hands.

The hostess was still screaming that they'd been robbed, and it was obvious the two teenagers had darted in, grabbed several pizza boxes off the carry-out table, and raced back out the door.

Determined to intervene, especially at the thought of his table companion being a possible target out on the street, he navigated through the crowd. Passing the hostess stand, he finally made it to the door and dashed outside. He caught a glance of the teenagers as they rounded the corner at the end of the block, and he ran in that direction, pursuing them relentlessly, ignoring the stiffness in his leg.

As he approached the corner, fast-approaching footsteps heightened his senses. He rounded the end of the building and was suddenly struck by a flying figure hurtling toward him. A high-pitched squeal hit his ears, and his arms wrapped around the person. Unable to keep from falling, he twisted his body to cushion the fall, landing on the sidewalk with the other person on top. Continuing to roll to pin them underneath him, he looked down, stunned to see that he had his dining companion instead of one of the teenagers. His body was prone on top of hers, and even though he'd taken the brunt of the blow from the fall, her delicate curves were trapped underneath him on the hard pavement.

Just as he was about to inquire if she was all right, distant curses hit his ears. His gaze snapped toward the end of the alleyway, where a gated fence impeded the escape progress of the two teenagers. They were struggling to climb with the pizza boxes clutched in their hands. Oliver disentangled himself from the woman and pulled her to her feet, offering a hasty apology. Turning, he darted after the teens who were halfway up the fence while precariously balancing the pizza boxes.

Racing forward, he closed in on them and shouted, "Stop!"

The older boy dropped to the other side and tried to assist the smaller boy, who was still struggling with the one box he was carrying. The older boy set his boxes on the ground and then lifted his arms toward the younger boy.

Oliver heard a female voice call out, "Stop!" and jerked around to see the woman running up behind him. Her gaze was initially fixed on the teenagers, then shifted to him.

Worried for her safety in case the teens pulled out a weapon, he ordered, "Get out of here. Go back. I've got this."

"No!" she argued, her gaze still on him before she looked over at the teens.

Furious she was putting herself in danger, he barked at her again. "Go back!"

Ignoring him, she stepped to the side with her hands on her hips and stared at the two boys. "I've seen you before. I know where you used to hang out. Stealing isn't the way. The last thing you want is to get picked up by the police."

The younger boy gasped, his eyes wide, looking between the other teen and the woman. The older teenager grabbed the smaller one, tugging him to the ground. As they stood on the other side of the tall chain-link fence, he bit out, "Why? We can't arrive empty-handed. Anyway, we only get a few bites before we have to give it up."

Oliver's gaze darted among the three people around him. His training had him keep his eye on the teens, yet the woman's presence drew him in. He was fascinated and had no idea how she fit into their little trio.

With a tight-lipped, determined expression, she reached into her shoulder bag and retrieved the plastic bag with the boxes from the pizza parlor containing her leftover slices and the breadsticks. "Come on. If you have to share with anyone else, at least take something just for the two of you."

Neither boy spoke. They watched in silence as she popped the top and showed that there was plenty of pizza for both boys.

The younger boy stared at the plastic boxes from the restaurant, his eyes growing big, and it was obvious his loyalty wavered between the food held out in front of him and what he thought he needed to do.

The woman tied a knot in the bag and tossed it over the fence. As the older teen caught it, she said, "You know where I am. Come whenever you want."

The tension was palpable in the dimly lit alley as the teenagers' gazes darted back and forth nervously between Oliver and the woman. Indecision played out on the older boy's face before he gave a subtle nod to the younger one. Oliver's muscles tensed as he prepared to take action when the woman's gaze rose to meet his.

Under the soft glow of streetlights, her wheat-blond hair shimmered like a halo around her head. Her eyes, the color of dark honey, locked onto his face as though she had completely forgotten about the two miscreants.

The retreating footsteps echoed in his ears, but Oliver knew he could easily scale the fence and still catch them. Just as he was about to turn, her hand snapped out and gripped his arm while pleading, "Don't! Please."

He lowered his gaze to meet her intense stare and then glanced at her fingers, which had now slid down to wrap around his hand, anchoring him in place. A current passed through their touch, as though she had a hand buzzer as a prank. "What the hell?" He wasn't sure if his question was about the inexplicable current zapping through him or why she was pleading for the boys.

"Please," she implored. "Don't go after them, and don't call the police."

Narrowing his eyes as suspicion settled in his mind, he asked, "Why not? Are you in on this with them? Is that your arrangement? Do you scout out a place and then give them a call? I watched you… you knew they were there. Did they watch you leave the restaurant, knowing there was food by the door, and then they try to rob them?" His gaze flicked to the side where the teenagers had now rounded the corner of the next building, their footsteps fading away.

Frustrated with her silence, he propped his hands on his hips and glared down at her. She was only about five foot four inches, bringing her head to the top of his shoulders. *Just where it would tuck under his chin if she were close to him.* Shaking his head, he wasn't sure where that thought came from.

As his gaze roamed over her, he noted her flushed cheeks and the tendrils that had fled her braid. Her chest heaved with each breath. Her eyes glowed, no longer dancing with the mirth and ease they had in the restaurant. She was even more beautiful than he'd thought when he first met her.

However, the days when he might be completely taken in by a beautiful face were over. Right now, all he saw was a woman who may have been entangled in a scam. "Well?" His voice was rough and felt like gravel as his breath came out in a ragged exhalation. Without thinking, his hand lowered to rub his aching thigh. "Are you going to tell me what the hell you're doing here?"

She held his accusing gaze but took a cautious step backward, slowly shaking her head. "No," she replied softly. "I don't think I will." Glancing down at his hand on his leg, she added, "I'm sorry you're injured." With that, she turned and hurried out of the alley until she was back on the sidewalk.

He followed her without understanding why but was pulled along by a magnetic thread that seemed to keep him from walking away. She turned around, her expression carrying a deep sadness. He blinked as he looked around, realizing they were back outside the pizzeria. She threw open the door and walked inside.

Now, curiosity taking hold, he followed her with a purpose. As he stepped inside, his feet stuttered to a halt as he watched her talking to the hostess.

"I heard what happened, and I feel terrible for the people who paid for their pizza that was taken. I'd like to pay for what was stolen."

The hostess's brow crinkled as she scowled. "You want to pay for the pizza those thugs stole?"

"No. I want to pay for what those *kids* took."

A barking scoff left the hostess's lips. "What's the difference? Thugs or kids?"

"I'm not going to argue semantics with you. I just want to pay." She handed her credit card to the hostess, who Oliver noted had no problem taking it while they were still arguing.

"I don't know what semantics are, but I do know a dirty thief when I see one." She ran the card, then handed it back to the woman.

Tucking the card into her purse, the woman turned while unsuccessfully hiding an eye roll from Oliver. She stepped to the door, saw him standing there, and her eyes flew wide open. "Are you following me?"

"I was curious about what the hell you were doing."

They held each other's gaze for a moment, and she sighed. "Did you think I would come in here and steal pizza?"

It was on the tip of his tongue to offer a quip, but the expression on the woman's face had the words die on his tongue. As he stared at her pensive expression, he slowly shook his head, realizing that, regardless of not understanding her motives, he knew she wasn't going to steal.

She pushed past him, walked through the door, and stepped out onto the sidewalk with her phone in her hand.

Following once again, he hastened until he was walking beside her, careful not to have her too closely. "Why are you doing this? What those kids did was illegal, and you helped them get away with it."

"The pizza has been paid for. The restaurant is not out any money."

"True, but only by the goodness of your heart. I still don't understand why you let them get away with it."

He was standing close, and she took a step back, her phone still in her hand.

He wasn't about to terrify her. He was pissed, but not an asshole. Trying a different tactic, he said, "It doesn't matter what you were doing with those kids. All they managed to get was pizza, which looked like they could use. But you shouldn't be out here after dark. Where do you live?"

She barked out a laugh, having pulled out her phone. "You must be crazy if you think I'm telling a strange man where I live." She glanced at the screen and then looked up the street.

Knowing she was right caused his frustration to boil over. "Look, you've got two kids running around, playing a dangerous game."

"First, they're not *my* kids," she exclaimed, lifting her hands in front of her. "What they did was wrong. It's just that right now, all I can see are the two scrawny kids standing next to you." She waved her hand up and down toward him, and then her cheeks pinkened. "You have to admit, you would've been a formidable adversary for them to fight."

"It makes me wonder what they were thinking—"

"I don't think they were thinking." Sadness coated her words as her expression fell. "I think they were just hungry."

"Then why don't they just go home?"

A wall dropped over her expression. "Don't talk to me about something you have no idea about. It's easy for you to walk around and judge other people when you have no clue what happens in the world."

Her words pissed him off, and he drew himself up to his full height, looking down at her. "Lady, I served as an Army Ranger all over the world. Don't tell me I don't know what goes on. I've been in shit holes you could never even imagine."

If he thought she was going to be intimidated, he was wrong. She also drew herself up to her full height, much shorter than he, yet he felt as though she was looking down on him.

"You may know what goes on in those *shit holes*, as you call them." She pointed at the ground with a jerking motion and added, "But you need to educate yourself on what goes on right here in your own backyard."

He opened his mouth to refute her claim but couldn't find any words. For a moment, they simply stared at each other. He wished he could say he didn't notice the way her chest moved as she breathed heavily, and he couldn't deny that he was interested. Right now, everything about the woman equally frustrated and fascinated him. "Then educate me." The words slipped out before he could think them through.

Her shoulders slumped as she slowly shook her head. "I'm not sure there are enough hours in the day to educate you." Her voice was now soft and filled with what sounded like a touch of exhaustion.

Once again, frustration filled him, and he scrubbed his hand over his face. Then, he decided to end that discussion and go back to basics. "It's getting dark. Please, let me see you safely home."

She shook her head. "I have someone coming to give me a ride. Thank you for the offer."

He was surprised when she started walking down the street. With only a few strides, he caught up to her. A car slowed down on the other side of the road, and she raised her hand to wave. He twisted his neck and spied a car with a woman behind the wheel.

The woman rolled down the window and called out, "Girl! I thought you needed a ride, but it looks like you found a tall cowboy for the night. Good for you!"

He looked back at the woman near him and watched her face blush deeply as she threw a narrow-eyed glare toward the car and shook her head. She lifted her gaze back to him and spoke softly. "Thank you for not hurting the boys." She pressed her lips together as she tilted her head. "I hope your leg is okay. And by the way, your chivalry was noted and appreciated, but my ride is here, so I'll say good night."

"Can I know your name?" The question slipped from his lips, but curiosity got the better of him. She was the most intriguing woman he'd met in a long time, and he wanted the chance to know her better. He pressed his luck when she didn't immediately deny his request. "After all, I didn't hurt anyone."

A faint smile graced her lips, and a small snort erupted as she hurried across the street. When she got to the passenger door, she looked over her shoulder. "It's just charity," she said before gracefully slipping into the vehicle.

As the car drove away, he watched as she twisted around and looked out the back window at him until she was out of sight. *Charity... great. She thinks I was chivalrous and let the boys go because of charity.* "Hell," he mumbled to himself, thinking of the blond hair and light brown eyes holding him spellbound. "I didn't do it for charity, that's for sure."

Heading in the opposite direction toward his SUV, he left behind thoughts of the teens. The feel of her soft curves beneath him and her face illuminated by the street lights lingered in his mind.

7

"Girl, please tell me you got that man's number!"

Charity Whitlock rolled her head to the side to observe the wide grin on her friend's face. She heaved a sigh, knowing Paula wouldn't like her answer. "No, I didn't."

"Why not? You had a man who could hold any woman's attention, and you just let him walk away from you?"

"No… I allowed myself to be picked up by my friend and driven away from him."

"Stop arguing," Paula groaned.

Despite the strange occurrences in the past half hour, Charity couldn't stop from grinning at Paula's frustration. She'd first met Paula when the irrepressible woman came in to interview for a job where Charity worked. But where Paula was free-spirited, fun to be around, and never had problems finding a man to spend time with, Charity was the quiet one who preferred a good book, warm flannel pajamas, and a glass of wine by herself than dressing up and going out.

"Let's just say that I didn't find him to be a very empathetic person. Too judgmental. Too quick to act before finding out facts. Too... too... just too everything!"

Paula's brows lifted. "Wow, that was a lot to discover in such a short time. And talk about the pot calling the kettle black!"

She whipped her head around. "Are you implying that *I'm* being too judgmental?"

"No... well, sort of... maybe... yeah, I guess I am."

"Paula, you've always been better in the romance department than I have. Not that I'm looking, of course."

"That's not true!" Paula retorted. "Plus, I'm not looking for romance. I'm looking for a good time, and that's all for right now. But you, sweetie, are looking for more, and that man looked like he might just be the one to romance you."

She rolled her eyes. "A man who looks like that would hardly be looking for romance with me. I saw him in the pizzeria. He had two women's phone numbers given to him before he'd ordered." She looked at Paula, daring her to refute what she thought was the irrevocable truth.

Paula slammed on the brakes as they pulled over to the sidewalk in front of Charity's door. "Geez, you don't have any idea how gorgeous you are! Any man would be honored to be with you!"

They were silent for a moment, and then Paula pushed, "I heard you tell him your name was Charity."

Scrunching her nose, she sighed. "Yeah, that was a momentary lapse in judgment. At least I didn't give him my last name."

Paula's face softened as she reached out to wrap her fingers around Charity's hand. "I think any man would be lucky to have you. Romance is important to you, and that's exactly what you deserve. Nothing less. And one day, when I'm ready, I hope I also find a forever love. But, you're right– until you find that special man, don't settle for anything less, even if he is the hottest thing I've seen around this neighborhood!"

Charity laughed, her heart lighter. "You do know I love you, right?"

Paula winked. "What's not to love, babe?"

Shaking her head, Charity climbed out of the car and started to close the door. Suddenly, she stopped and leaned down to peek inside. "I hope we both find what we're looking for."

Paula nodded, then stretched across the seat to grab Charity's hand on the doorframe. "Don't assume that because a man looks like the way he did, he's not the type to go for romance. You never know what you'll find, so be willing to give someone a chance."

Charity unlocked her door and then turned to wave. She knew her friend wouldn't drive away until she entered, so she walked inside and turned to secure the locks behind her. Her neighborhood wasn't dangerous, but her door didn't face the street. The small entrance hallway led straight up the stairs, and her apartment was the only one there. Once she'd climbed up to the landing, she unlocked the door leading directly into her apartment.

She shrugged off her coat, hung it on the coatrack, and moved farther into her cozy apartment. Although not spacious, it was home. A small living room was warmly decorated with colors of hunter green and burgundy. A doorway led into the eat-in kitchen, where she'd maintained the same color palette, only making them brighter with pale green and rose accents. Her space was rounded out with a bathroom and bedroom, both surprisingly sizable.

With no leftovers to store in the refrigerator, she simply filled a glass with wine before returning to the living room and settling onto the deep cushions of her sofa. Instead of turning on the television, her mind drifted back over the past hour's events as she took slow sips.

When she'd left work earlier, she realized she had missed lunch, and the thought of a microwave dinner since she hadn't grocery shopped this week was far from appealing. A pizza craving filled her thoughts, and while she didn't eat out often, she'd given in to the urge to indulge.

Dining alone might be unpleasant for many people, as our society is so geared to couples or groups. Eating alone can feel like standing out. But Charity never minded sitting alone when having a meal. In the past, she'd been approached by men who felt sure she desired company when, in reality, all she wanted was to be left in peace to enjoy her meal.

However, as she thought about the lone man she'd spied several tables away in the restaurant this evening, it hit her that if he'd come over to ask if she'd like to eat with him, she might have been tempted to say yes. *But only tempted.* After seeing him gain two women's numbers, even though he appeared not to want them, she'd chuckled aloud, then ducked her head to keep him from seeing her mirth.

He was tall and possessed captivating features. His physique was fit with defined muscles outlined in a long-sleeved T-shirt. His dark hair was trimmed shorter on the sides, and when seen up close under the lights, a slight reddish tint to the thick waves was revealed. A neatly trimmed beard and mustache framed his angular jaw, and his arched eyebrows gave his stare an intense and appraising gaze. But his smile held her attention—it gave him an impish expression.

When she'd landed on top of him, and then he'd rolled them over, she'd stared directly into his face, which was only a few inches away. She then discovered his eyes were green, ringed in gray that became darker toward the outer edge. And even though it sounded like a cliché from a romance novel, she felt she could drown in his eyes with a single glance.

"Good grief," she moaned aloud, downing half the glass of wine in one large swig. "I'm sure that Mr. I-could've-walked-away-with-a-date-with-the-server-or-the-hostess would have no interest in a short, decent-looking workaholic whose pay rarely allows for more than the occasional pizza night out."

Her words weren't self-deprecating but simply

stating a fact. There was nothing wrong with her girl-next-door looks, but they rarely caught the attention of a man like him.

When she'd gone to dinner, she had no idea how complicated the evening would become. With a heavy sigh, she dropped her head back and rested it against the soft cushion as she stared up at the ceiling.

She had recognized the teenagers across the street as soon as she saw them. They hadn't come to the center yet, but she had no doubt of their identity nor that they were up to something—probably something dumb. She'd finished eating and placed the leftovers in the plastic bag provided but had waited, hoping to keep an eye on them. As a crowd had walked across the street toward the restaurant, she knew that continuing to take up a table when she was finished with her meal wasn't the right thing to do.

She was half a block away when she'd heard the scream and, turning around, had spied the boys racing away with several pizza boxes in their hands. Determined to catch up to them before anyone else did, she'd sprinted forward, darting into the alley where they'd disappeared. Heavy footsteps echoed behind her, and she'd turned swiftly, her heart racing. Running back toward the open end of the alley with her hands flung out to the side, she'd slammed into someone large and powerful. As his arms banded around her in mid-fall, they managed to twist so that he took the brunt of the impact on the concrete.

When he'd rolled them over, she found herself sprawled on the sidewalk, staring up into the eyes of the man she'd shared a table with. The breath was knocked out of her, but he'd jumped to his feet and hauled her upward. With no other words, he'd started after the boys again. His mannerisms had screamed law enforcement, and she was terrified he'd grab the boys before she could stop in.

Now, leaning forward on her sofa, she shook her head. *Someone like him would never understand why I didn't want him to take them into custody.* "Ugh," she muttered before turning up her glass and draining the rest of her wine, barely tasting it. Dragging her fingers through her hair, she eventually stood and began flipping off the lights.

With each light extinguished, the darkness crept in behind her as she made her way to the bedroom. The room lacked a picturesque view, so she'd placed a long, narrow table in front of the window and filled it with plants. It had taken her a while to keep her little garden going, but seeing it each evening always made her smile. Her mother used to have a small garden in front of their house, and they'd spent many hours digging in the dirt, laughing and talking as they planted vegetables and flowers.

After watering the plants, she indulged in a soothing shower. Once dressed for bed, she braided her hair to keep it out of her face and enjoyed the results each morning when soft waves were easy to style. It wasn't much of a beauty regimen, but considering she had little time, it worked for her.

Climbing into bed, she left the lamp on her nightstand and pulled out her eReader as she leaned against the cushions next to the headboard. Romances were her go-to read to forget about the woes of the day.

Normally, her days were filled with relentless work and countless reports– everything from compiling statistics, writing grant proposals, checking on the facilities, or counseling the ones in her care. She loved her job, but it left little time for anything else.

Snuggling against the soft mattress and squishy pillows, she surrendered herself to the imagination of the romance writer who made her always believe in a happily ever after.

8

The next morning, dressed and ready for her day, she poured her coffee into one of her large mugs. It was a routine of her morning that she refused to give up. She had a collection of mugs with different sayings on them. Each morning, she stood and stared into her cabinet, choosing the mug of the day carefully as though it had magical powers. She always set her alarm early enough to sit in her kitchen and inhale dark roasted coffee, sweetened liberally with flavored creamer.

Today's choice was a blue mug with ***Here we fucking go again... I mean, Good Morning.*** Grinning, she savored her first sip, her eyes drifting closed as the warm, creamy deliciousness hit her taste buds. When she finally drained the last drop, she glanced at the clock on the stove and hurried to rinse her cup, eager to start her day.

As soon as she stepped into work, there would be fires to put out, emergencies to deal with, and problems to rectify. She grabbed her coat, looped her purse and computer bag over her shoulder, then locked the doors as she left her apartment. She walked down the stairs and, ignoring the door leading to the outside, unlocked another door that led into her workplace.

Living in such proximity to her job was convenient and cost-effective. Several small apartments were set up for on-site staff when the old school was turned into Bright Futures Home. Two were for the house parents —one on the girls' side and another for the boys' side. An additional apartment was tucked away next to the main building. While she wasn't considered to be part of the twenty-four-hour staff, the reality was that her presence was occasionally needed at all hours. Plus, it gave her affordable housing, allowing her to save for her eventual dream home.

"Hey, Paula," she greeted as she entered the lobby. "Anything from the evening?"

Each morning, Paula would receive a report from the night guard as to any new information. The house parents would've called Charity if there had been a major problem, but she liked to know everything that happened at the Bright Futures Home.

Paula shook her head, her curls bouncing as she smiled a welcome greeting. "Nope, not here. Can't say the same about you and Mr. Holy-moly-gorgeous from last night."

Charity widened her eyes, making a playful face, and shook her head. "I'm not talking about that!"

"Fair enough," Paula huffed before adopting a more

serious tone. "The night guard said it was all quiet." Her brow furrowed as she looked back down at the paper in front of her. "Although, he noted two teenagers who walked by the front door several times but never approached."

Charity wondered if it was the two boys from last evening's pizza theft fiasco. Her shoulders rose in a slight shrug. "Well, hopefully, they'll muster up the courage to try us out if they need a place." She walked behind the reception desk and into her office. Whereas her apartment was her calm and organized sanctuary, her office usually resembled organized chaos.

Piles of folders were stacked on her desk. The bookcase to the side held binders filled with information concerning the center, forms, laws, studies, and various needs to run the center.

At the top of the files on her desk was one titled Security system: analysis and implementation. She was grateful for the center's funding, but there had been a call for more security. Several months ago, someone tried to break in the front door after hours. The evening guard had stopped them, but they ran away. With the call for more electronic security, she'd had no idea how she would be able to afford more. She had applied for another grant but had not heard back. Money was a precious commodity since there was never enough and always a need for more.

It was then that one of the older men who worked at the home had spoken to a friend of his. George told her that he knew of a security company that would take certain cases if needed, and the company could make it happen. She had appreciated George's diligence in attempting to speak to his friend but promptly placed the idea out of her head, assuming no one would want to donate the money and time to secure a place like the center.

Just when she was out of ideas, she received a call from the man George had recommended. Carson Dyer's company, Lighthouse Security Investigations West Coast, offered various services, including the study of security system needs and the installation. She listened with interest but needed to make sure Mr. Dyer understood that the center could not pay. Or at least not until she determined whether she could receive grant money for the need.

It was then that he had dropped his amazing offer to her. They did several jobs each year pro bono for the community. After the recommendation had come from a reputable source and they'd completed their own investigation, they wanted to do the work for the center... at no cost.

She was floored at their generosity, especially having looked at the high cost of the system he was proposing. The initial plans were created after she met with Mr. Dyer and a few of his employees. While much of the technical terminology was unfamiliar to her, she was confident they would do an excellent job.

At the sound of a knock on her doorframe, she jerked her head up and smiled at the sight of two of the dearest women she could ever imagine working with—Helen McCabe and Mary Tobiasson. When the center began, she needed the assistance of full-time employees who would agree to live on-site. Having studied other homeless youth centers, the use of house parents was common. What was more difficult was finding individuals who would agree to this type of employment and could also pass the stringent background evaluations.

George McCabe and Robert Tobiasson had been friends since they'd been in the military many years before. Once out of the service, they both worked various jobs before retiring. Robert's wife, Mary, had been a teacher in the local school system for many years and found retirement too dull. George's wife, Helen, had been in retail for many years, eventually moving into human resources for a large company. When they heard about the center, both couples applied for the position of house parents.

They were not only employees at the center but had quickly become very good friends and, in many ways, surrogate parents to Charity.

Seeing the women standing at the door with their arms crossed, she tilted her head to the side. "And what brings you to my door so early?" She leaned forward, and her muscles tensed. While the two women's countenances didn't give evidence of a problem, Charity tried to be prepared for anything in dealing with teenagers every day. "There's nothing wrong, is there?"

"No," they said in unison as the two women walked in and sat down in her office. "We just wanted to check on you. We didn't see you later yesterday and hoped that maybe you had a date."

Barking out laughter, Charity shook her head. "A date?"

"Well, Paula mentioned..." Mary's words faded as she sighed.

"I'm not sure I remember what those are."

Mary and Helen shared a look before returning their worried expressions to her.

"That is exactly what we're talking about," Helen said. "You can't devote everything to your job."

Rolling her eyes, she sighed. "Isn't that the pot calling the kettle black?"

Neither woman cracked a smile, and then Mary added, "We may live and work at the center, but we are both married and have had our share of living."

Charity opened her mouth, but Mary threw her hand up, palm out, halting the words ready to burst forth from Charity's mouth.

"I know what you're going to say," Helen exclaimed. "We're not implying that you need a man, or a woman for that matter, to be fulfilled."

"Absolutely not," Mary agreed. "We just mean that we have something else in our lives besides our work. And that's all we want for you. Go out with friends. Have a date with someone. Go for a walk or a run that doesn't just involve looking for kids in need and trying to help everyone."

She understood their words came from a place of love, but she had no idea how to pack anything more into the twenty-four hours of each day. Last night flooded her mind, and her cheeks pinkened.

Mary leaned forward, her eyes eager. "What's that

look for?"

"Well, I did go out to eat last night." Both women's eyes lit up. "Granted, it was by myself."

"Good for you," Helen said, her smile wide.

Before they had a chance to grill her further, Paula popped her head through the doorway.

"Sorry to barge in, but a new teen has just walked into reception."

She stood and grabbed her tablet. "Sorry, ladies, but you'll have to hear the rest of my story later."

"We'll hold you to that!" Mary said before she and Helen headed down the hall.

Stepping into the reception area, she smiled at the sight of the younger boy from last night. Quickly scanning the lobby to see if the older brother was with him, the young boy appeared to be alone. "Hi," she greeted with a smile. "It's nice to see you again."

His lips were tightly pressed as his gaze darted around the room before returning to land on her.

"Would you like to sit and talk for a little while? I promise it will just be you and me. This is a safe place for you."

He shrugged, then jerked his head up and down. "We can talk. Yeah. That'd be okay." His eyes widened as he sucked in a quick breath. "But I don't want this gettin' back to nobody."

She nodded her affirmation. "Just you and me. I have a small conference room right here that we can go in."

He ducked his head and followed her into the small room. There was a table with four chairs, and she let him pick where he was most comfortable sitting. He opted for the chair in the corner, away from the visibility of the door. She kept the door partially open for safety reasons and then slid into a seat across from him.

"I'm going to let you tell me what you want to tell me," she said. "I'm not going to ask you for more than you want to say."

His gaze roamed around the room, looking at everything except her.

"I really would just like to get to know you better." She waited patiently, knowing that sometimes it took a lot of silence to build trust before one of the young people explained their needs.

Finally, he looked at her and sighed. "Thank you," he whispered.

She continued to wait patiently but nodded. Often, adults fill the silence with too many words for kids. She had found that most kids just wanted to be heard, not lectured to.

"You didn't have to give us your dinner. We had the pizzas. I'm sorry you went hungry."

"I had already eaten my dinner," she explained. "What I gave you was extra."

He nodded, seeming to give great thought to her words. "It was nice of you to do that."

She remained silent, a soft smile on her face.

With trust building a little more, he continued. "I was scared. I thought if that man caught us, we'd surely go to jail."

She nodded encouragingly. After a moment, she asked, "Did you have any questions for me? Are you interested in seeing what we might be able to do for you?"

He hesitated, and she could feel emotions pouring from him. It was tangible, a feeling radiating from him so hard she wanted to reach out and take his hand. But she held back, giving the power to him.

"I wouldn't want to be here without my brother."

"Your brother seemed good to you last evening when he helped you over the fence. He didn't just run away and leave you."

The young man's eyes widened, and he shook his head quickly. "He'd never leave me. He always says, 'Whatever happens, we do it together.'"

"It's really nice to have somebody like that in your life. Someone who will help you. Reach out and hold your hand when you need it."

He offered a tiny smile for the first time, and she felt that straight to her heart. "By the way, most people around here call me Charity."

She waited, and after another moment, he said, "My name is Ramzi."

Smiling, she stuck out her hand. He left her hanging for a moment and then, blushing as he dipped his chin, put his hand in hers. She gave it a firm shake. "It's nice to meet you, Ramzi."

Taking a chance, she pressed forward as easily as she could. "Last night, you mentioned that you'd only get a few bites before having to give it up—"

He immediately stiffened, and she tried a different tactic. "I assumed you were sharing your food."

His lips pinched together into a thin line, then he

just shrugged. He stood, his gaze once more darting around before landing on her. "I just came to thank you. That's all I need."

"Okay. I appreciate you coming by and hope I get a chance to see you again sometime."

His brow furrowed, and he looked around as though expecting someone to jump out from the corners. Finally, lifting his gaze back to hers, he asked, "You're not gonna try to talk me into staying?"

"Not at all. I can give you all sorts of reasons you'd be safe here, can go back to school here, and learn how to take care of yourself in a way that's legal and safe. I can show you around the cafeteria where there are meals every day. But my job is not to drag you in here kicking and screaming. My job is to be here if this is where you want to be."

He seemed to ponder her words for a long moment, then started toward the door. She followed him, and they crossed through the reception area and stopped at the outer door.

"Keep in mind, Ramzi. Sometimes you can turn things around by simply accepting a helping hand. And, since you and I now know each other, I hope you'll stop by occasionally to say hello whenever you find that it's time for home."

He held her gaze, this time not looking away. Then he jerked his chin up before slipping through the door. She watched as he looked both ways before walking down the sidewalk.

As she had so often with others, she stayed as they

left, staring at the closed door for a few minutes. Finally, Paula wrapped her arm around Charity's shoulders.

"You can't make them want a home, you know?"

Paula often said the same thing to her when she stared at the door after a session much like she'd just had with Ramzi. In truth, it happened almost every day. "I know. But that doesn't keep me from trying or wishing."

9

A week later, Oliver drove onto the winding driveway that meandered through trees, finally emerging at the LSIWC parking lot near the lighthouse. The initial anxiety he'd felt the first day was gone, but the excitement over new possibilities still lingered.

Today would be the first day that Carson had him out in the field. He would accompany Poole and Tricia as they finalized the installation plans for the security system they had designed for the center. He had visited the city when he'd first read the file on the center. He shook his head at the memory of encountering the woman who'd continued to fill his mind. *I still can't get her out of my thoughts.*

Carson explained that this pro bono work was recommended by a friend of Teddy's, who had contacted him to see if the Keepers could do anything for the facility. Since Oliver had nothing special to do over the weekend, he had looked over the design, gaining an understanding of what he would be seeing.

He eagerly anticipated going out in the field with Poole and Tricia. Riding with them, he attentively listened as they discussed the center's needs. He asked questions and threw out suggestions when appropriate, for which they appeared to be grateful.

"Did you spend all weekend studying the files on this?" Tricia asked, turning around to smile at him from the front seat.

He shrugged. "I wanted to ensure I fully grasped the plans and how to secure the center."

"You stayed in all weekend?" Poole chuckled. "You definitely need to get out more!"

"I did have a break," Oliver defended. "Our parents came to visit on Saturday for dinner, so I wasn't studying the whole weekend."

At that, Poole looked into the rearview mirror, lifting a brow as he caught Oliver's eyes. "Did Natalie do the cooking?"

Shaking his head, he chuckled. "My parents were prepared. We had a cookout—Leo handled the barbecue, my mom brought the side dishes, and then Natalie baked homemade cinnamon rolls with cream cheese frosting."

"Damn, and she didn't make extra to bring into work today?" Poole grumbled.

"I'm afraid we didn't leave any leftovers. As far as the weekend, while I'm in Leo and Natalie's house, I try to give them as much privacy as possible. I mostly just kept to myself and looked over the files. It's pretty impressive what this center does."

Tricia nodded her agreement. "Teddy's friend and

wife are both retired and are house parents on the boys' side. Another retired couple is the house parents on the girls' side. There is staff plus volunteers during the day and security both day and night."

He nodded, having already read that information in the files. The building they were going to had once been a small, private school that had gone out of business and was taken over by a nonprofit organization that offered housing, education, and counseling to homeless teenagers. He didn't admit that he'd never thought of homeless kids, not with parents. A flash of memory hit —the intense gaze from a fearless, petite blonde and the words she aimed toward him. *"You need to educate yourself on what goes on right here in your own backyard."* He had no idea who she was or what she was referring to, but her words rang true.

His attention was diverted as they arrived and parked outside the center. As they stepped out of the SUV, he surveyed the nondescript brick building with an intense gaze and renewed scrutiny while thinking about Poole's security plans. He noted the placement of the outside lights and identified the areas where Poole wanted to install additional lighting.

"You're looking at things differently, aren't you?"

Jerking his head around to see Poole and Tricia smiling at him, he nodded.

Poole continued, "Most people barely notice a building unless something catches their attention, and then it's usually the aesthetics. But considering the safety and security of those inside, we have a different outlook. You're already seeing things you wouldn't have considered before."

Oliver's time in the Army had trained him for missions and certainly heightened his sense of security. But once home, he'd never fallen into the mental space of seeing enemies everywhere. He'd had fellow Rangers who'd succumbed to the PTSD terrors or even some who scoped out every building as though the enemy was ready to pounce. While security conscious, Oliver had always segregated the real from the overly cautious.

"You're absolutely right. If I hadn't studied the plans you designed, this is the kind of building I would've driven by and never given a second thought. But now, I'm considering who is on the inside, what their needs are, and what we can do to enhance their security."

"That's perfect," Tricia chimed in. "That's exactly the mindset you need to have in this field."

They entered the building through the front door, stepping into a warm reception room. Comfortable seating arrangements with a sofa and several chairs offered casual relaxation. A reception desk was to the right, with a woman smiling as soon as her eyes met theirs. She stood and walked over, her hand extended. "Welcome to Bright Futures Home. I'm Paula, one of the day receptionists."

"It's nice to meet you," Poole said, his voice equally as pleasant. "My name is Frederick Poole. This is Tricia Burrows Poole and Oliver Parker. We're here from Lighthouse Security Investigations."

"Yes, Ms. Whitlock told me that you would be here today. It's nice to have you with us. My understanding is that you will be walking around the premises and making final notes and observations as you assist us with our security needs."

"That's exactly right," Poole said.

"I'm afraid Ms. Whitlock was called away and isn't here today. But I have your visitor badges ready and ask that you return them when you leave. I hope you don't mind, but our regular daytime security team member, Elliot Salsbury, will walk around with you. Because we work with teenagers, we want to protect everyone."

Poole nodded as he reached out to take his badge. "Understood."

Tricia had taken her badge and slipped the lanyard around her neck, and Oliver followed suit.

Just then, a man walked from the back and looked at the three of them.

"Elliot, these are the security visitors Ms. Whitlock told us about," Paula said.

Oliver quickly sized Elliot up. He appeared to be in his mid-fifties and physically fit, wearing a uniform of navy pants and a navy polo with Bright Futures Home embroidered over his left chest. He stepped forward and shook their hands, a smile on his face.

"If you'll follow me, we'll get started," he said. "Do you have a particular place you want to view first?"

"We'd like to look at the common areas, then take a look at the setup for the dorms," Poole said.

With Elliot leading the way, the Keepers left the reception area and moved down a hall that led into a large multipurpose room.

"This is both our dining area and gymnasium. Like

the school that occupied this building when it was first built and had to make multiple uses of space, we find this accommodates us in the same way."

As Elliot stood to the side, Oliver walked with Poole and Tricia, absorbing their conversation. They looked around the area to see if they thought where the security cameras would be most efficient on the floor plans would work in actuality.

"Do you usually find that you have to make many adjustments from floor plans to being in the buildings?" Oliver asked.

Poole nodded and pointed up to one of the corners near the ceiling. "There's a good example. I thought a security camera in that corner would give the best view, but as you can see, a pole is used to hang banners. So I need to consider that when I'm looking at where to place the camera."

Oliver had to admit he was fascinated after having previously wondered if this kind of assignment would be boring. In the military, all of the planning for the mission had already been completed by the time he set boots on the ground. But here, he would be actively involved in the initial designing, evaluation, and then the reevaluation of the original plans.

"What you should do is make notes on your own based on our drawings, then we'll pull them together to see what the best plan will be," Poole advised.

With a nod, he walked around the room and began making notes on his tablet. From the common area, they moved through a door on the right that led them to the boys' dormitories.

"The security needs are especially high in the hallways," Elliot said. "It's important for the young people to feel that they have a sense of privacy and safety in their own rooms, but at the same time, we have to be able to discover anyone's attempt to abuse those privileges."

Once again, the three Keepers moved up and down the hall, making notes of the best placement for security cameras.

They moved through the common area, then through an identical door on the left, finding the female dorms. After that evaluation, they headed into the commons area again, this time making their way through four classrooms.

Elliot continued, "The dining times and classrooms are coed. For everything else, we keep the boys separate from the girls."

"I understand a couple lives full-time on each dorm side?" Oliver asked.

"Yes, sort of like dorm parents. They are trained by social services in counseling as well as security. Their job is also to ensure the on-site safety." Elliot heaved a heavy sigh. "Some of these kids come from rough backgrounds. We want to make sure that none of our kids under our roof are assaulted. Male and female nighttime security guards are also available. A female daytime security guard works part-time with me."

"That sounds like a lot of dedicated people," Oliver said.

"If you want to talk about dedication, wait till you meet Ms. Whitlock. She lives in and breathes the

Bright Futures Home and all the kids who pass through here."

Thanking Elliot, the Keepers walked back to the reception area, where they began their work in earnest.

The next several hours were filled with thorough exploration as Tricia, Poole, and Oliver walked around the entire building perimeter. They continued to jot notes into their tablets, exchange ideas, and compile a list of LSIWC's proposed security enhancements for the center.

As they finally pulled out of the parking lot, Oliver cast a parting glance at the building and reflected on the stark contrast between his childhood teen years as opposed to the teens receiving assistance from those inside the center. His parents had showered him and Leo with loving support and unwavering dedication. He and his brother had their share of squabbles, but they always had each other's backs. School had been fun, and high school sports had given Oliver a chance to understand real camaraderie before joining the Army.

Snapping back to the conversation between Poole and Tricia, he stopped musing and listened as they discussed the intricacies of the center's security needs. Diving into the topic, he grinned with enthusiasm, glad to be part of the team.

10

"She came tear-assing up the alley as I got around the corner. We slammed into each other—"

"Damn, that had to have hurt her."

"She just kept going after me to get to the boys."

Oliver was in Leo's living room, lounging on one of their comfortable chairs with a ball game on the widescreen TV. Leo was on the sofa, his long legs stretched out with his feet resting on the coffee table. Natalie perched beside him, her shorter legs resting on Leo's.

Oliver was in the midst of regaling the others with his escapades from the week before. Initially, he'd kept the incident a secret, especially about getting bowled over by the much smaller woman. However, with plans to return to the area with Poole and Tricia as the ongoing security installations continued, he decided to share the tale. He couldn't help but laugh at how a slip of a woman thwarted his pursuit of the boys. Leaning forward, he rubbed his thigh.

"What was she trying to do?" Leo asked.

"Hell if I know," he replied as his mind returned to the feel of her pressed against him. He'd been in too many battles to have felt any pain when taking her down but was man enough to immediately recognize that she was unlike any adversary he'd ever tangled with. He had admitted that he'd seen her in the restaurant but left out the part about how he was interested—well, interested until he suspected her of assisting the boys to grab the pizza and then get away.

"And your leg?" Leo asked.

"It'll take more than a run down the street chasing a couple of teenage thieves to stop me."

"How's the center's security assignment going?" Natalie asked.

"I looked at all the diagrams and just started reading more about the center."

"You gotta learn everything you can about a place that you are planning security for," Leo said, holding his gaze. "Whether you're providing a security escort for someone or helping to design a security system. You need to educate yourself on exactly what they do so that you know how to take care of their needs."

As the game held the others' attention, Oliver's mind stayed firmly on the woman. *You should educate yourself.* She had essentially said the same thing as Leo.

Determined to show his commitment to learning everything he could about the various types of assignments and missions that LSIWC was involved in, he had thrown himself into looking at the center's blueprints and equipment installation plans. But he hadn't looked up to see what the center did other than knowing it was a place for homeless youth to gather.

While the game continued, he pulled up his laptop and typed in Bright Futures Home. He read how they served runaways, homeless, and trafficked youth. The shelter provided residential resources, as well as crisis counseling, case management, community referrals, and coordination of services. They operated a twenty-four-hour crisis hotline, as well as anger management classes, a licensed safe place, and community outreach.

His eyebrows lifted to his forehead as he continued to read, falling down the rabbit hole of online sites that gave him more information.

He was startled when Natalie plopped her feet on the floor, stood, and stretched her hands over her head. "I'm gonna make some sandwiches and grab some chips before the next game."

"Thanks, babe," Leo said. "I'll come help."

"That's okay, I've got it."

Oliver looked up, and the expression on his face must've been one of incredulity because Leo stared at him and then asked, "What the hell is wrong with you?"

"I've just been reading what the Bright Futures Home is about. I hadn't taken the time to research what they offer, and now I feel pretty stupid."

Leo waved his hand dismissively. "Look, little bro. You were chosen to be a Keeper because you come with a skill set from the military that's important to Carson. But you're in a different career now and have new things to learn. Give yourself a break."

Oliver wasn't content with that explanation. "It's not

just that, Leo." He sat up straight and held his brother's gaze, pulling his thoughts together. "I've had a world view based on where I was and what I was doing. You know the drill... often in places you couldn't wait to get out of. Figured everything was better back home. But now that I'm back in California, I need to understand better what's happening here. Right here in my own neighborhood, so to speak."

Leo set his beer on the coffee table and held Oliver's gaze. "What's brought this on?"

"It was something that lady said the other night. The one who wanted the kids to get away. She told me that I needed to be more educated about what was happening around me. And you just said the same thing about becoming educated on our assignments."

Nodding slowly, Leo looked up as Natalie came back into the room and sat on his lap. "What did you learn?"

"I thought it was just a center where kids could come and hang out if they wanted. Hell, I didn't even think about they needed dorm rooms." He shrugged. "I don't know... kind of like the boys club where you and I used to play basketball after elementary school, remember?"

Leo chuckled and nodded. "When Teddy brought this assignment to Carson, I remember hearing it was for homeless youth, right?"

Oliver nodded. "Yeah. The site had previously been a private Catholic school. They have a boys' dorm and a girls' dorm. They offer counseling, emergency services, job training, mentoring, as well as a shit ton of other things."

"Sounds like the kind of place that Carson would spend tens of thousands on pro bono security," Natalie said. "I'm glad you get a chance to see the work we can do there."

That night, Oliver lay on his bed in the guest room, unable to shake the image of the woman he'd had dinner with and then collided with. Grinning as he rolled over, he punched his pillow. *Maybe spending time near the pizzeria will bring her back into my sights.*

Their morning meeting began as Carson reviewed their current cases and upcoming assignments. He looked over at Oliver. "I'll have you remain with Poole on the center's security installment designs for a few more days. After that, Tricia will have the necessary equipment and will begin the actual installment. Then I'll shift you to another Keeper and allow you to work with them on a bodyguard assignment."

Oliver nodded, eager to work on anything Carson wanted to throw his way. "Sounds good. Thanks."

After the meeting concluded, he walked over to Poole. "I'll be ready to head out whenever you are."

Poole glanced over and caught Tricia's eye. "You have anything to finish before we leave?"

"No, we can leave now. That will give us time to check out a few more things before we meet with Ms. Whitlock."

Poole and Tricia rode in Tricia's company's electrical van, and Oliver drove his SUV. He was quiet for most of the drive and even had the radio off. His mind was filled with the woman from the restaurant. Before he knew it, he was pulling beside Poole outside Bright Futures Home. Suddenly, he remembered something from the building's blueprints and security plan. As they climbed from the SUV, he pointed at a door down the sidewalk from the center's main door.

"I wondered about this. It wasn't on our plans."

Poole nodded. "I asked about that when we first began this project. I was told that it leads to an apartment that's not officially part of the center."

"So we ignore it?"

Tricia walked past him toward the front doors. "We're going to talk to Ms. Whitlock today about it. A door leads from the center to the apartment, so we want to learn more about it. It's not safe for the center to have someone living there who has access."

"I wonder who lives in an apartment so close to this establishment. You'd think it would be noisy with kids all the time."

"Maybe it's just a really cheap rental," Poole added as he followed Tricia through the center's front doors. "All the more reason to find out more about it."

Once inside, the receptionist greeted them again. "You're Paula, right?" Tricia asked with a smile.

"Yes! Ms. Whitlock is making her rounds. The local schools have a teacher workday today, so we've got a full house. You'll probably see her somewhere even before your scheduled meeting time."

Thanking her, they walked toward the common

area. Folding tables had been set up, and when Oliver glanced at the time, he realized it was almost time for lunch. Two men about the age of Teddy were setting the chairs around, and Poole called out to one of them. "Hey, George!"

The man looked up, then smiled widely and made a gesture for the other man to follow him as he walked over. "Poole, good to see you again." He shook hands with Poole, then introduced, "This is Robert McCabe. He and his wife, Helen, live on the girls' dorm side."

"Nice to meet you," Poole greeted. "This is my wife, Tricia. Her company will be completing the security installation. And this is Oliver Parker."

Oliver remembered that George was Teddy's friend and the originator of the request for the security installation at the center.

A man wearing a white apron over pristine white pants and a matching T-shirt emerged from the kitchen, rolling a cart containing platters of sandwiches. Two women followed him, each pushing carts filled with large bowls of fruit and cookies.

George looked over his shoulder. "Sorry to cut this short, but we all jump in to help wherever possible. Usually, the kids are in school, so we only have lunch during holidays, weekends, and the summer. Today is a teacher workday for the city." Turning, he hustled over to one of the women. "I'm sorry, honey. Let me get that for you."

Robert followed George, and the Keepers were introduced to Mary Tobiason and Helen McCabe. As soon as the doors opened from the back hall, kids began streaming into the room.

They were exuberant but orderly as they grabbed paper plates and formed a line, eagerly piling their plates with sandwiches, chips, fruit, and milk or water.

Taking in the scene, Oliver noticed kids who appeared as young as twelve up to what he assumed was upper teens. In truth, he wasn't sure the exact ages that the center would accept. *All of these kids are homeless.* Watching them eat and converse with each other, he winced, realizing that he'd never thought about homeless youth who weren't with their families before learning about the center. The words runaways and trafficked youth became real as he tried not to stare at the faces in front of him.

A thin girl with a wide-eyed, shy expression walked into the room accompanied by a woman whose head was bent as she whispered to the young girl. Oliver's gaze was drawn to the woman as sunlight streamed through a window, illuminating her golden hair pulled back into a ponytail. His heart raced. *No way.* But as the woman stood, the air rushed from his lungs as he realized who he was looking at.

George called to the woman, who turned with a radiant smile. Oliver knew the instant her gaze landed on him. Her eyes widened, and her mouth opened slightly in surprise.

"There's Ms. Whitlock," Poole said, inclining his head toward her.

Oliver's head whipped around. "She's the one who runs the center?" Incredulity dripped from his words.

"Yes, that's our amazing Charity," George said.

Oliver's brow furrowed. "Charity?" He watched as she escorted the young girl to the tables to ensure she had others to sit with before walking toward them. Her gaze darted to him before she stopped in front of their group and smiled at Poole.

"Mr. Poole, it's nice to see you again," she said, reaching her hand out while her gaze flickered briefly to Oliver.

"It's just Poole, ma'am. And I'd like to introduce you to my wife, Tricia, and Oliver Parker."

She continued smiling as she shook Tricia's hand as well. She then stepped over to Oliver. "Hello. I'm Charity Whitlock."

"Your name is Charity?" he asked, feeling foolish. When she'd given him her name, he'd misunderstood, thinking she referred to it as charity to let the boys go.

She tilted her head to the side and scrunched her nose. "I told you that when you asked, but I guess I was too far away for you to hear me."

"No," he admitted honestly. "I heard you, but I... well, I've never met anyone whose name is Charity before, so I made the wrong assumption."

She nodded slowly, and her lips curved softly. "Don't worry. It's a common mistake that lots of people make."

He suddenly hated being grouped in a category with lots of other people. "Seeing you here... well, it makes your actions of that night understandable. I'm afraid I owe you an apology for all of my suppositions."

"No apology is necessary, Mr. Parker—"

"Oliver."

She gracefully dipped her head. "All right. No apology necessary, Oliver. Given the situation, your assumption was based on observation, which made sense."

Warmth moved through his arm, hitting him in the chest. Looking down, he realized that her hand was still in his. The feel of their touch was so natural that it never dawned on him to simply shake and let it go. As though she became aware at the same instant, they both jumped slightly, then looked around to see the other adults standing with lifted eyebrows and grins on their faces. Sure that the tips of his ears were burning, he released her hand and cleared his throat.

Thankfully, Poole jumped into the awkward abyss and said, "We're a little early for our meeting. We can look around."

"Yes!" she rushed out, her head bobbing as she nodded. "I need to assist with lunch—"

"No!" Mary and Helen nearly shouted out in unison. They looked at each other, and then Mary continued, "We have lunch in hand. Why don't you walk around with them as part of your meeting time?"

Before Poole had a chance to respond, Oliver said, "That would be helpful. I'm still learning about the security installation, and having the center's administrator walk around with us would give me more insight." He glanced at Poole and Tricia but ignored their wide grins and focused on Charity's face.

The blush deepened on Charity's cheeks, but she nodded her agreement. "If I can be of help, then, of course, I'll be glad to walk with you." She waved her hand to indicate they should proceed. "I'll let you lead since you know specifically what you might be looking for when it comes to security."

Poole and Tricia started down the hallway leading to the girls' dorm while Oliver stepped behind them and walked beside Charity. Knowing she championed the teens in need, he still couldn't reconcile why she allowed the boys to get away even though he no longer suspected her of being an accomplice. Keeping quiet, he hoped to gain more insight as they walked around.

Poole turned around and said, "Tricia will be here for all of the installation, but she's the only female electrician in her company. She has one other who's interning, but the others are male."

Tricia turned toward Charity and said, "What conditions do we need to work around, or what schedules should we be aware of?"

"As you can imagine, we need to be able to see what is going on in our center. I'm in the process of hiring a female security person full-time. She's worked for us part-time, but I'm hoping I can move her to full-time with the new funding.

"The kids are all expected to be up every morning, dressed and ready to go by breakfast. George and Robert check the boys' dorm rooms, and Helen and Mary check the girls'. After breakfast, they get on the buses to go to the local high school, middle school, vocational training, or GED tutoring. So from breakfast on, the electricians will have full use of the dorm halls to handle the installations. Some of the older kids may be in one of our classrooms for money management, counseling, looking for affordable housing, and job applications. The buses bring the kids back by three thirty, and then they are in the common room to use it as a gym, for crafts, and for games. There's also a lounge with TVs and computers, and counseling groups are meeting in the conference rooms. Our security and the house parents make rounds to ensure everyone is safe."

Tricia nodded and made notes on her tablet.

She shrugged. "So basically, your installers can work freely wherever they need to. When the kids are here, plenty of people will be around during the day. All I ask is that you let me know each day where they'll be, and then I can have our security keep an extra eye out in case something is needed." Shaking her head, Charity winced. "I've given you so much more information than you asked for."

Tricia smiled warmly. "Not at all. It's good for me to know all this so I can schedule my guys' work times appropriately."

They stopped outside a door with no identification plate on the outside.

Poole inclined his head toward the door. "We know you lease a small apartment through here. It's our understanding that it stays locked and isn't part of the security installation."

A blush graced Charity's cheeks once again. "Actually, that's my apartment."

Oliver startled and quickly shot his gaze toward

Poole and Tricia, discerning from their expressions that her response was a surprise for them, too.

"Oh!" Tricia exclaimed. "I was under the impression that no security was needed for that."

"There's not!" Charity rushed. "It was originally part of the school years ago. I think one of the administrators lived there. But since I'm the only one who lives there, even though it's part of the building and could be considered part of the center, it didn't feel right for me to have security out of the grants and donations."

Oliver wanted to demand that she be as protected as anyone else in the building but didn't feel like it was his place to say so. But lifting his gaze to Poole, he offered a wide-eyed look, hoping the other Keeper felt the same.

"Ms. Whitlock," Poole began.

"Charity."

"Right, sorry. Look, Charity, if you live here, in what is essentially part of the building, you need to have the same security," Poole continued.

Charity stopped in the middle of the hall and dragged her tongue over her lips before pressing them together, rubbing them back and forth. "I don't feel like I'm in danger, and it seems excessive."

Poole rubbed his chin. "Would it be okay if one of us took a look at the apartment to see what could be added?"

She lifted her arms and nodded. "Sure."

Oliver's gaze shot to Poole again, but he hid his grin as Tricia said, "Why don't you go, Oliver? It will give you a chance to map it out, and then we can review it together."

Poole ducked his head as he also tried to hide his grin. "We'll check out the classrooms and then come to your apartment."

"That's fine," she agreed easily as her gaze and smile settled on Oliver's face.

As Poole and Tricia walked back down the hall, Oliver inclined his head toward the door and waited as she pulled out a key from her pocket and unlocked it. Stepping through, she said, "I use this entrance when going to and coming from the school. Otherwise, I use the outside entrance for my personal use."

They stepped inside a small hall with another door that he assumed led to the outside and a staircase that led upward. He followed her as she ascended the stairs and tried to keep his eyes off her ass. She wore navy pants and a pale blue blouse. Neither would have been noteworthy on their own, but on her, the outfit couldn't hide her curves. She used a key at the top of the stairs and opened the door leading into her apartment.

"Do you always lock the outside door and this one, too?"

"Yes. I'm very careful about that. I would never want to leave any part of the building at risk, so I lock the outside door, the door to the school, and the door to my apartment."

"Good," he said, noting her smile as she peered up at him.

Her clear eyes held his gaze, and he had to forcibly divert his attention before he committed a completely unprofessional act, like leaning down to see if her lips were as soft as they appeared.

Clearing his throat, he forced his body to turn and allowed his curiosity to roam freely through her apartment. Small but neat. Simple but complete. The small living room featured a worn but comfortable-looking green sofa that faced a brick wall with a modest flat-screen TV. A dark red armchair sat at an angle. He caught a glimpse of the kitchen through a wide, arched doorway. A hall extended past the kitchen, and he assumed a bedroom and bathroom lay at the other end of the apartment.

"It's small, but it's home."

Her words broke his silent perusal, drawing his gaze back to her. Her eyes held a glint of uncertainty, and he chuckled. "It's great. Hell, it's more than I have."

Surprised, she blinked as she stared up at him.

Running a hand over his beard, he confessed, "I live with my brother and sister-in-law. I've only been out of the military for a short while and working for LSI for a few weeks. So bumming a room is a lot less than what you have here. This is nice."

A smile tugged at her lips as she nodded. "Thanks. I like it, and it suits my needs for now. Do you need to look around?"

He had glanced at it on the blueprints but hadn't paid attention to it at the time since it wasn't part of the original security plan. Now, he found that he not only wanted to look for security issues, he wanted to see more of her home. Her beauty had caught and held his attention, but today, his interest was based on more. He was curious about the woman who ran a center for homeless youth, raced after two kids who'd stolen pizza, and tackled him to keep him from interfering with their getaway.

She tucked a wayward strand of hair behind her ear as she looked around as though trying to see her place through the eyes of a stranger. "Well, this is obviously the living room. The place isn't very big, so I'm unsure what security it would need. As you can see, it's on the second floor, with only a window in the kitchen and another in the bedroom."

Images of many missions he'd undertaken as a Ranger where he'd scaled buildings easily to get in through windows crossed his mind. While he didn't want to scare her, he felt compelled to warn her of the dangers. "Windows can always be a point of entry, even on the second floor."

"Oh… yes, I'm sure… I just never thought about it." Her brow furrowed, then she quickly added, "I also keep them locked."

A grin slipped across his face. "Good. Sounds like you're very security conscious." Suddenly, her safety felt like it was of utmost importance. Before she had a chance to respond, he continued. "But, you need your windows to be alarmed just like the rest of the center. If not, then you're leaving a potential weak spot in the entire building."

She nodded slowly, her gaze never wavering from him. "Okay. I hadn't thought of that. I'll let you do whatever needs to be done here."

He understood her intention, but her words ignited images of what he'd like to do to her here. And it would start with a kiss. They stood with their bodies close, surrounded by a charged current that swirled around.

"Hey, Oliver!" Poole called from the bottom of the stairs. "Are you good up there?"

Startled, both Oliver and Charity jumped back. Her cheeks pinkened with a rosy hue, but as an embarrassed smile crossed her lips, all he could think of was that he was definitely *good* up here with her.

11

Charity found herself standing in her apartment, gazing into the eyes of the man who had occupied her thoughts since their eventful meeting over pizza and then the chase down the alley. In fact, it had been his eyes that she had conjured up in her mind as she drifted off to sleep each night in the bed they were standing close to.

The situation felt oddly surreal to have him in her personal space. Not because it wasn't presentable to a stranger—she didn't have underwear tossed in the corner of the bedroom or a bra hanging over the shower curtain. She'd grown up in such cramped quarters that she'd learned to keep her living area neat as a way to maximize the space. It was a lesson she carried over into adulthood.

She appreciated her small apartment more than most people could understand. It perfectly suited her needs and was more than what she had growing up. Working with people who had less continued her deep gratitude for what she had.

What made the situation so awkward was realizing that who we were was often reflected in the things we had in our private sanctuary... the pictures on the walls, the scented bath oil sitting on the side of the tub, the colors of the curtains chosen to decorate. And when Oliver stopped to look at the window in the bedroom and stared down at her small garden of potted plants, she felt an odd sense of vulnerability, as if the air in the room had grown thinner.

Crossing her arms around her middle, she stepped back, unconsciously creating distance between them until she could breathe easier.

He turned around to face her and smiled. Her knees quivered, and then she inwardly shook her head to regain her focus. Drawing herself up to her full height, she forced a smile on her lips. But in truth, all she wanted to do was rush from the room.

How many women would love to have this gorgeous man standing in their bedroom? And all I want is for him to leave!

Determined to return to her professional armor, she sucked in a cleansing breath. "Do you have everything you need?"

He stepped closer, his smile still intact as he looked down at her. "Not quite."

Her lips parted, and she wondered what he meant as he neared. His gaze dropped to her lips, and for a few seconds, she wondered if he would dip his head to kiss her.

Surprised at the ribbon of anticipation wrapped around her body, she jolted when he leaned past her and picked up the tablet he'd laid on her bed. Looking down, he began tapping into the notes he was taking. A mixture of relief and disappointment speared through her, slicing through her anticipation.

Turning on her heels, she walked out of the bedroom and called over her shoulder, "I need to get back to the center." She didn't want him to stay in her apartment, and now that she'd shown it to him, she knew he could complete his job without her presence. It suddenly dawned on her that workers would be in her apartment in a few days when they added security.

As she halted in the hallway, her shoulders slumped as she looked down at her feet. Rubbing her forehead as it ached, she hadn't realized Oliver had walked up behind her until his voice was very close.

"Hey, Charity. Are you okay?"

She was startled and turned to see him right next to her. Wincing slightly, she said, "This all seems a bit overwhelming."

"Just think how much more secure your center will be when the security measures are in place."

"Oh, it's not that," she rushed to explain. "I'm thrilled for any of the security available for the center. The kids and the staff need to feel safe."

"And what about you?" He walked to stand directly in front of her.

She had to lean back to keep her gaze on his face, then tilted her head slightly. "I don't understand. What about me?"

"Don't you deserve to feel safe?"

Her brow furrowed, and she admitted, "I've never felt unsafe here."

"There's a fire escape outside, connecting your two windows."

"Yes, but the ladder is pulled up from the ground. No one can reach it."

His chin jerked back, and he lifted a brow. Without him saying anything, she squirmed. "Okay, that was a dumb thing to say. Obviously, someone could stand on boxes, grab the bottom of the ladder, pull it down, and then climb up the fire escape. And yes, I keep the windows locked, but someone could break a window."

His lips quirked as he nodded. "You're right. I'm not implying that you've done anything to make yourself unsafe. I'm saying that you have to think like someone who wants to do harm. Someone who's looking for a way to get in. Believe me, you can find a way to get into a place that's not secure."

Now, her chin jerked back slightly as she listened to his tone. "That sounds suspiciously like you know what you're talking about."

"I might be new to this type of security company, but I was an Army Ranger. It was often my job to figure out a way to get into a building."

She nodded as understanding moved through her. "So when you examine something like a window, a fire escape, a door with only one lock… you see a way for someone to exploit that."

Relief seemed to spread over his face. "Exactly. Granted, I would have team members with me who had already scoped out the area. But often, in the heat of battle, I had to learn quickly how to get in or out of a situation." He looked around her living room. "So as lovely as your home is, it could be used as a way to get into the center."

A gasp slipped from her lips at the reality of his words. "I understand now. Thank you." She heaved a sigh, and her shoulders slumped. "There is no way that I or the center can pay for any of the security your team is looking at, and I'm so grateful for what Lighthouse Security is doing for us." She hefted her shoulders in a little shrug. "I just wanted to try to save money. I never wanted to be a weak link."

"Charity, in the short time I've known you, you could never be a weak link. Your apartment? That's a different matter. But you? Absolutely not." His assurance was accompanied by a warm smile that struck her core.

A multitude of thoughts raced through her mind. She wanted to thank him but longed to express what the center meant to her. She wanted to learn more about his time as a Ranger and how he came to work for the security company. She even harbored a desire to invite him to dinner, hoping it wouldn't end up with him running down the street after a couple of teenagers.

As though he could read her mind at that instant, as his gaze held hers, he asked, "Why did you stop me? That night in the alley… why did you let them go?"

Time seemed to crawl as the universe slowed. Oft buried past memories flew at her, now threatening to burst forth. Blowing out a breath, she focused on his gently asked question. "I didn't know them. Not really. But I'd seen them around… and talked to them before.

And I knew they were brothers. I see others like them every day, and I knew they were hungry."

"They could have been armed. Desperate. Willing to do anything—"

She shook her head and stopped him with a hand on his arm. He looked down, and she jerked her hand back, stunned she'd touched him. Quicker than she could imagine anyone moving, he snapped his arm up and wrapped his fingers around her wrist, stopping her hand from pulling away. His thumb gently rubbed where her pulse beat wildly underneath his touch.

"I'm not stupid, Oliver. I wouldn't put myself at risk, but I... I knew they weren't dangerous."

He simply held her gaze, and she pulled her hand from his and mumbled, "I suppose we should get back for our meeting with Tricia and Poole."

His lips quirked on one side. "Yeah. I suppose we should."

She stared at the quirk, and her mind blanked of anything but wanting to see that expression again. "I know you're here for work, but you're more than welcome to come by and see how things are going. Um... if you ever get a chance or..."

His smile widened, and he continued to nod. "You can count on it. Even if I'm assigned to other jobs over the next several weeks, I'd love to come by."

As glad as she was for his reply, she realized she framed the question for him to check on the work. What she had really wanted to say was that she'd specifically like to see him more. Keeping her smile steady, she started to turn away when he reached out his hand to touch her shoulder, and then hesitated. She turned her eyes up to him in question.

"Perhaps, when I'm here, we could grab lunch."

She nodded, her smile widening. "I'd like that."

Turning, they walked back out of her apartment, where she locked her door, then went down the stairs and through the door into the center.

Entering her office a few minutes later, she realized her mistake. As neat as her apartment was kept, her office was chaotic. And with two large men, Tricia, and herself, there was no way it would work. Turning quickly, she said, "Perhaps we can meet in the intake room. It's a little more roomy."

Paula was just passing and quickly shook her head. "I'm sorry, Charity. David has taken someone into the conference room since you were busy."

"An intake?"

"Yes."

She pressed her lips together. "I'm sorry. If a young person has come in for help, I don't want to displace them to another room and make them feel unwelcome. Let me see if I can—"

"Please don't worry about us," Poole said. "Your office will be more than adequate."

Nodding, she led the way in. "I'm sorry it's so small." She moved around her desk and then noticed that Tricia and Poole sat in front of her while Oliver stood, leaning against the now-closed door. "Oh, Oliver, I can get—"

"I'm fine. Don't give me another thought," he assured. He crossed his arms over his chest, and she let out a shaky breath.

She knew his assurance was that they should proceed with the meeting and not worry about a chair for him, yet there was no way she wouldn't give *him* another thought. In fact, how he looked now guaranteed he would take up residence in her mind.

Forcing her gaze down to the new additions to the plans, Poole walked her through what would be needed for her apartment based on Oliver's observations.

"I know this means you have to order more equipment," Charity said. "But I would prefer that you go start on the center. I don't want to be the reason anything gets held up."

Tricia waved her hand dismissively and smiled. "Oh, don't worry about that. The extra cameras in the hallway outside your apartment and the security on your windows are the same as what we'll install in the rest of the center. We always order more since we never know if we might make a change or if equipment might need to be replaced. So we can get it all done at the same time."

Pleased with that assessment, she reviewed the provided paperwork. Before she signed as the administrator, she held the pen in her hand, her fingers shaking slightly as she hesitated. Looking up, she locked her gaze onto Oliver, and he stared back with curiosity in his eyes. Her top teeth bit down on her bottom lip as she worked to settle her nerves.

Dropping her gaze from him to Poole and then to Tricia, she admitted, "I'm sure this seems ridiculous to you—my anxiety." She winced as she shook her head.

"The fact that your company is donating time, equipment, and labor that I know would cost more than I could ever imagine… it means a great deal to me. It means a great deal to the staff. And while they may not understand it, it means the world to the youth who come through the center."

Oliver dropped his arms to his side and leaned away from the door, his expression now one of concern. For a second, she thought he would come to her, but Tricia spoke first. "Charity, LSIWC is more than honored to do this for you and the center. Please don't feel indebted. We're impressed with this facility and what you're doing for these kids."

She closed her eyes for a moment, and no one spoke. She appreciated the chance to work through her emotions. Finally, looking up, she continued. "Do you know who some of the most vulnerable population of our country is? It's the children and young people who have no home. Too young to really take care of themselves. And some would prey upon them. I can't stop all their suffering, but I want to give them a safe place to come so they can become adults caring for themselves and others around them. The fact that your company, you're generous boss, and each of you is doing this for us means the world to me. Thank you."

Blinking to hold back the tears that threatened to fall, she dropped her gaze back down to the paper in front of her and signed her name with a still-shaky hand. As they stood, Oliver opened the door and stepped out, allowing the others in her office to follow. She escorted them to the front door and extended her hand. With a lighter heart, her smile came from deep inside. Tricia shook her hand, and then the two women pulled each other in for a warm hug.

"I'll be back in two days with my workers," Tricia promised. "I'll be here every day to oversee the work. You'll also have other Keepers stopping by to check on things."

Tricia stepped back, and Poole moved forward to shake her hand. "Tricia was honest when she said it's our honor to work with you." He then turned to Oliver and said, "We'll see you later, Oliver." They walked through the door, and she realized he must have driven separately.

Standing in the reception area with people milling around, there was no privacy, yet she felt they were the only two souls in the room. Taking Oliver's extended hand, she loved the feel of his rough palm and the way his fingers wrapped around her smaller hand. The strange tingling she'd felt when he touched her the first night they met returned, and she couldn't imagine why she had that feeling with him and no one else.

"I know you have other…um… duties, but I do hope I will have the chance to see you again," she said.

He didn't release her hand as he smiled down at her. "As a new employee with LSIWC, and I'm sure my boss will have plenty of work for me. But he'll also want me to see how this project goes, and it's not that far from where I'm living, so it'll be easy to stop by."

Glancing down at their still-held hands, she was uncertain what to say, but he didn't appear to have that difficulty. "Anyway, we need to have lunch… or dinner. That is if you're still interested."

"Absolutely!" She rolled her eyes at her enthusiastic reply. "And I promise that I'll try not to chase anyone when we're out."

He leaned until his mouth was close to her ear as his hand squeezed hers slightly. "It would be fine if you chased me."

Unused to flirting, she blinked up at him, staring at the twinkle in his eyes. Chuckling, she slid her hand from his. "We'll see." Her simple reply must've surprised him.

He threw his head back and laughed as he stepped back. "That sounds like a challenge, Charity. And I love a challenge." He started to step back, then pulled out his phone. "Would it be possible for me to get your phone number?"

She nodded and pulled her phone from her pocket, rattling off her number. He sent her a text. "Now, you've got my number, too."

He offered a chin lift toward the reception desk, and Charity was reminded that there were other people around. He then turned his attention back to her and said, "I'll see you soon."

She nodded and watched as his lips curved before he walked out the door. Turning, she spied Paula, grinning widely at her, both thumbs up. Rolling her eyes, she walked back toward the classrooms.

The rest of her day was spent checking on her staff and the residents, and completing paperwork. Bright Futures Home was part of a statewide initiative to assist homeless youth. They were one of the newer shelters to open, and she was grateful for the guidance the state and local directors gave. And even though she had a top-notch staff of counselors, support, staff, and house parents, she still wanted to be involved. It was a fine line not to make the professionals underneath her feel like she was constantly watching over their shoulders, but she couldn't sit back and just do paperwork.

So she spent time every day with each staff member, and unless she had a meeting out of the building, she checked on the kids as they left breakfast and headed to the school buses and also greeted them when they came in from the school buses at the end of the day. She was glad that most of the work would be done while the younger kids were at school and the older kids were either at job sites or training.

At the end of another busy day, she did a final sweep through the dorms, checked in with security, then headed through the door to her apartment. She'd just made it into her living room when her phone buzzed. Looking down, she blinked at the number.

Oliver? Tapping on messages, she looks at the text.

I don't think I can wait until next week. How about dinner Friday night? Unless you've got a better suggestion, I hear there's a great pizza place near the center. Or anywhere you say.

She couldn't help the grin that spread across her face. At twenty-nine, she could hardly act like one of the sixteen-year-olds in her care, yet she felt a giddiness, knowing that he was serious about taking her to dinner.

She quickly tapped out a response. **Dinner sounds**

good. Pizza is always perfect. What time should we meet?

I don't think you have to worry about me knowing your address anymore. Let me pick you up.

He was right. Her usual reticence and refusal to give her address no longer applied. **I can be ready by six. My door or the center?**

Since this is a date, I'll pick you up at your door.

Labeling this as a date puts a lot of pressure on me. We better make it 6:30 so I can be sure to have the time to run a brush through my hair and find a pair of shoes that will squish my feet appropriately for date night.

She waited as the three little dots danced, surprised at how her anticipation ramped up with each message.

With brushed hair and fancy shoes, you've now just upped my pressure. I'm wondering if a pizza joint isn't the right location for such an elegant date.

Laughing out loud, she walked farther into her apartment and plopped down on the sofa. Kicking off her shoes, she tucked her feet under her butt.

I think in honor of the place we first met, the pizzeria will be perfect.

Perhaps you should leave off the fancy shoes in case the opportunity to run down an alley presents itself.

Rolling her eyes, she had a feeling he would never let her live that down. As soon as that thought crossed her mind, she jerked, realizing she'd just anticipated having a relationship lasting long enough to have a *How We Met* story to retell. Tapping out another message, she hit send.

I promise not to run down any alleys unless a serial killer is chasing me. I assume you aren't a serial killer since you work for a security company and were in the Army.

On my honor, I am not a serial killer. And I will give you no reason to have to run down an alley. So bring on the fancy shoes, and I'll see you on Friday.

She held her fingers over the keys but hesitated, realizing that while she'd dated, this was the first time in a while that she was really looking forward to one. Finally, she typed **Can't wait.** After hitting send, she wondered if that made her sound too eager. Tossing her phone onto the coffee table, she sighed.

Oh, Lordy. I am so in over my head.

12

Oliver knocked on the outer door that led up the stairs to Charity's apartment. As soon as his knuckles rapped on the metal door, he realized that he wasn't sure how she would hear him since the sound would need to travel to the second floor. That led him to ponder how she would respond to any knock on the door if she weren't expecting someone. Then he began to wonder how she would know who was outside since there was no security peephole.

Frustration washed over him for not considering this when he initially assessed her apartment. He made a mental note to ensure these concerns were added to the security plans. Scoffing, he felt sure that Poole had already thought of those details. Lifting his hands to knock again, he was surprised when his phone vibrated. Looking down, he spied the text. **Is that you at the door?**

Smiling, he typed a return text. **Yes. It's me and not a serial killer**

He heard the quick footsteps of someone descending the stairs on the other side of the door before it was flung open. He opened his mouth to talk about the security plans needed for her front door when all thoughts vanished as she smiled up at him. Her glossy hair flowed down her back in thick waves. Her makeup was subtle but highlighted her eyes and long lashes. The tinge of blush on her cheeks was so natural that he wasn't sure if it was makeup or a sign of nerves.

Her lips were tinged with a soft pink gloss, and he had to resist the urge to see if they were as kissable as they appeared. His gaze continued downward. Her clothes were hidden behind a green coat, belted at the waist, flaring out over her hips. Her feet were encased in low-heeled boots. She lifted one leg and wiggled her foot. "Not great for distances, but I could run in a pinch."

He chuckled and extended his elbow for her to take. She locked her door, then turned and slipped her arm through his.

"It's not far, but we can drive."

She nodded her agreement and allowed him to assist her up into his SUV. It was only a five-minute drive, and then he parked near the restaurant. Once inside, he ignored the appraising look of the same hostess he'd avoided when he was here before. He only wanted to look at one woman, and his hand rested on the small of her back as they walked to a booth near the back.

Comfortably seated, their order was taken, and he leaned his forearms on the table and fixed his gaze on the woman who was such an enigma to him.

A crease furrowed across her brow, and she lifted her fingers to her chin. "You're staring at me in a funny way. Do I have something on my face?"

He reached over and wrapped his hand around hers, pulling it down while shaking his head. "No! Not at all!" he felt the tips of his ears heat and wished he had a way to keep his embarrassment from showing. "I was just thinking how beautiful you are."

Her lips curved as her cheeks blushed. "Thank you."

"I'm sure you hear that a lot."

She had sipped her water, and her eyes widened before she could swallow. Coughing, she finally shook her head and laughed. "I'm afraid it's been a while since I've been on a date." Tucking a strand of hair behind her ear, she amended, "And I should warn you that it's been even longer since I've made it to a second date."

"That's hard to believe. There must be something wrong with any man who wouldn't want to ask you out for a second date."

"Don't make assumptions too early, Oliver. I might be really terrible at dating." She tried to hide her grin as she rolled her eyes toward the ceiling and ticked off her imaginative list with her fingers. "You could discover that I'm narcissistic, or a gold digger, or a self-absorbed influencer, or maybe order the most expensive thing on the menu." She suddenly dropped her mirth and held his gaze as she shrugged. "Or maybe you'll be bored out of your mind and discover I have little life outside of work."

He gently rubbed his thumb over her knuckles. "I've already seen where you work and know what you're passionate about, even though I want to hear more. I've already witnessed you chasing teenagers down an alley and watched you give away your leftovers. I've met your coworkers and can tell by the look in their eyes that they think you're amazing. So even though this might be our first official date, I don't doubt that I'll want a second date."

They were interrupted by the server bringing their pizza. When ordering, he'd been pleased to discover they liked similar toppings—meat lovers with extra cheese. Digging in, they slowed their conversation as they both ate heartily.

She ate two pieces of pizza, then leaned back against the booth cushions and patted her stomach. "I'm so full! You're going to have to finish it."

He looked down at the platter on the table between them. Normally, he'd have no problem polishing off the rest of the pizza, but remembering her carrying home leftovers, he hesitated.

She shook her head as though she understood where his thoughts had gone. "Seriously, Oliver. Please, eat whatever you want."

He took another slice. "The first time we met, I asked you why you wanted to save those kids. You told me I needed to educate myself."

She winced. "I'm so sorry, Oliver. That was incredibly rude of me."

He shook his head with it. "No, it wasn't. You were exactly right. I was looking at the world through my military mission optic, but not what was happening around me when I wasn't on a mission. I was fairly single-purposed in my focus."

"I can only imagine what you needed to be to survive as a Ranger. And we all owe you a debt for your service."

He waved away her praise. "That may be true that I did what was necessary to survive, but I'm no longer in the Army. I'm a Keeper, and I need to understand the community around me. And that's what I've tried to do in the past couple of weeks. I've looked at the news and read some reports, so I'm much more aware of youth homelessness." He leaned closer and added, "And I want to understand you better. How did you get involved with the center?"

She stared at him in silence for a long moment, and he wondered if she would speak. "I was fortunate enough to earn a scholarship to college. It was the only way I would've been able to attend. I earned a master's in social work and completed a residency at a homeless shelter. It was an area of interest for me, and I worked with students and families at a local high school who were homeless, connecting them with the services in the area."

"And Bright Futures Home?"

"There is a huge need for shelters and services for homeless youth and teens. The state is working to open more, and I spent a year working at one before being offered the position of helping to start the one here. I'm young to be the Director, and it's not false modesty to say that I really shouldn't be. I'd like to be more hands-on with the kids, but no one else wanted to take the leadership position. The last thing I wanted was for the services not to reach the kids because no one would step into the leadership position." She shrugged in a self-deprecating manner. "So here I am. I'd do anything for those kids, so stepping out of my comfort zone to become the director has also been good for me."

"Until I started reading about the issues, I had no idea of the scope of the problem. And I know I've only touched the surface with what I've read."

She squared her shoulders and stared straight into his eyes. "Every year, over four million youth and young adults experience homelessness in this country. Almost one million of those are considered unaccompanied minors. They're not part of any family or accompanied by a parent or guardian. Do you know what that equates to?"

Mesmerized by her voice and words, he shook his head.

"Almost one in thirty youths between the ages of thirteen and seventeen will experience homelessness every year. And that amount is probably greatly underreported due to the challenges with contacting them. Often, they don't go to shelters, or they transition by sleeping on sofas and floors of friends or acquaintances. And if you think this is an inner city problem, it transcends rural, suburban, and urban communities at the same rates."

The slice of pizza he started now lay unfinished on his plate as he listened. Hearing the words from Charity gave so much more emotion to the subject than just reading them from the website article. "I can't believe how prevalent it is."

Her face was tense as she held his gaze. "Oliver, the ramifications are horrendous. Food, shelter, and clothing are our most basic needs. And when those aren't being met, most people will do anything to obtain them. One in three teens on the street will be lured into prostitution within forty-eight hours of leaving home. Almost forty percent of homeless youth report using alcohol, and almost fifty percent report drug problems."

He leaned back, his appetite now waning, and the food he'd eaten now felt like a rock in his stomach. "Fuck," he breathed. "That's heartbreaking."

She glanced down at his plate, and then her eyes darted up to his as she grimaced. "And, now you can see why I rarely make it to a second date. My dinner conversation is depressing. Although, I've never had anyone on a date ask me *why* I do what I do. Usually, we don't get past them asking what I do. As soon as I tell them I work with homeless youth, either they don't know what to say, try to make a joke, or tell me that it's not society's place to care."

He jolted, his mouth dropping open. "You can't be serious! Charity, the problem with the date isn't with you. The problem is the pricks you've met."

Laughter bubbled up from her, and he grinned. She was beautiful as she spoke passionately about the needs of young people. And she was breathtaking when her eyes were lit, and the sound of her laughter filled his ears.

"Okay, change of subject. Tell me about becoming a Ranger." She crinkled her nose. "To be honest, I know nothing about special forces other than what I see in the news. I'd love to know what made you want to join."

It hit him that she didn't ask what he had done or where he had gone. She wanted to know *why* he joined. He was sure no previous date had ever asked him that.

"I have an older brother. Leo. He was only eighteen months older than me, so sometimes we seem more like twins than just brothers. My parents were great about not comparing, but as the younger one, I looked up to him. And while he was a wonderful big brother, I also felt a certain competitiveness."

He thought for a moment, then shook his head. "Not a bad competitiveness, like I had to try to be better than him. But it's just that I often fell into doing many of the same things that he did. Looking back, I suppose that could've been bad if he'd been a negative influence. As it was, he was a fucking amazing brother. So we did a lot of the same sports. Since I was two grades below him, I had my own friends, but we also shared many. He joined the Army and then went through Delta training. It's not like I didn't consider anything else for a career or thought I had to follow my brother blindly. It's just that I was interested in the same things he was. So I joined the Army, too, but decided to become a Ranger."

Her eyes twinkled. "Still a bit of competitiveness?"

"Oh, no," he said with great exaggeration while pressing his hand over his heart. "Rangers are clearly more badass than Deltas."

A beautiful smile curved her lips. She took another sip of wine and asked, "What made you decide to get out?"

"Leo was injured in an accident, which had him decide to leave the service. He joined Carson as a bodyguard to the stars when Carson started that business. Believe it or not, he was the bodyguard for Hollywood's sweetheart, Camilla Gannon."

Charity gasped. "You're kidding. She's no longer an actress, is she? In fact, I think I read she lived in a little beach town on the East Coast."

"Yep. Believe it or not, she and Leo are still friends. She's married now and is satisfied to be away from the LA madness." As he settled into his story, his gaze stayed on the way her eyes sparkled in the candlelight on the table. She seemed to listen with her whole being.

"Carson hated that business, so he joined forces with a company in Maine that dealt with security and investigations and opened an office in California. Leo was his first employee. I was still in the military, but I loved the direction Leo had taken with his career. He kept telling me that I'd have a job as soon as I wanted to leave the military. An accident also had me get out sooner than I thought, but I was lucky. I interviewed with Carson and got hired." He grinned as he placed his hand over hers. "And I met you on my very first assignment as a Keeper."

She looked down at their joined hands and smiled. Then lifting her head to hold his gaze, she asked, "What exactly is a Keeper?"

He thought about the newest tattoo that he'd just gotten on his shoulder and smiled. "It's everything."

13

Oliver recognized that his response to Charity's question needed more explanation. The only problem was that he was such a new LSIWC employee he felt inadequate to give it the proper definition.

"When I was in the military, it was about brotherhood, doing whatever the mission required, and figuring someone above us directing our actions had a cause for our country that made it all worth it." He hesitated, and when he looked up, her head was tilted to the side, and her attention was riveted on him. He sighed heavily. "For the most part, I think it was."

She leaned closer. "And now... I sense a doubt in you."

He swallowed deeply, relinquishing hold of some of the protective layers shown to most people. "Sometimes... the mission was to take out someone our government deemed a threat. And then, you realize that the person who takes their place is worse, but their politics might align with whoever our leader is at the time." He leaned back and scoffed. "I was in long enough to see us take out someone only to turn around and take out their successor down the line. After a while, it fucks with your head."

"Was it always like that?"

"No," he said quickly. "Thank God. Many of our missions were rescues."

"And now?"

"Keepers." He stated the word, thinking how to describe it without sounding ridiculous. His breath hissed through his teeth as they pressed against his bottom lip. "It started with the original owner of Lighthouse Security Investigations based in Maine. According to Leo, Mace Hanover's grandfather used to tell him stories about the lighthouse keepers of old. He developed an appreciation for how they risked their lives to guide sailors to safety. Mace had been in the Army Green Berets and knew Carson back then. When he separated from the military and started his business, he nicknamed his employees Keepers. I think it's a reminder, every day, of who we are and what we're trying to do. Guide people to safety."

Her hands squeezed his as she leaned closer. "I think that's wonderful, Oliver. And I think that's exactly what you are."

He slowly shook his head and rubbed his fingers over her delicate hands. "I'm not the only one, Charity. You're a Keeper to those kids."

Their eyes remained locked on each other until the server cleared her throat, causing them to swing their gaze up to her.

"Do you want me to box up the rest of your pizza?"

He knew what Charity's answer would be and went ahead and replied, "Yes, please."

She laughed. "I told you that I wasn't going to chase anyone tonight. What will I do with all this pizza?"

"What were you gonna do with the pizza from the first time I saw you?"

She crinkled her nose. "I was going to put it in the refrigerator. I don't like food to go to waste, so if I can't eat everything during the few times I eat out, I make sure to take home the leftovers and eat them later in the week."

As he stood, he reached out, loving how her palm felt against his. He looked at the now crowded restaurant, and instead of guiding her with his hand on the small of her back, he led the way so that his larger body would naturally cut a path for her while keeping their fingers linked.

He held her coat at the door so she could slip it on. After she tied the belt, she looked up at him and smiled.

Once outside, a chilly wind swept past, and he wrapped his arm around her shoulders. He pulled her in closely as they hustled down the sidewalk to his vehicle. Soon, they were parked in front of her door. He wanted more time with her but didn't want to seem presumptuous.

Hurrying around the front of the vehicle, he helped her down. As soon as they stood at the door with her keys in her hand, she turned and looked at him. Placing one palm on his chest, she lifted on her toes and kissed the edge of his mouth. The electricity that shot through his body was more than he'd felt with any other full-on-the-lips kiss. He could only imagine what that would be like, but before he had a chance to find out, she smiled as her heels settled back onto the concrete.

"Would you like to come up?"

Those six little words caused the breath to rush from his lungs, and he couldn't respond fast enough. "Oh, hell yeah."

She laughed and handed him the keys while wrapping her fingers around the leftover pizza box. She walked through and led him up the stairs. Again, he unlocked the door to her apartment, and they stepped through.

After she moved into the kitchen, he heard the refrigerator door open, then the rustling of the leftover bag as she placed it inside. "Would you like something to drink?" she called out.

"Absolutely," he replied, following her melodic voice into the kitchen.

She graced him with a smile as she looked over her shoulder. "I have wine, although not expensive. I have a beer, but it's a craft one that I got at a local shop, so it might not be to your taste. I also have iced tea or can make hot tea." She looked back into the refrigerator, then over at him. "I'm afraid that's all I have."

"Beer is fine. Any kind."

As she retrieved a beer from the refrigerator and poured a glass of wine for herself, he couldn't help but notice her innate caregiving nature. It was as though taking care of others was an integral part of who she was. So intrigued, he wondered about her upbringing.

What were her parents like? Was she raised nearby? The questions danced on the tip of his tongue, ready to be voiced, but then he suddenly decided to hold back.

They had covered a multitude of topics for a first date, and he was eager to have a second date. Deciding to save her background for the next time, he stepped forward as she handed him the beer. He took her free hand and led her back into the living room, where they settled on the sofa.

Sitting beside him, she bent down and gracefully slipped off her ankle boots. He twisted to face her, and his heart raced when she leaned closer. He cupped her face, utterly captivated and desperate to taste those irresistibly kissable lips.

As soon as their lips met in a gentle, longing kiss, electricity seemed to fire between them, settling first in his chest before shooting straight to his cock. He angled his head, and as soon as her lips parted, he slipped his tongue into her warm mouth. She didn't hesitate to guide her velvety soft tongue over his, and his arms banded around her middle as he pulled her tighter.

She shifted, throwing one leg over his until she straddled his thighs, her dress now hiked up to her ass. The urge to lay her back on the sofa, unwrap the dress like a present, and rip her panties off so he could plunge his already aching cock deep inside was strong, but his self-resolve was stronger. He had already acknowledged he wanted a second date, but the truth hit him—he wanted a lot more. He had no idea how long they might last, but Charity Whitlock was worth finding out how far they could go together.

Her fingers clung to his shoulders, her short nails digging in slightly through his shirt. As one of her hands slid to the back of his head, her fingers slowly dragged through his hair. His already sensitive skin tingled, and a shiver ran down his spine. His actions mimicked hers, and he discovered the golden tresses were just as silky as he'd imagined.

The kiss flamed hotter and grew wilder, and she began to rock against his crotch. He was driven mad by the movement, and the need for more than friction coursed through his veins. Just when he wasn't sure he could hold back, his hands moved to her shoulders, and he gently pushed enough to separate their lips. Her eyes were closed, but the cool air moved between them, and they fluttered open before widening.

Her cheeks flamed pink, and she gasped. "Oh my God! I'm so sorry. I was practically dry-humping you! I'm so sorry!" She tried to scramble off his lap, but he held fast and shook his head.

"Don't think I don't want this, Charity," he said, his voice rasping as he tried to catch his breath. "I haven't had a kiss like that affect me so much since I was probably a teenager."

A snort slipped out, and she slapped her hand over her mouth. Unable to stop the giggle, she said, "I have a hard time imagining you as a teenager."

Still rocking from the roller coaster of a kiss, he blurted, "I knew Leo kissed his first girl when he was fourteen years old. Not that it was a great kiss, according to him. But still, I had something to live up to. So when I was almost fifteen, I knew time was running out."

She laughed aloud and shifted slightly so that she was still straddling his thighs but no longer pressing against his erection. He hated not having her body so close but knew it was for the best if he was going to continue his embarrassing story.

"I was desperate. The clock was running out. The only girl who had shown an interest in me was another fourteen-year-old. Sonya Maxwell. Jesus, I can't believe I remember her name."

Charity rolled her eyes and shook her head. "I hardly believe that! You probably had more girls than just lucky Sonya lined up, ready to kiss you!"

"Nope! I was tall, and even though I ate all the time and played sports, I didn't have a lot of muscle yet. Leo was already sixteen and done with pimples, but not me. On top of that, I still had braces. And my ears stuck out."

Charity was full-on laughing aloud. "Keep going. I have to hear about this kiss!"

Now wondering if he was crazy for admitting this to her, he plunged onward. "I was two days away from my fifteenth birthday, and I passed her a note, asking if she wanted to kiss. She passed me another note in the hall and agreed. So at the end of the day, we waited at our lockers until no one else was around and stared at each other. I wanted to be so suave but had no clue how to be. I grabbed her shoulders and brought her forward, terrified she was going to slap me. She didn't and leaned forward, too. But I closed my eyes too soon, and our noses bumped. I opened my eyes, but she was right there looking like a cyclops since she was so close."

Charity snorted with laughter as she wiped the tears from her eyes. "Keep going. Surely, this kiss gets better."

He nodded, barely able to speak through his chuckles. "Finally, our lips touched, and I had two thoughts in my head. One... I thought I'd feel it in my dick, but I didn't, probably because of the second thought."

"What thought was that?"

"It was a kind of slimy kiss that I really didn't want to repeat."

"And what about poor Sonya?"

"I don't think she liked it any better. She looked at me, blinked, and then ran off. She didn't talk to me again for the rest of high school."

Still laughing, Charity reached up and cupped his jaws, her thumbs dragging over his beard. "Well, I'm sure you've had thousands of kisses between then and now, each giving you more practice. But for the record, Mr. Parker, I felt our kiss run straight through my whole body, settling deep inside and making my panties wet."

"Fuck," he breathed. "I'm trying to do the right thing here, Charity, but you say something like that, and I feel the caveman coming out."

"What does the caveman want to do?"

"Throw you over my shoulder and drag you off to my lair."

Their mirth slowly ended as they continued to stare into each other's eyes. Slowly, she slid off his lap and reached her hand out. He stood, and they moved toward each other until she leaned her head back and offered her mouth. He bent to kiss her, forcing himself to keep it gentle.

"I'm going to go now, sweetheart. I want another date with you as soon as we can arrange it."

"I'd like that," she whispered before lifting on her toes and kissing him lightly.

He adjusted his crotch and then led her to the door. "I hate that you have to go down the stairs, but you need to lock up after me."

She nodded, and they walked to the outer door, where they kissed goodbye again. He waited outside until he heard the lock click, then jogged back to his SUV. She didn't leave his mind on the entire drive back to Leo's house. And he grinned the entire way.

14

Kofi strode past the pizzeria, well aware he couldn't hit the same place again so soon. His gaze snagged on a woman sitting at a table near the window. He recognized her, then his gaze shot to the man sitting across from her, and he sucked in a hasty breath. It was the man who'd chased him and Ramzi a few weeks ago with the woman from the center. His initial glare softened as the memory resurfaced. He had to admit that the man could have caught them or called the police. But she'd stopped him, and the man allowed her to toss them some food without reporting them.

Kofi's stomach rumbled, a painful reminder that he hadn't eaten since yesterday, and his meal had only been a slice of bread and some cheese. He couldn't stand the thought of eating when Ramzi wasn't able to.

He hurried away from the pizzeria, avoiding any chance of being seen by anyone who might recognize him from his previous visit, especially not with the woman or the man inside.

Regret gnawed at him for foolishly deciding to steal the pizza. There was too much he had to lose, and it could've made things a hell of a lot worse for Ramzi. He snorted as he dropped his chin against the wind and shoved his hands into the pockets of his jacket. It was hard to imagine things getting worse, but sometimes, there was no choice.

As Ramzi's older brother, it was up to him to ensure their safety, and he'd failed. Ramzi had taken another risk on his own, grabbing money from an older man, and had come dangerously close to being caught.

Eliza and Cory Halston were infuriated by the incident, and for the past two nights, they had locked Ramzi in the basement cell. Kofi had begged them to let him take the punishment, but the Halstons weren't about to give any mercy. It was how they maintained control. Ramzi was enduring his punishment without making a sound, knowing that crying for help would end in a beating for Kofi.

The Halstons appreciated having siblings work for them. Most people could ignore the bond of someone they didn't share blood with because, when push came to shove, it was truly a dog-eat-dog world.

Kofi had already completed his assignment this afternoon, placing a skimmer and camera on his targeted ATM. That would get him his regular payout from the Haltons, but if he could score big tonight, he could earn a reprieve for Ramzi and get him out of the basement cell early.

Kofi didn't know how Cory Halston figured out how to steal from ATMs—all Kofi knew was that Cory made the kids working for him do all the dirty work, then he'd sit at his computers all day and night, moving money from one account to another.

Kofi sighed. He and Ramzi earned very little from the Halstons. *Not enough to ever get ahead and away from them.*

Walking along, assuming the appearance of a kid just trying to stay warm, he spotted the man dressed in ragged jeans and an old Army jacket. The man had alighted from a shiny, black pickup truck and walked into a laundromat known among the street people to be more than just laundering clothes. Kofi had no doubt the man was getting ready to launder drug money.

Slipping around to the side alley, he waited until the man came out of the laundromat and passed him by. Desperation drove him as he jerked his knit cap down over his face, exposing only his eyes and nose. He grabbed the man and jerked him back into the alley, shoving his face against the brick wall. Digging his hand into the man's coat pocket, he prayed he didn't encounter any drug needles. Thankfully, he wrapped his fingers around the packet, jerked it out, and then shoved the man to the ground before turning and running as though the hounds of hell were after him. For all he knew, they might have been.

He ran for blocks, moving in and out of alleys before finally slowing and pulling his cap off his face. He jerked off his coat and turned it inside out, changing the color of his jacket from black to green. He didn't stop to count the money until he got closer to home.

Home. That's a joke. He once heard that home was

where the heart was. That was where Ramzi was, so he supposed it was as much a home as any place. He went around the back of the dimly lit house, where secrets and power played a dangerous game. His normal confidence was missing, knowing he held his brother's fate in his hands. Moving through the back door, he stopped in the kitchen. It was clean because Eliza made sure the kids kept it that way. But it stank with age-old cigarette smoke that was etched into every crevice.

Eliza sat at the kitchen table, her over-bleached blond hair teased out and sprayed until it never moved. But then, she rarely did either. She was almost always sitting at the kitchen table, ruling her little kingdom from the room where she could keep an eye on everything and everybody coming and going.

Her eyes narrowed to slits, landing on him until her gaze dropped to the packet in his hand. "Tell me no one saw you. Tell me this isn't gonna come back on you." Her gravel words had to filter through her pack-a-day cigarette habit.

"No one saw me."

"Where'd you make the hit?"

He licked his lips, uncertain if he could get away with lying. She'd be pissed that he hit a place she hadn't sent him to. But then, he hoped she'd be satisfied with the amount. Glancing at the packet now in her hand, he began to doubt what he'd done.

"I asked you a question, boy," she said, slowly standing. Her bone-thin body with her head of blond teased hair made him think of a matchstick, always ready to ignite. And with her volatile temper he'd witnessed many times, she could go from calm to blazing inferno in an instant.

"I hit the laundromat over on Market Street."

Her eyes narrowed first with doubt, followed by a flash of anger. "Are you fuckin' shittin' me?"

As the tension thickened, the heavy stomp of boots coming down the hallway announced the arrival of Eliza's better half... or rather just her other half. If Kofi had to decide which was better, it would be a complete toss-up. Both were equally as vicious.

Kofi's heart quickened its rhythm, beating in sync with each footstep reverberating down the hall until the large man entered the room. Cory Halston might have been fit in his prime, but he had succumbed to the years of hard living and a mostly sedentary job. His gut protruded, and his physique was more flab than muscles. But his meaty fists could instill fear and obedience. His dark gaze moved from Kofi over to Eliza, down to the package in her hand, and back to Kofi. "What the fuck is going on in here?"

With a cigarette held between her fingers, she jerked them toward Kofi. "This asshole hit the laundromat on Market Street."

Kofi had never seen surprise written on Cory's face, but his wife's words caused him to jerk slightly and then blink as he looked at Kofi.

Quickly, Kofi said, "No one saw me. No one followed me. You said if I scored big, I could get Ramzi out of the cell. So I was smart. Followed the rules that you taught me. And I think you'll find that"—he inclined his head toward the package clutched in Eliza's hand—"to be just what you need."

Still holding her cigarette with the ash threatening to drop, she used her long fingernails to slice through the paper and unwrapped a stack of ten-dollar bills. Even with limited experience, Kofi knew she was holding a thousand dollars. Eliza plopped her ass back onto the chair and managed to drop the cigarette expertly into the ashtray while keeping her fingers around the money.

"Plus, I got the skimmer on the ATM at Garden Street. The one near the department store," Kofi rushed to explain.

Eliza's thinly plucked brows lifted. Kofi wanted to beg that they let Ramzi out of the basement immediately. He also wanted to beg that they give them the percentage that they promised. But he'd learned that there was a time to stay quiet, and considering he'd taken a big risk in getting the money where he did, he didn't want to give them a reason to back out of any deal.

That was one thing about the Halstons. They generally kept their promises because they knew if they screwed over the kids in their care, they wouldn't get very far. Allegiance was the best way for them to stay safe.

His heart continued to pound, and sweat trickled down the side of his face. But he waited quietly, giving them the respect they demanded, even though they hadn't earned it. Everything Kofi did, he did for Ramzi.

Eliza cleared her throat and looked up first toward

Cory and then at Kofi. "Okay." Looking back up at Cory, she said, "This buys Ramzi out."

Cory rubbed his chin and eyed the money before shifting his gaze to Kofi. "You did it, so we'll uphold our end of the bargain." Then he leaned forward with a mean glint in his dark eyes and added, "But remember, you're responsible for his training. I don't want any more fuckups, or we'll decide you're not worth the risk."

"Understand, sir," Kofi said, working to keep his voice steady. He hated to give the title to a man like Cory Halston, but he knew how to play the game. His gaze dropped to the money still in Eliza's hand.

She picked up her cigarette and took a long drag before exhaling along with the bitter breath that almost made him gag.

"You know that you won't get a full cut. Part of your cut goes for Ramzi's freedom."

"Yes, ma'am."

She snickered, then ended up in a coughing fit.

Cory shook his head. "Those fucking things are gonna give you cancer and kill you one day."

"Everyone's got to die somehow," Eliza sneered.

Kofi's face remained blank, but he couldn't help but think the world would be better when those two were gone.

"Your cut is five percent," she announced, skillfully peeling off the bills. It struck him that she handled money like an expert, but that was probably the only thing she'd ever worked hard at.

With a mixture of excitement and relief, he pocketed the fifty dollars she handed him, discreetly hiding the surge of joy that threatened to overcome him. What he'd just brought in was more than what any of the other kids ever stole, yet he'd only been given half of what he normally would have earned. Yet the fact that he'd succeeded in securing Ramzi's freedom caused the tightness in his chest to ease.

Kofi was different from the other kids in this grim house. He had a talent for saving his earnings, spending only when necessary. He taught Ramzi the same principle, knowing the money they saved was their key to escaping the Halstons' clutches. Many people wouldn't understand his choices—robbing someone and then saving the money as though it was a good thing. He knew it wasn't right, but trapped in a life he didn't know how to get out of, taking care of a sibling he would die for, he was doing the best he could.

He followed Cory down the basement steps, the dank smell and dim light making his fists clench with the desire to wrap his hands around Cory's neck and squeeze the life out of him. Fighting to control the urge to rid them of the abusive asshole, he stepped into the basement. The space was divided into smaller cells, each made of wooden boards with wooden doors, so the world was dark for the days you were punished. Cory unlocked the padlock and threw the door open. Kofi noticed no one else was in confinement. While he was relieved that no one else was imprisoned in these foul conditions, it also meant that Ramzi had had no one to talk to. His brother stumbled out, eyes red from crying, and his clothing rumpled.

Ramzi's gaze blinked as he looked in fright at Cory,

and then his eyes shot toward Kofi. Ramzi opened his mouth, and Kofi knew his brother would assume he was trying to take his place. Not wanting him to say anything to anger Cory, he quickly shook his head, and Ramzi's mouth snapped shut.

"Hope you learned your lesson, you little shithead," Cory chided. "Learn from your brother. In fact, from now on, stick with him. Don't make any dumbass decisions on your own and bring the law down on us. That's the fastest way you could end up with a bullet in your head."

Ramzi nodded, his eyes wide and fearful.

Kofi jerked his head to the side, indicating that Ramzi could follow him. Neither spoke as they ascended the stairs. In the kitchen, Eliza barely spared them a glance as she muttered, "Get a piece of bread if you want something to eat."

Ramzi seemed frozen in place, so Kofi walked over and grabbed several slices of bread and cheese. The two boys turned and hurried out of the kitchen. Kofi wanted to get away from the Halstons as quickly as possible. They moved to the stairs of the house and headed up to the second floor.

Glancing into one bedroom, Kofi saw the two prone figures moving under a blanket as the sounds of grunting filled the room. One of the girls offered herself for an extra percentage of money. Kofi hated what she felt like she needed to do and never took her up on the offer.

Steering Ramzi away from that bedroom, he looked in the next one, but it was filled with kids already sleeping. At the end of the hall was a large closet with a mattress on the floor. There wasn't a window, and it was next to the bathroom, so the room would sometimes fill with unpleasant odors when the toilet backed up. However, it was the one place where Kofi and Ramzi could be alone.

Nodding for Ramzi to sit on the mattress, Kofi walked into the bathroom and grabbed a handful of toilet paper before returning to the closet. He handed it to Ramzi to let him wipe his eyes and blow his nose. Sitting with his back against the wall, he kept the door partially open to ensure he would be aware if anyone was out in the hall. His brother leaned into him, finally letting out a long sigh.

"I'm sorry. I didn't mean to fuck things up and make it harder on you or get thrown into the basement," Ramzi apologized.

Kofi's heart ached. "I'm sorry, too, little bro. I should have been with you. From now on, we stick together." Heaving a great sigh, he shook his head. "I'm sorry I couldn't protect you."

Ramzi jerked around, his eyes filled with guilt as he shook his head. "It's not your fault. You're the best brother anyone could ever have."

Kofi snorted, thinking how far from the truth that statement was.

After a moment, Ramzi spoke in a low voice. "That's what I told the woman at the shelter."

He startled at Ramzi's words and looked down at him. "The shelter?"

"The woman who didn't let the man come after us

when we took the pizza. The one who works at the shelter."

"What are you talking about?"

"I told her about you."

Icy-cold fingers gripped him as he wondered what his brother might have disclosed to the woman. "Why the hell did you talk about me?"

"No, no, it's okay," Ramzi reassured. "I didn't say anything bad. I just told her you were the best brother anyone could have, and you've always cared for me."

Twisting on the mattress so that he was facing Ramzi, he stared, dumbfounded. First, that Ramzi would have had the guts to go to the center, and second, that he'd told her that his brother was a good person.

Ramzi shrugged. "It was after that night. Do you know the name of it? Bright Futures Home. I thought that sounded nice. I'd seen her go in there before when some kids were getting off a bus."

Kofi knew the place and knew the woman who ran it. If ever there was a name of a place to draw in someone, that would be it. "Why did you go there?"

"I wanted to thank her for… you know. She gave us leftovers." Ramzi ducked his head and shrugged. "Not a lot of people do stuff for us without asking anything in return. I just felt like I should do it."

Unlike the irritation he'd felt a few minutes ago, Kofi was overwhelmed by a surge of emotions. Shame crept in, settling in his gut. His brother had done something that he should've done. Sucking in a deep breath, he exhaled slowly. He leaned back against the wall again and placed his arm around Ramzi. "You did the right thing."

They shared the bread and cheese and cups of water filled from the tap in the bathroom.

"How did you get me out?" Ramzi's voice was barely a whisper as though afraid of the answer.

Kofi chuckled softly. Shoving his hand into his pocket, he pulled out the fifty dollars Eliza had given him. "I made a big haul. It was enough to get you out and also get this."

His brother's eyes were wide. Then he lowered his voice again. "Are we close?"

He knew exactly what Ramzi was asking. They'd been saving their money for the past year to get a small efficiency apartment somewhere that was theirs. He'd be eighteen and could get a job that might not pay as much but would be legal. "We're getting there."

After a moment, Ramzi's eyes began drooping, and Kofi assumed his brother had almost no sleep for the past two nights. Sighing, he said, "You know it's not right to steal?"

Ramzi hesitated, then finally admitted, "Yeah, I know."

"I promise I'll get us out of this place," Kofi said fiercely. "And when I do, we won't steal ever again. But for now, don't make a move without me. We gotta be smart. We gotta stay safe."

"Okay, whatever you say, Kofi. I promise."

Ramzi fell asleep, but it didn't come for Kofi. He'd never imagined this would become their lives. Stealing money for a little percentage. The Halston's giving them just enough to keep them dangling on the hook. He'd accepted that prison might be in his future. But now, looking down at his slumbering brother's sweet and innocent face, he knew he couldn't live with himself if something happened to Ramzi.

Making up his mind, he lay down next to the door on the mattress so no one could get to his brother without him knowing. Getting out of this fucked-up situation would feel like freedom. Maybe, just maybe, it would be a bright future.

15

Charity hustled through the door leading into the center. She couldn't believe of all days, today was the day she was late. But she and Oliver had talked on the phone long into the wee hours of the morning.

In fact, they'd talked every night since their pizza date. He had been given other assignments to work on and hadn't been back to the center, but today was the day everything would start happening.

Rushing into her office, she called out to Paula. "Coffee! Stat!"

A few minutes later, Paula came rushing in with a large mug of coffee. Grabbing it, Charity couldn't help but laugh when she saw the words emblazoned on the mug. ***Lack of planning on your part does not constitute an emergency on mine.***

Lifting a brow, she said, "Listen, when it comes to coffee, everything is an emergency!"

"Well, I would've had some ready, but you usually have it at home before you come."

"Sorry! I didn't get much sleep and was running late, and the security electricians are coming today."

Paula's brow furrowed. "Are you worried about it? Is that why you couldn't sleep?"

She blushed but remained silent as she took another sip of coffee. Thank God Paula knew how to make her coffee sweet and creamy.

"Oh, I get it. You've been staying up too late with Mr. Badass Security Guy, right?"

"Yes, but not the way you think. It's only texting or phone calls." Seeing Paula's smile droop, she continued, "But hopefully, he'll be here tomorrow, and we'll have another date this weekend."

"I hope date equates to rocking sex."

She laughed. "Well, I don't have a particular number of dates before I put out—"

"Girl, when was the last time you put out?"

Charity huffed. "Who has time for sex when they're trying to run this place?"

"I would always make time for sex. But we're not talking about me, we're talking about you. So maybe this weekend?"

"I prefer to be spontaneous. So I'm not going to plan."

Paula lifted her brow. "So you're not going to shave, moisturize, pluck, put on that sexy underwear, and do everything else to be ready just in case?"

"A girl can be ready without planning."

Before Paula had a chance to respond, Helen popped her head into the office. "There you are, Paula. The security people are in the lobby."

"Oh, damn," Paula said, turning to hurry out of the office. "Our boss distracted me with talks of sex!"

Helen looked over at Charity, who sputtered into her coffee. "I was not." Realizing she sounded like she was twelve, she set her cup down on her desk and rushed out into the lobby after Paula.

She spied Tricia waiting in the lobby, with six men standing just behind her. Hurrying over, she exclaimed, "I'm so sorry I wasn't here to greet you. Would anyone like some coffee?"

"No, that's fine," Tricia said. "My guys know to tank up before they come!"

She met each electrician and noted Paula had given them all visitor badges. Elliot met them in the lobby. "He's part of our security team and will need to be familiar with all the equipment."

"Once we start working, we'll quickly take care of things," Tricia said. "We should be finished with installations late Wednesday or early Thursday, and then we can do our testing Thursday and Friday. If all goes well, we'll be out of your hair by the end of the week."

"We're just so thrilled that you're here and can do this for us," Charity enthused.

For the next several hours, she darted around the building, taking care of her normal duties as well as popping out and walking the halls, checking to see what was being done. She was so impressed with Trish's team as they efficiently placed cameras and alarms in all the agreed-upon areas.

She wondered when they would get to her apartment, but a text from Oliver had assured her that he'd be there the next day when they would be in her personal space. She hated that she wasn't going to see him today, but as frazzled as she was, she thought the distraction of him would be too much.

Checking at the end of the day, she was amazed at how each work area was now clean and all the tools and equipment were put away. By the time the kids alighted from the school bus, it was as though no one had been there.

The next day, she set her alarm for thirty minutes earlier and managed to have her coffee in her apartment even though she was bleary-eyed. She took several long breaths between sips and smiled at her mug. ***Badass Boss Bitch and Princess... deal with it.***

Hurrying down the steps, she once again rushed through the center and into her office. She barely had time to look at the files on her desk and open up her laptop when Paula popped her head through the doorway.

"I looked outside, but it appears that everyone is sitting in their trucks and vans. Even Ms. Poole."

"Thank you, Paula. She told me yesterday that they would wait until the kids had loaded onto the buses." Glancing at our clock, she said, "I'll head outside now for the kids."

To keep the reception area from becoming too crowded in the mornings, especially if someone was looking for an intake, the kids used the door leading from the multipurpose room out to the sidewalk where the buses picked them up. There were many eyes on it for security—the McGabes, the Tobiassons, Elliot, and any other staff available. Charity always made it the habit of being there for the goodbye. The best way for a child to have a good day at school was to start with breakfast and then someone who cared about them enough to wish for their day to go well.

As soon as they got to school, things might go downhill, but she was determined to make sure each child in her care had a chance to have a great day with a guaranteed good start.

She hurried to the multipurpose room where the kids were lining up. The teenagers heading to the high school were the first to be picked up, followed by the middle schoolers.

Stepping outside, she smiled widely as she said goodbye to each teen, making sure they had their homework, backpacks, and school supplies. The kids were eligible for the free lunch program, and she wanted to ensure they had a water bottle and snacks if they wanted them.

"Have a good day, Tim," she said as she shook the hand of the first teenager in line. "Jon!" she called out as she practiced the complicated handshake he'd taught her.

"You've almost got it, Ms. Whitlock," he said, laughing.

"I'm just not very coordinated," she complained with a smile.

Carol and Sue were two teenage girls who had become best friends at the home. Both threw their arms around her and said, "Bye, Miss Whitlock."

Her heart was warm at the way the two girls had

bonded, encouraging each other. She knew from their counseling sessions that neither girl had come from a nurturing environment, and they'd never had another female they could count on.

More high schoolers came out, heading for the alternative education school. These were the ones who decided that they didn't have enough time or interest to work for a high school degree and wanted to earn their GED. The city's alternative school had teachers just for those who wanted to pursue this avenue. Shaking the hands of each one, she also wished them a good day.

Another van pulled up that would take some of the older teenagers to the job training vocational school that the city offered. With a wave, she watched them drive off.

As the high school bus pulled away from the curb, she jumped up and down, throwing her hands over her head in a wild wave. Some of the kids on the bus laughed, and some rolled their eyes, shaking their heads. She knew it was just a laugh but hoped the smile they rode away with would last them throughout the day.

Helen escorted the middle school kids out, and Charity allowed herself to be a little bit more silly with them. Sometimes, she attempted a rap song using their names but was horrible at it. They didn't seem to mind as they laughed, giggled, or chuckled, but once again, each left with a smile on their face and a hearty goodbye.

"Goodbye, Robina. Have a good day, Latifah. Tamaria,

good luck with your English test. Timothy, you know you can ace the math. Pat, you got this!" Once again, with the precision of a practiced routine, she leaped into the air as the middle school bus pulled away from the curb. Her hands waved wildly in the air, a joyful display that never failed to elicit laughter from the kids onboard.

Turning around, she spied her smiling staff enter the building, with Helen glancing over her shoulder toward her, a grin on her face.

"Look behind you," Helen whispered loudly, as though sharing a secret everyone else knew.

She spun around and gasped. As she blinked in stunned silence, a group of people standing on the sidewalk stared back at her, unable to hide their laughter. Tricia and Poole stood with several other men she didn't know, but based on what she was learning, she had no doubt they were also Keepers. Trish's electricians were behind this group. And right in front was Oliver, his stance exuding confidence. Legs spread, arms crossed over his chest, and crinkles emitted from his eyes as his smile widened.

She'd never minded any passerby seeing her whacky morning routine, but as her face heated, she was sure it was flaming red. She marched toward them, adopting the most professional expression possible under the circumstances. With eyebrows raised, she calmly greeted, "Good morning."

The attempts at restraint were abandoned as the group erupted with laughter. Owning the situation, she performed an impromptu curtsy before burying her face in her hands as her shoulders shook with embarrassed laughter.

Strong arms enveloped her, and she peeked through her fingers to see a pair of boots right in front of her. She didn't need to look up to know who it was, but the excitement she'd felt when she had awakened intensified. Lifting her head, she sucked in a quick breath at the handsome face so close to her. So familiar yet still surprising. "Hey," she whispered.

"Hey to you," he said, his smile wide. "I liked the morning performance."

"I want to give the kids a chance to start their day off in a good, if albeit goofy, way."

"I could go to work with a smile every day if I'd had you cheering me on."

Her teeth nibbled her bottom lip as she considered his words. They had only kissed, but the idea of being with him at the start of each day, preferably after having a great night together, raced through her mind. "Yeah..." she breathed.

"I have some people I want you to meet."

Poole, Tricia, and the electricians followed Paula into the center. That left three men and one woman. There was a twinkle in his eyes, but assuming she was meeting his coworkers, she could handle herself.

Oliver said, "I'd like you all to meet Charity Whitlock, Director of Bright Futures Home and cheerleader extraordinaire for the going-to-school ritual."

The others grinned widely, and before she could elbow Oliver in the gut, he continued.

"And here are a few Keepers. This is Jeb Torres and Adam Calvin."

She shook their hands, welcoming them to the center before they left to follow Tricia and Poole inside.

"And these two are more Keepers. This is my brother, Leo, and this brilliant beauty is his better half, Natalie."

As soon as he mentioned the word *brother*, her eyes widened. *Shit! This is a big deal.* She turned to them and managed to straighten her wobbly smile as she forced out the words of welcome. "Hi! It's nice to meet you."

"It's nice to meet you, too," Leo said, his eyes twinkling.

"You have no idea how nice it is to meet you," Natalie added. "By the way, I'm not here to work today. I'm here to see who snagged Oliver's attention 'cause I've been just waiting for him to get caught by someone."

"Natalie…" Oliver's low voice carried a warning tone despite his obvious affection.

Putting his arm around his wife, Leo pulled her into his side. "Babe, chill."

Natalie sent a narrowed-eyed glare up to Leo. "Hell, I put up with teasing for years. Little ole baby brother can stand me poking fun at him." She turned back and graced Charity with a smile. "Honest to God, he's great. But I'm here to check you out and fill your head with stories about him that would curl your toes."

Charity blinked at the fireball in front of her, not knowing if she was friend or foe. Or a combination of both.

Oliver wrapped his arm around Charity but kept his gaze on Natalie. "I'm warning you—"

"Oh hell, like I'm scared of you!" She turned to Charity. "Come show me around."

"Charity has work to do—" Oliver continued to argue.

Charity looked up at him and lifted a brow. "I'm perfectly capable of showing Natalie around my center and having what I'm sure will be an informative chat." Looking at his sister-in-law, she smiled. "Ready whenever you are."

Natalie laughed. "Charity, you've got brains and beauty, and other than Oliver, you have good taste. But I have no doubt you can cure whatever ails him."

She snorted and knew she and Natalie were going to get along well.

"Are you finished now?" Oliver asked, his hands planted on his hips.

Natalie patted her slightly protruding tummy. "Baby Parker and I are going to keep Charity company without you and Leo." She stepped forward and looped her arm through Charity's. "Come on, let's get acquainted."

Walking into the lobby, she glanced over her shoulder, her eyes wide. Leo was laughing, and Oliver simply lifted his hands in defeat. "You'll be fine.

"I know you've got work to do, but don't mind me as I shadow you today. You can tell me everything about this place and keep an eye on the electricians."

"Okay," Charity agreed easily, leading the way into her office. This day was going to require more coffee.

"I told Carson that I was coming today. I was honest about just coming to see who was already taking up residence in Oliver's mind. He laughed and told me not to worry about it. And then Rachel told me that since I was working the *Welcome-to-the-Keepers* committee, I was still here officially."

Charity was still trying to unpack all that Natalie had said when she plopped down in her chair. She looked around, but it seemed Paula had already absconded with her mug.

Charity jumped up before Natalie had a chance to sit. "I need coffee."

"Um… okay."

"I have herbal tea in my apartment."

Natalie grinned. "Then let's go."

She hesitated, knowing she had a full day of work to finish, but since she needed to be in her apartment sometime with the electricians and she really wouldn't get any work accomplished with Natalie shadowing her, she nodded. "Follow me."

Once they were in her apartment, she ushered Natalie to her kitchen, put on the kettle, and popped a pod into her coffee maker. She moved to get the creamer out when Natalie made herself at home and reached for a mug from the dishwashing rack.

She held one up. "Is that your cup?"

Charity looked over to see her holding the **Badass Boss Bitch and Princess… *deal with it*** mug. Nodding, she laughed.

"Did someone from your staff give you that?"

She shook her head. "Nope, I got that for myself."

A smile curved Natalie's lips. "Why did you get that one?"

She stopped and looked at the cup for a long moment before lifting her gaze to Natalie. "Because it's true. Knowing who we are and who we want to become is half the battle. So once we decide what we want, we need to remind ourselves often. So that mug is my reminder."

Natalie pinned her intense gaze on Charity. "Well… I already know what I need to know. You and I are going to get along great, and you'll be able to keep Oliver in line when he's an ass." She held up a finger and added, "Not that he's much of an ass… but he is a man, so there's only so long they can go before a bit of *assery* comes out!"

She blinked and then burst out laughing, taking what was an obvious compliment to heart.

16

"Your wife is crazy," Oliver groaned. "And if she says anything to upset Charity, I swear I'll—"

"Give me a fucking break!" Leo laughed. "The ten years that Natalie and I were friends, you constantly rode my ass about claiming her. And every chance you got when you were around her, you flirted just to drive me nuts. So if Natalie is going to spend some time with Charity, you've got to suck it up and deal with it."

"Hey! I was always trying to get you and Natalie together. How do I know that Natalie won't say or do something that will send Charity running?"

Leo turned his exasperated expression directly toward Oliver. "Seriously, bro? Natalie has wanted you to find someone special for as long as you've known her. And from everything you've said, Charity sounds perfect. So give your sister-in-law a chance to get to know the woman who just might become our sister-in-law."

Oliver's feet stumbled, and he stared at his brother

with his mouth hanging open. "You do realize that she and I have only been on one date, right? I hardly think it's the time to start talking about her becoming a sister-in-law!"

By now, they'd made it into the large common area, and Leo looked around with a smile. "You're right. This reminds me of the boys' club we used to hang out at after school."

Chuckling, Oliver nodded. "That's the first thing I said to Charity when I saw this room." He looked around as the electricians were working with Tricia, Adam, and Jeb, testing the equipment as it was installed.

It appeared that Leo and Natalie had come merely to meet Charity. And, it seemed, to give him grief.

"Do you remember Dad talking about Mom?" Leo asked. "He always said that it didn't take long for him to know she was right for him. He used to tell us it was her beauty he first noticed, but her personality had him hanging around wanting more."

Oliver grinned. "I remember."

"I get that," Leo said. "When I first met Natalie, she knocked me on my ass. She was gorgeous, funny as hell, and a badass. All we ever could be were friends since we were on the same Delta team. I knew what I felt for her was a lot deeper, and honestly, if we hadn't had to deal with regulations against dating, I would have claimed her not long after I met her."

"So what are you saying? After one date, I should claim Charity?" Even as the words left his mouth, he had to admit the idea was not foreign to him.

"No, that's not what I'm saying. But you've heard us

say it takes someone special to be with a Keeper. I've listened to you talk about her since you met her. I've read up on the work that she does here, and my wife is getting a chance to check her out."

Oliver rolled his eyes but remained quiet.

Leo continued, "You've had years to chase a lot of tail." He threw his hands up. "Hell, I did, too. I'm just saying that when we find it, go for it."

Tricia walked over, interrupting their brotherly chat. "Sorry to interrupt, but I have some guys ready to add the equipment to Charity's apartment. I know she and Natalie are already there." She laughed. "I'm sure that Natalie has Charity well taken care of." Tricia winked and walked off laughing.

"We better get up there fast!" Oliver said.

"Lead the way."

It only took a moment to get to Charity's apartment, but they took the time to check out the security camera installed at the bottom of the stairs leading up to her apartment. One of the electricians was also alarming the door leading to the outside, and another was working on the door leading straight into her apartment.

As he mounted the stairs with Leo right behind, he could hear the sound of female laughter, and his shoulders relaxed. He loved Natalie, and while he felt sure that she wouldn't do anything to harm his budding relationship, she could be a loose cannon. As they got upstairs, he heard their voices coming from the kitchen.

Another man was with them as he alarmed the window. Natalie had lined up all of Charity's coffee mugs and was howling with laughter over the sayings prominently displayed on their sides. He'd only seen a few of them and had to admit, it was a funny quirk of Charity's.

He walked straight over, hugged her, and whispered, "You doing okay? I can send them packing if you need me to."

She leaned back, held his gaze, and smiled. "I'm good. And I really like your sister-in-law."

"Just so you know," Natalie said, with a brow lifted. "I've given her the third degree, exposed all her skeletons, and then filled her head with stories about your Playboy days."

"Shit," he groaned.

Charity laughed, then looked around the room. "I should be working, not hanging up here in my apartment. But, I admit, while it feels like I'm playing hooky, it's nice."

"I know you have a full day of things to do, but let's face it... you need to be here to see what's installed and how to make it work. Just like you would anywhere else in the center."

She lifted a brow. "What about you all?"

He stood tall, adopting a serious, official-looking expression. "I'm here in a supervisory capacity."

Amid the shared laughter, they returned to the living room. He made himself comfortable on the sofa, his arm naturally finding its place around Charity as she nestled in beside him. Leo eased his tall, large frame onto her comfortable chair and pulled Natalie onto his lap.

Leo regaled her with hilarious and sometimes embarrassing childhood stories of the two Parker boys, making sure to focus on his brother. Oliver also managed to get in a few hair-raising stories about Leo. Natalie continued to retell brotherly escapades from when they were in the military.

It struck Oliver that he was so comfortable with Charity, it was as though they'd been together longer than just knowing each other a few weeks.

She laughed and engaged easily in conversation, her smile unrestrained. But he realized she wasn't sharing any childhood stories of her own. He wasn't sure why but didn't want to pry, especially not in front of an audience. Glad that Leo and Natalie showed similar restraint, they talked and laughed until Tricia popped up into the apartment.

"Hey, guys. My men radioed and said they were finished, so I'm going do a check."

"We need to head out anyway," Natalie said. "This guy promised to buy me and baby Parker lunch."

Leo and Natalie said their goodbyes and headed down the stairs. After Tricia checked the work the electricians completed, she reviewed the security codes and information with Oliver and Charity. He wanted to make sure she was comfortable with the system.

Finally, they went back into the center, and he knew he also needed to say goodbye. He was surprised when she grabbed his hand and dragged him into her office. She closed the door and then, with her hands on his shoulders, pushed until his back was against the door, and she was pressed against him.

"I know I'm at work, and you need to leave, but if it's going to be a couple more days before I can see you again, I really want a goodbye kiss that will last."

"Damn, girl!" He barely got the words out before her lips landed on his. He hoisted her into his arms and turned so that her back was against the door. She instinctively wrapped her legs around his waist,

The kiss was smoking hot, and he felt her core against his erection. He knew he'd walk out with a hard-on, but at that moment, he didn't care. All he wanted was his lips on hers and the feel of her soft curves pressing against him.

His tongue slipped in, tangling with hers. The taste of flavored coffee flooded his senses. Their faces twisted back and forth as their noses bumped, and their teeth occasionally clicked together. The kiss was wild and crazy, with no finesse but a hell of a lot of heat.

Finally, coming up for air, they barely separated. She was panting, and with each breath, her breasts pressed firmer against his chest. She slowly unwound her legs from his, and he held her until her feet were steady on the floor. Her hair was mussed from his hands, and her lips were slick and slightly swollen, and her chin had a little beard burn.

They slowly stepped apart, and he willed his dick to relax. Finally under control, he heaved a great sigh. "I'll be back on Friday," he managed to say.

"Okay," she said, her voice breathy, as she still breathed hard.

"I'll take you to dinner."

She slowly shook her head. "I'll cook dinner." He

lifted a brow, but she hurriedly added, "I'd like to spend as much time alone with you as possible. Dinner out has too many people around."

He grinned, loving her explanation, and nodded. "We can call out for food."

"It's okay. I like to cook, but cooking for one isn't a lot of fun. Sometimes I'll cook more and share it with the McGabes and the Tobiassons. But mostly, it's just me. So I'll love having a chance to cook for you."

"I'll bring wine and beer."

She smiled. "Perfect."

They stared at each other for a moment, and then she dragged in a ragged breath and let it out slowly, never taking her eyes off his. "If you want… plan on staying the night after dinner."

He couldn't believe she put it out there but loved her honesty. And with a wider grin than he knew he could even possess, he nodded. "Count on it."

Walking out, he'd mostly managed to get his erection under control, but with the taste of her still on his lips, the memory of the kiss at the forefront of his mind, and the anticipation of the next weekend had him smiling as he climbed into his vehicle.

He thought about Leo's words and had to admit his brother was right. Gorgeous women were a dime a dozen, but Charity was one of a kind. It didn't matter how long you knew someone… you just had to know that what you felt was right.

17

Charity walked through the lobby of Bright Futures Home after having sent the kids off to school and welcomed the electricians. She'd chatted with Paula for a few minutes and then was heading to her office when the door opened behind her.

She schooled her expression into one of calm and did not leap with excitement when Ramzi walked in with his brother right behind him. The older boy's gaze darted around as he thought he was expecting someone to jump out and grab him.

Walking over, she smiled. "Ramzi, it's so nice to see you again." Turning to the taller boy, she said, "Hello. I'm Charity Whitlock. You must be Ramzi's brother."

The older boy held her gaze, his eyes slightly narrowed. "How do you know?"

"The two of you look so much alike."

Ramzi grinned widely, pride showing in his smile. "This is my brother, Kofi."

"It's nice to meet you, Kofi. What can I do for you two today?"

The boys exchanged glances, then Ramzi asked, "Can we talk? Like you and I did the other day?"

"Absolutely. Would you like to go to my office? Or would you like to walk around the center while we talk?"

At her last suggestion, a spark of interest ignited in Ramzi's eyes. Taking her cue from his expression, she smiled. "Let's do that. Let's walk around a little bit, and then we can end up in the kitchen. I don't know about you, but I'd love to get a snack."

She lifted her hand to gesture the direction they would go and began to walk, glad when both boys fell in step with her. She decided to share information about the center as they strolled, hoping that becoming familiar with the center would make them more comfortable.

Their curious gazes took in the multipurpose room and peeked into a few of the classrooms where the older students were practicing for job interviews. They ventured into the TV and computer lounge and then walked into the boys' dorm area.

George and Mary were in the process of helping one of the volunteers with laundry, and both looked up with kind smiles as they greeted the boys.

Retracing their steps through the hall that led to the multipurpose room, she overheard Ramzi whispering to Kofi, "Told you it was nice."

She smiled at hearing his enthusiasm and silently hoped it rubbed off onto his brother.

Assuming they might be hungry, she stopped just inside the kitchen. "I've talked a lot as we walked around and am thirsty. Would you like a snack and something to drink?"

Ramzi looked at Kofi for guidance, and Kofi held his brother's gaze and then nodded. Ramzi smiled and also nodded. "Yes, ma'am."

She opened one of the large refrigerators and pulled out milk, hiding her smile. The two boys obviously showed great affection, with Ramzi looking up to his brother and Kofi fiercely protective.

She handed them the glasses of milk and directed them toward the counter, where there were several stools. "Hop on up, and I'll see what else I can find."

Before she had a chance to prepare anything, their cook, Sebastian, walked in, wiping his hands on a cloth. Crinkles emanated from his eyes as he smiled at Charity and then greeted the boys. She and he had a silent conversation with just a simple shared look, and he said, "I don't know about you three, but I could use a sandwich."

"That sounds great. Thank you, Sebastian," she said. Looking toward the boys, she added, "Sebastian makes fantastic sandwiches."

She was quiet as Sebastian got to work, noticing the boys kept their eyes on the cook. Sebastian dominated the conversation as he talked through what he was making. It not only made them feel more at ease but he also created a teaching moment.

"Everyone thinks you have to only use butter outside of a grilled cheese sandwich. But I always smear a thin layer of mayonnaise on the outside. It makes it extra crispy."

Sebastian expertly laid out the thick slices of bread with two kinds of cheeses, a slab of ham, and some bacon. Before putting the sandwiches together, he toasted the bread in the frying pan, adding a tomato slice and lettuce in the middle. Then he left them to toast a little bit longer before sliding them onto the plates. Charity added apple slices and some potato chips.

"That's a whole lot of food for just a snack," Kofi said, his voice holding a hint of suspicion.

"Yeah!" Ramzi agreed, his enthusiasm eagerly showing as he stared at the fare.

Sebastian was already digging into his, and Charity took a bite of her sandwich. After swallowing, she said, "Come on, guys. Eat up." Then with her eyes on Kofi, she softened her voice. "This isn't a bribe. This isn't a trick. I was hungry, and since I hadn't had breakfast and hate to eat alone, this was just a time to eat something with new friends."

Kofi regarded her, his expression a mix of contemplation and evaluation. She hoped he'd find what she wanted him to see, and he finally nodded. "Thank you, ma'am."

"Around here, everyone calls me Charity."

Kofi was in mid-bite when his brow lowered. "Charity?"

She laughed. "Believe it or not, it's the name my mama gave me."

Kofi grinned, and Ramzi joined in with a snicker.

Minutes later, they finished their meal, and Sebastian reached for their plates.

Kofi intervened. "We got this. Thank you for the meal." He stood and jerked his head to the sink, and Ramzi followed him dutifully. Sebastian started to move forward, but Charity shook her head.

Sebastian nodded, and with a hearty goodbye, he headed out of the kitchen. Charity wanted to give the boys their dignity. The center had provided a meal for them, and their ability to clean up afterward was their offering. She watched as they worked side by side, even wiping down the counters when they finished.

"Okay, then. Thank you. Let's head to one of the rooms where we can chat for a while."

They passed some of the electricians as they walked back down the hall. She waved and greeted them, then noticed both boys stopping in the hall, their attention captured by what the men were working on.

Ramzi turned to her with curiosity in his eyes. "What are they doing up there?"

"They're installing security to help us keep everyone here safe."

Ramzi's eyes were wide as they passed by a few of the workers on ladders, and while Kofi's expression was wary, Charity noticed his eyes held interest even if his mannerisms were cautious.

They had just entered the lobby on their way to a conference room when Oliver stepped through the door. The footsteps of the boys came to a halt. Turning, she observed them staring at Oliver, their bodies tense and their stances ready to flee.

Her eyes widened, hoping to convey a message to Oliver telepathically. Fortunately, he offered a barely perceptible chin lift, then turned his smiling face to the boys. He walked forward and extended his hand. For a moment, it seemed Kofi was going to leave him hanging. Then slowly, Kofi reached his hand out and shook Oliver's.

"It's nice to see you here," Oliver said.

Charity explained, "We've had a tour of the center, checked on the electricians, had a snack, and are now heading into one of the conference rooms to chat."

Oliver nodded. "You can't find a better listener than Charity. She'll take care of you."

As they turned to move to a room, Kofi stopped and looked straight at Oliver, shoving his hands into his pockets. "Thank you."

Oliver held Kofi's gaze, also schooling his expression not to show surprise. Instead, he waited for Kofi to elaborate.

"For letting us go that night." Kofi's words were simple and straight to the point.

Ramzi nodded, his head bobbing. "Yeah, thank you. That was nice."

A meaningful silence slid between the four of them standing in the lobby, but Charity felt as though an important moment was happening and remained quiet.

Finally, Kofi broke the silence. "I know we were wrong. What we did was wrong. I can't expect you to understand, but… well… we're… I'm working on some things." He glanced down at Ramzi and sucked in a ragged breath. "I want more for my brother."

Oliver moved closer and held Kofi's gaze. "A man will make a lot of mistakes in his life." He scoffed and shook his head with a hint of self-reflection. "All men. But we make choices every day. Recognizing the ramifications of our choices and seeking a different way of doing things defines a good man. The fact that you've already made that decision at your age is damn impressive."

Kofi blinked several times, then turned to Charity. "Can he be there too?"

This time, she was unable to contain her surprise. "You also want him to come into the conference room?"

Ramzi's eyes were large as he stared at his brother, but Kofi turned his appraising gaze back to hold Oliver's eyes again for a long moment. He nodded slowly. "Yeah. Uh… yes, ma'am, I do."

She led the way into one of the larger rooms with a small sofa and several comfortable chairs. It was used for some of their smaller group counseling sessions. She inclined her head and gestured toward the sofa, and the two boys sat down, allowing her and Oliver to take the comfortable chairs facing them.

Turning to Oliver, she felt she should explain to make the boys more at ease. "Kofi and Ramzi came in today to talk to me. We haven't started any specific conversation yet. They did have a chance to meet Sebastian while enjoying a sandwich."

Oliver smiled and nodded. "Since coming here, I've had a chance to have some of Sebastian's special grilled cheese sandwiches."

"That's what we had!" Ramzi chimed in. "He uses mayonnaise on his grilled cheese sandwiches."

Kofi scoffed. "Grilled cheese? He put a lot more than just cheese on that sandwich."

"It was so good!" Ramzi exclaimed, still enthusiastic about his meal.

Charity's heart ached as it always did, knowing that it had taken both desperation and bravery for the two boys to come here. "Okay, gentlemen. Let's talk."

Without hesitation, Kofi said, "I want my brother to stay here."

Ramzi's eyes widened as he swung his head around to stare open-mouthed at his brother. "No! I'm not staying anywhere without you!"

"I need to get you somewhere safe," Kofi said. "We talked about this."

"But I thought you meant both of us. You want to leave me?" Ramzi's eyes welled with tears, and he struggled to keep them from falling.

Charity knew he'd be embarrassed to cry in front of all of them and discreetly leaned forward to push a box of tissues closer to him. This wasn't the first time she'd seen an older sibling, worn out from trying to take care of the younger ones, bring them to the center because there wasn't enough money or food to go around. They were willing for the younger sibling to have all the benefits of the center while they would continue to go without.

"Kofi, how old are you?" she asked.

"I'm seventeen. I'll be eighteen in a few months."

She leaned forward, her tone compassionate. "I

admire your commitment to your brother's safety. You also easily meet the age requirements for staying here. If you meet the qualifications, you can both stay here at the center."

Ramzi swiped at the moisture in his eyes and looked at his brother, hope replacing despair. "See? You don't gotta make a choice. You don't gotta leave me here. We can both stay here. We don't gotta go back to them."

Charity's body stiffened at the word "them," and the way Oliver's hands flexed, she was sure he caught the same inference. Deciding not to question Ramzi about what he was referring to, she waited.

Kofi shook his head and hissed, "I can't do that. It can make things worse."

Ramzi argued, "They might—"

"No!" Kofi bit out.

At his harsh voice, Ramzi pressed his lips together, showing how much he wanted to continue but respected his brother enough to remain silent.

Kofi lifted his gaze to Charity. "You said if he qualified. What does he have to do?"

"There's nothing he has to do. I'm going to ask a few questions and need your honesty. Okay?"

"Sure," Kofi agreed readily, nodding. His eyes, which had seemed cold since they arrived, now flickered with the warmth of obvious interest.

"Do you know the location of your parents or legal guardians?" She asked the question gently, knowing the answer could create stress.

"Don't got no dad. Mom ran off with her boyfriend about six months ago when he said he didn't want to be with a woman who had baggage. She said we were old enough to look after ourselves, so she took off. Haven't heard from her since."

"I'm sorry," she said in earnest. "And where have you been living since then?"

"We stayed in the apartment for about two months without paying rent because we kept telling the super that our mom would pay when she got back from work. But he found out she'd skipped out on us, so he kicked us to the curb."

"What the hell?" Oliver blurted. "Where did you go?"

She shot a glance his way, offering another wide-eyed expression, silently pleading for him to remain quiet. He sheepishly winced. Turning to the boys, she prodded, "What happened next?"

"I had a friend from school whose dad said we could stay in his basement for a few weeks. They had a sofa bed, and there was a bathroom down there, too—"

"We had a TV there!" Ramzi interrupted, smiling.

Kofi looked affectionately at his brother, and Charity felt her heart tug.

"They were all right, but by the end of the month, they began asking when we'd move out." Kofi shrugged. "Can't blame 'em. We didn't have no money to pay."

"She made good cookies," Ramzi said, nodding his head slowly before he let out a long sigh.

Charity smiled at him, giving him a moment to hang on to a good memory. She had a feeling that he had precious few of those. "Okay, and then where did you go to sleep?"

"Slept at the park for a couple of weeks, but there's a

lot of crazies out there," Kofi said, his gaze flashing with memories that Charity had no doubt weren't pleasant. Kofi vowed, "I didn't want them near Ramzi. I had to get him somewhere safe."

Oliver's hand was resting on the arm of his chair. The tension radiating off him was so strong she was surprised they all hadn't been zapped with his supersonic waves of anger. She reached over to discreetly place her hand on his. Her touch caused his fingers to twitch and then slowly unclench.

"And after the park?" she asked.

Kofi hesitated, and Ramzi looked up at his brother, anxiety drawing his face into a grimace.

Kofi cleared his throat. "We found somewhere to stay. Met someone who said we could live with them."

It didn't miss her notice that, for the first time, he didn't give any details about where they were staying.

"Well, both of you are qualified under McKinney-Vento for homeless services—"

"Mac who? What's that?" Ramzi asked.

She smiled. "The McKinney-Vento Homeless Assistance Act is a federal law that provides money for homeless shelter programs. It was signed into law by President Reagan way back in 1987."

"That's a long time ago!" Ramzi said, eyes wide.

Laughing, she agreed. "What's important is that the law makes sure that homeless persons, including children, have what they need. So we can do an intake, check out a few things, and then get you qualified so we can provide services."

"I want this for my brother," Kofi said, sitting up straighter, his voice filled with surety.

"But Kofi…" Ramzi begged.

"Not me… not now," Kofi argued. He turned to Charity. "I have some things to take care of first… to make sure we're both going to be okay."

Ramzi shook his head and grabbed Kofi's arm. "We haven't been apart one night in all this time. We're not gonna start this now and make things worse. We go back together, take care of what needs to be done, and come here as soon as possible."

The two brothers stared at each other for a long time. Charity witnessed emotions moving between them as tangible as anything she could touch.

Finally, Kofi sucked in a deep breath before letting it out slowly and nodding. Pulling his gaze away from Ramzi, he looked at her. "Give us some time… maybe a week at most. And we'll both be back."

Charity nodded, hoping they made it back to the center. Others had made the same promise yet had not returned. Her smile was tremulous, and she turned to look at Oliver, seeing the same fear on his face.

18

Oliver had barely raised his hand to knock on Charity's door when it flung open, revealing her anxious face. Without hesitation, her hand shot out, and her fingers curled in the front of his shirt. She pulled him forward, and he willingly allowed her to manhandle him. Stepping inside her apartment, the playful remark he was ready to speak faded as he registered the look in her eyes. She needed more from him than a joke.

The week had been long and taxing, with Charity on edge every day that Kofi and Ramzi did not come back to the center. Since he was now on other assignments, they had spent hours on the phone every night. He'd listened as her emotions bounced from worry to hope and back to worry again.

The overnight bag he carried with him dropped to the floor before he wrapped his arms around her back, pulling her close. He kissed the top of her head as her cheek rested against his heartbeat.

She didn't need to say a word. He understood the

depth of her concerns, and his protective instincts surged. But he knew it was Charity's caring nature to feel so deeply, and he wasn't about to take that away when it made her who she was.

She lifted her head and offered a small smile. "I know I've been a basket case this week with everything going on, but I really want us to have a good evening."

"Charity, honey, if you let me help you, I promise it'll be a good weekend."

Her smile settled firmly on her face. "Perfect."

He bent and took her mouth, wanting to take her mind off anything other than the feel of their bodies pressed together. His tongue slipped between her lips, delving deeply, and the anticipation of what was to come hit straight to his cock.

An alarm sounded from the kitchen, and she jumped back, ending the kiss too soon. Eyes wide, she exclaimed, "Oh! Dinner!" She turned and ran through the living room and into the kitchen.

He sighed, adjusted his crotch, then followed her. A glance revealed the table set for two with several candles lit in the middle. A delicious scent reached his nose, but his attention was on her ass as she bent over to pull the casserole dish from the oven.

She turned and held up the dish covered in a lightly browned crust. He had no idea what it was, but it smelled amazing.

"It's homemade chicken potpie," she announced. "I use puff pastry on the top and bottom, so it's really good!"

They were settled at the table a few minutes later,

their plates piled high with her home-cooked meal. The light had already faded through the window in the kitchen, but the candlelight sitting on the table flickered its illumination in her eyes.

He couldn't remember the last time a woman had fixed dinner just for him as part of a date. He quickly cast his mind back through the years and realized that tonight was a first. He'd never wanted a woman to arrange a scene of domestication when the only amount of time they'd be together was a few hours of sex.

But looking at Charity across the table, the candlelight casting a glow on her face, and eating the meal she'd cooked, he couldn't imagine a better start to a date night.

He lifted his beer. "Here's to our second date."

She laughed and shook her head. "As much time as we've spent together here at the center, and all the calls and texts, this doesn't really seem like just a second date, does it?"

He smiled and wholeheartedly agreed. "Then here's to the continuation of us."

She grabbed her glass of wine and clicked it against the neck of his beer bottle. "Now that's a toast I can celebrate."

"I hate to ask anything that's going to bring the evening down, but we might as well get it out of the way. Have you heard anything today?"

Her shoulders slumped, and she sighed as she put her wineglass down. "I haven't heard anything from them. I asked a few of the kids if they knew Ramzi or Kofi, but they didn't. One of the girls said she thought she remembered Kofi from several years ago in school. She said the only reason was because his name was so unusual." She looked up with worry lines etched into her face. "What do you think they're into? Do you think they're okay?"

He reached across the table and squeezed her hand. "Sweetheart, there's no way to know. It was obvious that they had moved in with somebody who was using them for something. Drugs? Stealing? Something that makes them vulnerable and feel trapped."

"Because I know it must be dangerous, I'm terrified. But I also know I've met many kids, and each has a story. Some came and stayed. Some came and left immediately because they couldn't handle the center's rules. Some had so many difficulties that the center wasn't right for them. But I can't help but think that Ramzi and Kofi would be very successful here."

"I agree, but only if it's what they truly want."

She nodded and let out a sigh. "You're right, and that's what I have to tell myself every day when I come to work. There's only so much I can do."

By now, the meal was finished, and they quickly cleaned the dishes and the kitchen. They linked hands as they wandered into the living room, where he sat on the sofa and pulled her down with him.

He cupped her cheeks and kissed her gently, then nuzzled his nose over her jaw, trailing kisses over her face. Leaning back, he asked, "Do you want to know what I thought of this week that I hoped for tonight?"

Her breath hitched underneath his kisses. "What?"

He held her gaze. "I know more about Ramzi and

Kofi's backgrounds than yours. I don't want to make you uncomfortable, but we're a little unbalanced for us starting out. You know about my family, the relationship I have with my brother, and you've met Leo and Natalie. Sweetheart, I hope you feel you can trust me with your story as well."

She held his gaze, her face easing into a soft smile. He breathed a sigh of relief, seeing that she didn't tense up or become upset.

Instead, she offered a little shrug. "There's not really much to tell. I don't have a terribly exciting story."

"I don't want you to tell me anything you don't want to share," he said, his voice gentle but filled with curiosity. "But I hope tonight will go the way I think we both want it to go. We're not just two people meeting for a night and then moving on. You absolutely fascinate me, and I'd like to know how you became you."

She pressed her lips together, a contemplative look in her eyes as she gazed around the room. He didn't feel she was avoiding looking at him, but more like she was just gathering her thoughts. He waited patiently, eager to receive the gift of knowing her better.

Finally, her gaze settled on him with a little smile playing over her face. "You know how most people have names that somehow meant something to the parents. My name meant something to my mom. And even though it might seem really awful to some people, I've always liked it."

He stared at her soft smile, thinking everything about her was beautiful, especially her name. "What did Charity mean to your mom?"

She shifted next to him, getting comfortable. "My mom was seventeen years old when she got pregnant with me. She was at the beach with friends and met some soldiers on leave. One of them seemed to like her. They hung out for most of the week he was there. And then he went back for an overseas tour. They sent emails back and forth a few times, but it wasn't long before they stopped. She was heartbroken, but more than that... she discovered she was pregnant. Her parents couldn't stand the idea that their teenage daughter was pregnant. She tried to let my dad know and finally got ahold of a friend of his who said he'd been killed in action. Her parents kicked her out of the house. She lived with a friend for a while, but they couldn't keep her and a baby, so she moved into a homeless shelter."

"Jesus, Charity."

"When it was time for her to give birth, there was a free clinic that provided services. She said she thought they would be judgmental and rude, but everyone there was so nice. When they placed me in her arms, she looked up and saw one of the signs on the wall that said *Charity begins at home*. She thought how much she wanted a home for her baby, so she named me Charity."

"Fuck, sweetheart," he muttered, his heart clenching at the thought of the origins of her name.

She shook her head gently. "No, don't you see, Oliver? I was named for all the people who had been so kind to her. My mom might've been young, but she knew enough to find people who could help her, and that's what she did."

"And after you were born? Was she still able to get help?"

"They encouraged her to get in touch with my dad's parents. She tracked them down, but they didn't believe her. They weren't interested in a paternity test, and she wasn't going to push. If they didn't want to know if their son had a child, then she always said it was their loss."

"So what did she do?"

"There was a shelter for moms with babies or small children. They offered childcare as long as the parent was working at least thirty hours a week. So she worked, and we stayed there until I was almost two years old. It was crowded, and she was determined to have a place of her own. She saved every dime, and when I turned two, she had enough money for a first month's rent and security deposit on a camper."

He was taken aback, barely able to maintain a steady expression, and hid his startle.

She sighed. "I know what you're going to say. A camper? I suppose it was more like a tiny mobile home. A woman who lived close by would babysit some of the kids as her way of making money. So Mom kept working as a server for another year. Then the woman convinced her that if she worked with her, they could do child care for more money than she was making in tips. Mom wasn't too sure at first, and she simply took night shifts and Sundays at the diner. But the woman was right. They made enough as an unofficial daycare so she could quit the diner."

"What memories do you have?" he asked, emboldened by her soft smile and desperately curious about everything she could share.

"Playing with other kids in the mobile home park and having Mom close by. She was always smiling and singing. And could bake the best sugar cookies." She smiled as her gaze shifted to him. "Mom and I would plant flowers and some vegetables outside the house. I loved our garden." Looking back at him, she admitted, "That's why I have plants in the bedroom near the window. It's my little garden."

Oliver tucked a wayward strand of hair behind her ear. He knew there was so much more to her story and was consumed by knowing every detail. He'd never felt that about another person before. Not his fellow soldiers. Not the Keepers he was working with. With Charity, he wanted to know everything—her memories, her secrets, what made her smile, and what made her cry. With her tears, he wanted to know how to keep them from falling. And if he couldn't, he wanted to be the one to wipe her tears away.

"I grew up poor," she continued. "The kids in the mobile home park traded clothes as we outgrew the ones we were wearing. We went to the same school, and while I don't condone violence, a few of the boys and some of the girls didn't mind swinging their fists if someone made fun of us for being poor."

She chuckled as if fond memories were flooding back into her mind. "Of all the wonderful lessons my mom taught me, do you want to know the one I think is the most important?"

"Charity, I want to know everything," he replied, his eyes locked onto hers with intensity.

Her smile widened, and she met his gaze head-on. "Mom would tell me that there was always someone worse off, and we needed to count our blessings. I came home one day after visiting with a friend who lived in a big home. I was kind of down about our tiny home. My mom reminded me that people who lived under bridges and on park benches would consider our small trailer a perfect home."

At the word blessing, he blurted, "I met a woman named Blessing at the USO in the Atlanta airport. She quoted someone I can't remember, but it was about comfort, good food, talking with someone, and how that makes a home."

Nodding, Charity said, "That sounds like what my mom would say. Home is being with the ones who make you feel good."

"What else did she tell you?"

"Every morning, when she woke me up, she hugged me." Charity began to blink back the moisture gathering, but a tear rolled down her cheek. "She would give me a hug and tell me that I could be anything I wanted. I had a bright future."

Oliver's eyes stung, and he felt his chest compress. *Charity. Bright Futures Home.* He swallowed past the lump in his throat. "Tell me more."

She closed her eyes, sucked in a deep breath through her nose, and let it out slowly. She opened her eyes and looked deeply into his. "When I was sixteen years old,

Mom went to the grocery store. That was the last goodbye hug I received. She was a victim of a senseless act of violence. A kid pulled a gun to rob the cashier, and my mom came around the corner, not realizing what was happening. He panicked, aimed toward her, and fired. The police said that when he saw what he'd done, he turned the gun on himself. Two lives were lost, so pointlessly."

Gutted, Oliver could barely hear over his heart pounding and wondered how Charity could share her story and keep breathing.

"She lived long enough for the cashier to rush over to her, and her last words were, tell my daughter that I love her."

"Her last thought was of you," he said, his voice shaky.

"That was my mom. She let me know she loved me every day of my life."

"Oh, baby, what did you do then?'

"I didn't have anyone tell me that I had to move out of the trailer because there was enough money to pay the rent. I kept going to school, and in the afternoons and evenings, I continued childcare and babysitting with our neighbor. I started out at community college on scholarships, and then went to the local college, still living in the trailer park." She shrugged. "In fact, I lived there until I earned my master's degree and started working."

"And your little home?"

"You might think that I'd be so glad to get out of it. But it held the memories of my mom, and even when she was gone, I couldn't stand the idea of living somewhere she'd never been. And then I realized that the rent was so cheap, I saved a lot of money by living there. But the mobile home park was changing. The old manager died, and the new people didn't care about the place. My first apartment was near my job, and while it was much bigger than the trailer, it never felt like home. When I was able to move in here, I can't explain it, but it felt more like home."

"Maybe it was just the right time. Maybe it was time for a home."

She smiled and cupped his face with her hands. "I didn't mean to dump all this on you. Believe me, I had other plans for this evening."

"I wanted to know everything I could about you," he said. "But, believe me, the night is young."

19

As Charity leaned forward and kissed Oliver again, he let her take the lead. Normally, he was more of a take-charge kind of man, always seeing to the woman's pleasure before his own, but other than the sex, there were no emotional conversations or cuddling afterward. But everything with Charity was different, and he wanted it all. The overnight bag he'd brought was a testament that he was more than willing to spend the weekend with her.

Now, after such an emotional delivery of her background, he didn't expect sex. Instead, he would've been more than happy just to sit and watch TV or listen to music, then go to bed and sleep with his body curled around hers.

But the kiss she was initiating shot straight to his dick. She swung her leg over his thighs and settled her core on the crotch of his jeans, where his cock was now threatening to hammer out of its confines.

She angled her head and thrust her tongue into his mouth, and her velvet touch sent tingles up and down his spine, zipping straight to his balls. Desperate to make sure she understood this wasn't necessary, he placed his hands on her shoulders and pushed her back until their eyes latched onto each other.

"You're stopping?" Her surprise was evident in her voice, and her eyes were wide.

"I only want this if you want this," he said. His mind told him that was the right thing to say while his cock was saying, "Come on, let's get in the game." His heart just wanted to take care of the woman he was coming to care for greatly. "I want everything with you, Charity. But if we do nothing more tonight than just kiss on the couch and go to sleep next to each other, I'll be happy."

She dragged her tongue over her bottom lip, which was already puffy from their previous kissing. It was so hard not to lean forward and let his tongue follow along the trail that hers had. Forcing his gaze to her eyes, he spied a twinkle dancing in their depths.

"Your mouth says that we don't have to do this, but the way your eyes are staring at my lips, and the way your dick feels pressed against my panties gives me a different story."

He chuckled and shook his head. "My dick is explained by pure biology. My words are because I care about you and don't want you to do anything you're not comfortable with, especially after such an emotional conversation. And yeah, my eyes are looking forward to seeing every bit of you without these layers of clothing, whenever that may be."

She threw her head back and laughed, and as always, the sound caused him to smile and his heart to squeeze.

She dropped her chin and stared into his eyes, sliding her hands from his shoulders up to cup both jaws. As her thumbs danced over his beard, she nuzzled his nose and said, "I'm not ashamed or upset over my past. My father might not have known me, but in my eyes, he'll always be a hero who died for his country. My mom was a true hero in my story. I am who I am because of her. So while the retelling bared some emotions, I'm not upset. What I do want is you. Tonight. Everything."

It only took a second for her words to strike straight through him, and he stood with one arm behind her back and the other covering her ass. She quickly snapped her legs around his waist and held on tight as he stalked toward the bedroom.

As soon as they were there, he turned sharply so that her back was to the wall next to the door. With his body tightly pressed against hers, he felt every curve. His hands were both cupping her ass, then he slipped one under her dress. He shifted his hips backward just enough to slide his fingers between them. His thumb slipped underneath her panties, finding her slick and ready. Fingering the bundle of nerves that was already taut, he felt her entire body shiver. He slid his thumb between her folds and into her sex and deepened the kiss. His tongue thrust in her mouth in tandem with his thumb tweaking her bud. Her fingernail scratched down his back, and he knew if he weren't wearing a shirt, she would've drawn blood.

Their heads moved back and forth as their noses bumped, and then she finally pushed him back enough to mumble, "Too many clothes."

Keeping her in his arms, he turned again and let her body drag slowly down his front as he lowered her. Before her feet even settled on the floor, she jerked his long-sleeved T-shirt out of the waistband of his jeans and started shoving it upward. Before the shirt was all the way off, she seemed to become sidetracked by the corded muscles of his abs. She dropped and started trailing kisses over his stomach, then worked her way up and kept pushing the shirt along.

She latched onto one of his brown, flat nipples, and he thought his eyes were going to pop out of his head. She wasn't tall enough to get his shirt over his head, but he was more than happy to assist.

With his shirt now decorating her floor, he grabbed her dress, bunching it around her hips before pulling it over her breasts. He continued to drag it upward, apologizing when he snagged the neckline on her nose.

She laughed, but it was quickly cut off as he bent and took her lips in another searing kiss. She reached behind her and unsnapped her bra, flinging it off her arms. As her breasts bounced slightly, the air stuck in his lungs as he stared at her perfection. She pressed herself against him, and now, skin on skin, his mind was blown away by how he responded to her. Sex had always been enjoyable but somewhat perfunctory. Now, he could barely catch his breath.

Her hands had gone to his belt buckle, but her

fingers fumbled, and he gently pushed them aside, deftly loosening the offending item. She had already shucked her panties before he had a chance to tell her that he wanted to do that himself. *Another time.*

Acknowledging there would be another time with her was not a surprise. He'd seen his parents' relationship and what Natalie and Leo had. In the past several weeks, he'd gotten to know the Keepers and observe them with their significant others. And that was what he wanted with Charity. *Anyone who says that it's impossible to fall hard and fast and sure had simply never experienced it.* He knew what he felt. He knew what he wanted.

"Hey! You were thinking and not kissing," Charity fussed.

He barked out a laugh as he shucked his pants and boxers after shoving off his boots and socks. "Not true. I was thinking about you. I was thinking about kissing you. Hell, I was thinking about kissing you for a really long time."

Grinning, she lifted on her toes. He grabbed her and, giving a little toss, plopped her onto the bed. She laughed as she fell backward and then leaned up on her elbows. Spread out for him to see, hell, for him to devour, he couldn't wait to explore every inch of her.

He bent down to snag a condom from his pocket, then tossed it onto the bed next to her. It was going to get used, but not right away.

He crawled over her, his smile widening with each inch of her body he explored. He lifted her feet, kissing each one until she giggled and wiggled, telling him what he had already discovered. Her feet were ticklish.

He continued kissing up her legs, discovering that behind her knees was also ticklish. The scent of her sex was driving him mad, and he quickly determined that she tasted as good as she smelled. He had planned on continuing his exploration but knew that he couldn't move away from her sex without discovering all her secrets there.

He licked and sucked her folds, nibbled on her bundle of nerves, and thrust his tongue inside before replacing it with his fingers. She wiggled more, and he wondered if she wasn't ticklish there, too. He spread her thighs wider and dove in like a man starved. In fact, now that he tasted her, he would swear that being without her was like starving.

Her fingers ran through his hair, her nails scratching along his scalp, sending tingles up and down his spine. Soon, she was crying out before she came on his fingers. He continued to lap until her quivers subsided and her legs flopped apart.

She was barely able to lift herself on her elbows again, but she managed to do so and stared down at him. "Damn, I can't even imagine how much practice you've had to be such a master at that."

The last thing he wanted to do was even think about any other woman from the past, and he sure as hell didn't want to have that conversation now.

"There's only one woman for me, and that's the one I'm with."

She laughed and shook her head. "Tell me honestly... did you use that line on everybody?"

She was smiling, but he could see a hint of uncertainty in her eyes. For a moment, he didn't answer her but instead kissed his way over her mound, her belly, between her breasts before taking each nipple and sucking deeply. Hating to leave those beautiful peaks, he kissed over her collarbone to her jaw. He ended up on top of her with his arms holding his weight off her chest.

In this position, his cock settled right between her thighs and nestled against her core. He peered down into her eyes and said, "I've had sex partners, but it was purely physical. I've never once found anyone who I even remotely had an emotional connection with. I'm thirty-two years old, and I've never spent a full night with a woman and certainly not a whole weekend. You asked for honesty, and I'm giving it. That wasn't a line, and I have never said those words to another woman."

He wasn't sure she was breathing as her eyes widened, and she stared, her expression warm as it soothed over him. "Breathe, baby."

The air rushed from her lungs, and her arms encircled his neck as she pulled him down for a kiss. There was no starting slow. There was no simple burn. A spark was lit between them, and fireworks already crackled around the room.

He hated to end the kiss but lifted his head. "Tell me what you want, Charity. I need the words."

Her arms tightened as her legs wrapped around his

thighs. "I want to see how fast you can put that condom on. And then I want you to use it."

He blinked, then laughed, their chests pressing tighter together. "Well, all right, ma'am. You want me? You got all of me. My dick, my soul, and my heart."

Then with no other words to say, he grabbed the condom and rolled it on faster than he ever had. From the look on her face, she was impressed.

20

Charity lay on her back, her body languid as she reveled in her orgasm. Yet Oliver once again kissing his way up her body and then lavishing attention on her breasts with his cock nuzzling the entrance to her sex had her full attention. It seemed he had the full attention of every muscle, nerve, and cell in her body. She shot from relaxed to tingling and lifted her knees to make her more accessible.

After he finally let go of one of her nipples with a wet pop, he guided his cock between her slick folds and thrust deeply.

The initial jolt of the invasion swiftly passed with each skillful movement. She'd had sex before but now learned there was a great deal of difference in how the partner made her feel. With Oliver on top, it could be thought of as basic vanilla sex. But he wrapped an arm around her leg and stretched her even wider. His cadence didn't slow, and she loved staring up at him as she felt each velvet plunge. She lost his eyes when he lowered his head and kissed her. At that moment, she couldn't have coordinated anything, but his tongue thrust in time with his cock, and she felt the coil deep inside tightened. There was nothing basic or vanilla about Oliver.

She'd also never had more than one orgasm during sex, and even that wasn't always guaranteed. She had one orgasm with his mouth and at first assumed this would be about him finding his release. That notion was obliterated as her own body readied itself for the second onslaught.

"Jesus, Oliver," she groaned, finding it difficult to speak.

"I want to come buried in you, Charity. But let's ride this out a little longer."

She had no idea what he meant, but her eyes popped open when he rolled to his back, dragging her body along with him. She ended up prone on top of him with his cock still buried. She looked down and spied the questioning expression in his eyes. Grinning, she used her hands on his shoulders for leverage and pushed up while drawing her knees up at the same time.

Now she was straddling him, and how she'd managed to get in that position without losing his cock, she wasn't sure, but she was damn proud of herself.

He chuckled, and she felt the movement from where they were connected straight into her core. As she looked down, her hair falling around them like a curtain, she asked, "What's so funny?"

"You are, babe. You had a look on your face that you

just earned a ten in the Olympics of changing sex positions."

Now it was her turn to laugh, and she realized that was another first. Her previous sex partners had seen to her needs, and then they got down to business for themselves. Oliver could make her laugh, bringing humor and joy into sex. At that moment, she felt closer to him than she felt to anyone.

"Well, let's see what other tens I can earn." With that, she lifted up, almost off his cock, and then plunged down again.

His eyes widened, and his fingers dug in tightly to her ass. She repeated the maneuver several times, each time watching as his eyes grew darker with lust. She soon found her rhythm, alternating her speed with the depth she plunged, and couldn't help but smile. There was a sense of freedom in being on top. For her, it wasn't about power, although that was an emotion she felt, realizing the pleasure she brought to him. It also wasn't about control since, in reality, it was his long, hard cock that she was riding.

It was about trust. Whoever was on top had power and control, but that meant the person on the bottom trusted her to care for their needs. With her fingers still digging into his shoulders, she rode him until her movement slowed. "I don't think I'm gonna get an Olympic ten on riding. I'm gonna need a hell of a lot more practice for that."

He grinned up at her with an expression that could be deemed boyish, which seemed ridiculous, considering his body was all man. "We can give you plenty of practice, but lift a little bit for now, and I'll take over."

She stayed on top, with her breasts bouncing in time to his thrusts as he moved his hips up and down. He had the stamina she lacked, and his hands moved from her ass up to cup her breasts. As he tweaked her nipples, she felt her core tighten again.

With her eyes trained on him, she could tell he was close. His face was red, his neck muscles tight, and the blood vessels swelling. One of his hands remained on her breast while the other moved between them, his thumb rubbing her swollen nub.

She tried to hold on until he came but flew apart, then realized that was what he was also waiting for. As her body vibrated from deep inside, clutching him tighter, he roared out his own release as he lifted his hips, thrusting even deeper. His movements slowed, and as her arms began to ache, she lowered herself to lay on top of him with her cheek pressed against his sweaty chest.

As she lay there and listened to his heartbeat, it struck her that sex was messy, sweaty, and, in some ways, not very dignified. Yet when it all ended with her body coming down from the high of an orgasm, and she could press her ear against his pounding heartbeat, it was so much more than just a physical act. She had no idea what they were and wasn't ready to put a label on it. But right now, with the hoofbeats of his heart resonating against her face, it was as comfortable as coming home.

Charity sat in her office, still riding the wave of her fun, get-to-know-more-about-each-other weekend with Oliver. Even the piles of files on her desk couldn't dim her post-sex high.

A knock on her door shot her gaze over to land on one of the girls at the center. "Latifa. Hi. Come on in."

Latifa walked through the doorway, tucking a strand of hair behind her ear and glancing around at everything but Charity. She sat down and sucked in a deep breath before lifting her gaze.

"What can I do for you?" Charity asked, noting Latifa's nervous behavior.

The pretty teenager looked behind her at the open door and then swung her gaze back to Charity. "Would it be okay if I closed your door, Ms. Whitlock?"

"Of course." Charity waited until Latifa had jumped up, closed the office door, and then took her seat again. "Sorry," she mumbled.

"There's no need to apologize. My open-door policy is for everyone to feel that they can see me anytime. But many conversations need to be private, so this is fine." She waited another moment as Latifa fiddled with the hem of her sweater. Finally, feeling the need to prompt her, she leaned forward, casually placing her arms on her desk. "Something is on your mind. Please, how can I help?"

Latifa nibbled on her bottom lip before finally saying, "You were asking some kids last week about Kofi. Kofi Jackson."

She tried to hide her surprise but felt sure her interest flared like a rocket. "Yes, yes, I was."

"I lied when I said I didn't know him. He and I were in school together a couple of years ago. He was... well, he was real smart. And cute."

A little smile slipped over Charity's lips. "Yes, he seems to be very smart and very nice-looking."

Latifa offered a soft smile, and then it fell from her face into a grimace.

"Do you know something about him?"

Latifa's lips pinched together, then she blew out a breath and whispered, "It... might not be a good idea for you to ask."

A trickle of fear slithered through her, ending with her coffee souring in her stomach. "Why not?" she asked just as softly.

"Most of the kids here wouldn't know, but a few have heard things."

"What kind of things, Latifa?"

"Like...like... he's involved in some serious shit."

Charity sucked in a hasty breath before it left her lungs in a shaky exhalation. So many things ran through her mind—drugs, prostitution, trafficking. "Honey, I need to know so I can help him. It's not just him but also his younger brother." She got up from behind her desk and walked around her desk to take a seat next to the obviously scared teen. Reaching over to place her hand on Latifa's, she begged, "Please. I want to help him."

Latifa held her gaze and nodded. "All I've heard is about someone who gets kids to live with them, and then they get the kids to do bad stuff. Mostly stealing, I think. But no one knows who they are or where they are. I never paid any attention to the rumors because they had nothing to do with me. Then I once overheard someone say Kofi's name. They said he was gone, working for…"

Latifa's face scrunched, and Charity squeezed her hand.

"I only heard one name, which didn't mean anything to me."

"What was the name, Latifa?"

"It was something like Fagin."

Charity blinked, her hand jerking slightly. "Fagin?"

"Yeah. But I don't know if it's a first name or last. It's really nothing."

Charity sucked in another breath. "It's something if you know Charles Dickens."

Now, it was time for Latifa to blink. "Wasn't he an author, Ms. Whitlock?"

She patted the girl's hand and nodded. "Yes." She closed her eyes as her heart ached. "Do you know anything else about Kofi or this Fagin person?"

"No, ma'am. That's it. I swear."

Standing, she smiled at Latifa. "Okay, you can go on back to your studies." She wrapped her arms around the young woman, and they hugged tightly. "Thank you," she whispered.

As soon as Latifa left, she closed the door behind her and grabbed her phone from her desk. Hitting the number for Oliver, she prayed he would be available. As soon as the call connected, she let out a sigh of relief.

"Hey, Charity," he greeted. "What's up?"

"Where are you?" she asked.

"At the work compound, why?"

"I might have found out something about Kofi and Ramzi, but I have no idea what to do with the information."

"Okay, give it to me, and I'll see what can be done."

She told him about Latifa's visit, ending with, "I don't know how much you know about the characters in Charles Dicken's *Oliver Twist*, but we may be facing a modern-day Fagin."

21

After Oliver hung up the phone, for a moment, he was unaware that all the Keepers in the room were staring at him.

"Bro!"

He jerked his head around to see Leo's gaze on him, concern on his face.

"What the fuck is going on?" Leo asked.

He glanced over to Carson and said, "I have a situation, but I'm not sure what to do."

"Bring us up to speed," Carson ordered.

Everyone in the room quickly gathered at the table except for Abbie, Jeb, and his girlfriend, Skylar, who stayed at their computer stations with their attention riveted on him. After meeting with the boys last week, he'd already expressed concern over Kofi and Ramzi to the Keepers. Now, he added, "From what one of the girls at the center said, someone is exploiting children to handle their illegal activities. She didn't know what was happening but had heard Kofi's name mentioned along with the name Fagin."

"Fuck," a number of the Keepers said.

He looked at Carson and didn't hesitate to ask, "Is there a way for me to see if I can find out from the police if they have any information on this real-life Fagin?"

Carson only took a moment to get his FBI friend on a video call. "Landon, meet our newest Keeper, Oliver Parker. Oliver, this is Landon Sommers, our FBI liaison."

"Good to meet you," Landon said. "Parker, huh? Don't tell me you're related to Leo?"

Nodding, Oliver said, "I'm Leo's much younger, much smarter, and much better-looking brother."

Natalie barked out a laugh as Leo shook his head.

Putting the humor behind, Oliver jumped in to tell Landon briefly about Charity, the youth homeless center, Kofi and Ramzi, and what they'd heard from the girl.

Landon listened, nodding as Oliver spoke, then said, "It's not as uncommon as you might think for an adult to use young people, even little kids, to run scams and steal. Usually, those situations are often families who use other family members. Obviously, gangs operating in the area would be doing the same—younger and new gang members would be used for the legwork and initiations involving robberies. But for someone to take in kids and train them to scam and steal takes more coordination and a lot of power to pull off. And usually a huge threat to hold over the kids' heads to keep them from leaving or talking. If someone even hints that they want to stop working for the leader, chances are they would be killed, drugged and sold off, or abandoned somewhere."

"Shit," Oliver breathed, his thoughts going to Kofi and Ramzi. "Kofi indicated that he wanted Ramzi to stay at the shelter, and Ramzi was adamant that it would go bad for Kofi if he didn't stay with his older brother."

"So they're probably both involved with the leader," Landon surmised.

Jeb called out from his computer screen. "I have several police reports dealing with gangs of younger kids. Three of them are with known gangs out of San Francisco. There's a report from two days ago of the arrest of a man and woman running a prostitution ring with underage girls based out of San Jose." He turned and looked over his shoulder toward Oliver. "There's nothing else showing up with the local police."

"Nothing from on the radar of the FBI?" Carson asked Landon.

"The only thing that's down near the youth center is a recent case an agent friend of mine is working on. He's looking into bank scams that might be linked to ATMs, but that seems too advanced for someone using kids. I hate to say it, but Kofi and Ramzi seem more likely to be involved in a gang. There are over forty known gangs operating out of San Francisco, many extending to San Jose and lower. But I'll look for more information closer to where the center is located."

As Landon signed off from the video conference,

Oliver looked at the others, heaving a sigh. "If Kofi is trying to get away from whoever has control over him, what is he facing?"

"Chances are they'll use Ramzi to keep Kofi under control. He would have done better if he could have gotten Ramzi to stay at the center," Natalie surmised.

Oliver nodded slowly, then asked, "And the center? Charity is desperate to get the boys to stay there. Would they then be in danger if this person wanted to get their hands back on Ramzi? Or also Kofi, if he comes there, too?"

The silence that followed made his gut clench in a way it hadn't since one of his last missions where they were drawing fire and one of his Ranger teammates was caught in a building. In that instance, the rest of the team knew exactly what maneuvers to take to get him out and complete the mission successfully. But with Charity and the center? He had no fucking idea how to make that happen against an unknown enemy.

"We've got security set up at the center, so the youth and staff should be well protected," Poole said, then winced as he held Oliver's gaze. "Of course, during the day when the center is open, anyone could come into the reception area. At night is when it is best protected."

"With the cameras set up inside as well as on the outside, including the sidewalk and a street view, we can increase the surveillance," Jeb said.

Oliver nodded, saying, "True, but unless the boys come to stay there, I think Bright Futures Home will be safe. And if they do come to stay, I'll see if they'll talk to me about what is going on."

"Have her contact us the instant one or both brothers come back to the center," Carson instructed. "We'll make sure we keep our eyes on them."

Oliver nodded, more than appreciative of the backing of the Keepers, but he was already thinking of a way to keep a closer eye on Charity and the center. That was… if she would agree.

22

"Where the hell do you think you boys are going?"

Kofi looked over his shoulder, tensing as Eliza sauntered into the kitchen. A cigarette precariously danced between her lips, the ember glowing at the tip. Her lipstick cracked around her puckered mouth, the lines created from years of inhaling the shit she smoked. Kofi fought to keep his expression blank and his voice steady. "Taking Ramzi out to get something to eat."

A derisive snort escaped, showing her disbelief. "You got money for that?"

"Got a little left over from a couple of weeks ago." The lie fell easily from his lips—he had squirreled away almost all of it, hidden from her eagle eyes when she searched the upstairs rooms.

"Good, 'cause you're not getting anything off me."

She stared at him through hawk eyes, and he kept his breathing steady not to give her a chance to see his wariness. She leaned over the table to deliberately tap the end of the cigarette into the ashtray before bringing it back to her lips and inhaling deeply. Exhaling, the smoke curled around her narrow face, and Kofi was once again reminded of a sleeping dragon that was always ready to strike, unleashing its fire on an unsuspecting victim. His heart threatened to pound out of his chest as he maintained his composed facade.

Eliza held the cigarette between her middle and forefinger as she pointed at Kofi. "I don't trust you, boy. You got a look about you that's getting too damn confident."

"Ma'am, I'm just trying to learn everything I can from you and Cory while teaching my brother. If we stop working, we've got nothing, so you don't have to worry about us."

Her response was to drag her tongue over her bottom lip slowly, her gaze remaining steadfast on him. "You remember who you belong to—"

A noise from the second floor shattered the tense standoff, and she turned to yell at whoever was up there. As she stomped out of the room, still yelling, Kofi took advantage of the break in her attention. He grabbed Ramzi's shoulder and nudged him out the door.

Ramzi remained quiet, letting Kofi lead him out into the labyrinth of alleys with practiced stealth. Once they were far enough from the house, they stopped. Ramzi's eyes widened slightly, with alertness and wariness radiating from him.

"Did you do what I asked?"

"Yeah," Ramzi said softly. "I got some of our stuff but left enough so it would look like we were coming back."

Taking a few seconds to smile at his brother, he jerked his head to the side. "Come on."

He led Ramzi out of the alley and onto the street. They hustled down several blocks, ducked into a few alleys, popped out on other streets, and made their way to their destination. Along the way, he spied two ATMs on which he had placed skimmers and wished he could walk over and snatch them off. With a tight grimace, he walked past, never looking over.

Kofi had spent the past week thinking of every possible way to disentangle him and Ramzi from the Haltsons. Each scenario he considered always came back to the knowledge that Eliza and Cory wouldn't let them go easily. And the last thing he wanted to do was put his brother in harm's way.

If they both disappeared and left the area, he had no idea how long their money would last before it ran out. He could get a job, but they would need travel money to get away. And there's no way he'd leave without Ramzi.

"You're not thinking about leaving me at the center and going somewhere, are you?" Ramzi asked as though he could tell what Kofi had pondered.

With a weighty sigh, Kofi replied, "I thought about it." He and Ramzi had never lied to each other, so he wasn't going to start now. "I keep trying to think of a way for us to get out of this safely. The only thing I can think of is for both of us to leave the area. We got money saved up and can get on a bus going somewhere else. Ms. Charity said that homeless law was federal. That means it's not just here. It's everywhere. So maybe we can go somewhere else and find help."

Ramzi nodded slowly but waited.

Letting out a long, slow breath, Kofi said, "But I gotta make things right."

Ramzi's eyes widened as he tilted his head slightly to the side. He reached out to grab Kofi's arm. "What do you mean?"

"Do you trust me?"

Time stood still as the two brothers stared without blinking at each other. Ramzi slowly nodded. "You know I do. You don't gotta ask."

"Then there's only one way I can see for us to make this right. Come on." He turned and led the way down another street.

Paula rounded the corner quickly, nearly running into Charity, who stumbled backward. "What the—? Good grief, Paula! Where are you going?"

Out of breath, Paula grabbed Charity's arm. "I knew you'd want to know they walked in!"

Eyes narrowing, she asked, "Who?"

"Those two brothers... Kofi and Ramzi. They want you."

"Thank you!" she gasped as she rushed down the hall. When she came to the corner that would lead her into the reception lobby, she stopped, took a deep breath, and let it out slowly. Calming her heartbeat, she walked around the corner, and her gaze fell upon the two boys. Unable to contain her enthusiasm, she hurried forward, smiling widely as she reached out her hand."I'm so glad to see you!"

Kofi took her hand, and she held it between both of hers, giving it a slight squeeze before letting go and turning to Ramzi. He smiled shyly when she shook his hand, and she could've sworn she witnessed a look of relief in his eyes.

She had a million questions but knew it was important for them to tell her why they were there and what they needed. "Do you want to go into my office?"

Kofi looked around, then jerked his head up and down. "Yes, ma'am."

"Call me Charity." She waved her hand in the direction of her office. Both boys nodded, and she led the way. Once inside, Ramzi sat quickly, but Kofi hovered near the door.

"Do you mind if I close this, ma'am... Charity?"

She shook her head, and he thanked her as he closed her office door, then took his seat next to Ramzi.

"Okay, Kofi. You two are here, but I don't want to make any assumptions. So why don't you tell me what I can do for you."

"Is it possible for you to call that man back in?" Kofi asked.

Startled at Kofi's unexpected request, she blinked as her chin jerked back slightly. "I'm sorry, what man?"

"The one who was here before. The one who was with you and talked to us."

She startled again as understanding dawned. "Mr. Parker. Oliver."

Kofi nodded quickly and said, "Yeah, that's the one. Can he talk to us again?"

Wanting to proceed cautiously, she nodded slowly. "Yes, I'm sure he wouldn't mind talking to you again, but he doesn't work here."

Kofi's brow lowered. "He was helping with security here, wasn't he?"

"Yes, he was. But he doesn't stay here at the center. He works for the company who was designing the system."

She watched Kofi's lips press together, and Ramzi stare at his brother, fear back in his eyes. Making a quick decision, she offered, "But I can call him. I can put him on speakerphone or video, and then you could talk to him that way. Would that work?"

"Nobody could overhear us, right?"

"Not unless you wanted them to." She picked up her phone and waited to see what Kofi would say. When she gained his nod, she quickly dialed Oliver.

He answered almost immediately. "Hey, Charity."

"Oliver, listen. I have Kofi and Ramzi here in my office. They just came in and wanted to talk in private. But they really wanted you to be here also. So I told them that I could put them on speakerphone or a video call, and they could talk to you that way. But only you, okay?"

"Absolutely."

She loved how he agreed without hesitation and tapped on the speakerphone icon before laying her phone on her desk. "Okay, Oliver. I have you on speakerphone."

"Kofi?" Oliver prodded.

"Yes, sir?"

"To start with, you can call me Oliver. Next, I want to ask you a question, but the answer is completely up to you. I'm not trying to get you to answer one way or the other, okay?"

"Okay."

It didn't pass Charity's attention that Kofi also agreed without hesitation.

Oliver continued. "I'm still at work, surrounded by some of the other men and women in this organization, who, like me, work to keep people safe. I have no idea what you want to talk about, but if we get to a point in the conversation where you'd like to get help, would it be okay if I let them hear our conversation? We can see you from the security camera in Charity's office, but her phone will let us hear you."

Kofi glanced up at the camera in the corner, and Ramzi jerked his head around, his eyes wide. Then the two shared a look, and Charity held her breath, waiting for their answer.

Finally, Kofi said, "It's just people like you? It's not a bunch of policemen there?"

"There are no policemen here at all, Kofi. It's just me and some of the people I work with. I'm really proud of you two boys coming to see Charity. We've been really worried about you."

Ramzi grinned at Oliver's words, and Charity could have sworn that Kofi's shoulders slumped in relief.

"Okay. You can put me on speaker."

"After a few seconds, Oliver said, "You're on speakerphone, and so are we. It's all secure, and nobody here will do anything you don't want or know about, Kofi. Agreed?"

He nodded.

"Charity," Oliver began. "Why don't you start the conversation, and we'll interject if we need to."

"Kofi and Ramzi, first of all, you've come into the Bright Futures Home, so please tell me what you are looking for from us."

"We need a place to stay. It's no longer safe for Ramzi to stay where we were. Probably not me, either, but I'm bigger and can take care of myself. In fact, I think that's probably why we've been left alone. But we need to make some changes, and to do that, we need a safe place to stay."

"I've already gone over some of the basic questions the last time I saw you. You don't have a permanent place to stay. By that, I mean where you lay your head at night. Other than this place you've talked about, which is not safe, and it's not with a parent or guardian, right?"

"That's right."

"We have emergency housing that we can offer while we determine your legal eligibility." Seeing his eyes widen, she quickly said, "That just means I have to check to see when you were in school last, your last residence, any bills you've been paying, and have you signed a declaration statement that you do not have permanent housing. We don't have to wait on that to be able to offer you a place to stay. We're almost at full capacity, but there is a bedroom on the boys' side that has bunkbeds."

"That'd be fine." Kofi nodded in haste. Ramzi glanced at his brother and began nodding, too. "If Ramzi and I had to sleep together in the same bed, it'd be fine."

"No, we have a bed for each of you. Now, there are certain rules that you have to obey if you're going to be staying at Bright Futures. Each of you will need to sign them after we go over them carefully, and the understanding is that the rules are for your safety and the safety of others. If you break those rules, then you can be sent away from this home."

"We got it," Kofi said, again nodding. "We understand."

"Now, with the basics out of the way, before we get to any of the paperwork and details, do you want to talk to Oliver and let him know why you wanted him involved in your intake?"

Kofi leaned closer to the phone lying on her desk. "Mr. Oliver? Are you still there?"

"Yes, I'm still here. My fellow coworkers are also sitting here, listening and watching. How can we help you?"

Kofi's hands were clasped in his lap, pressing tightly together. Charity could feel the waves of anxiety rolling off him.

Finally, he looked at his brother and then up to the camera in the corner. "I was thinking about what you said the other day. You said everyone makes a lot of mistakes in their lives. But we also make choices. And looking for a different way of doing things is what can define a good man. Me and Ramzi, we didn't have a dad, and Mom had a bunch of loser boyfriends that she finally left us for. Ramzi's got no one but me to show him how to be a good man. And I can't do that if I don't fix my mistakes."

"It sounds like you're well on your way to being a good man," Oliver said. "You've taken care of your brother, made sure he had food and was safe. And now, you're taking even more steps to make sure you're both in a good place."

"Yeah, maybe." Kofi shrugged as he sighed heavily. "I mean, I've done those things, but I haven't always made good choices. In fact, I've done some things that weren't legal. But I felt like I didn't have a choice."

Charity ached for the heavy weight that Kofi was carrying around. Leaning forward, she said, "Kofi, you're making decisions right now, right here, and they are going to change the direction of both of your lives for the better."

They were silent for a moment, and she was grateful Oliver didn't ply him with a bunch of questions.

Finally, Kofi admitted, "I met someone who told me I could make good money. I knew this guy had run drugs and figured that's what he was talking about. I didn't want Ramzi around that shit. So at first, I told him no. But he told me it didn't have anything to do with drugs. He said there was someone who had a place where we could stay. He said they had a place where we could sleep and they had food. I asked him what the catch was, and he said we had to learn to steal from rich people. He said it wasn't easy, that's why he thought of me. He said they don't take just anybody because they can't take a chance on somebody doing something stupid and getting caught. He said he was sure I was smart enough to make us some good money." He squeezed his eyes tight and shook his head, another sigh leaving his lips. "I was so stupid."

Ramzi grabbed his brother's arm and gave it a shake. "We were hungry. Don't you remember? We spent some nights in the park, and it was scary. You promised you'd try to find a place where I'd be safe and we wouldn't have to worry about food. And then this guy showed up talking to you, giving us hope. You weren't stupid, Kofi. We were just hungry and tired."

The two boys held each other's gazes. Tears pricked Charity's eyes, and she hoped Oliver and the other Keepers could witness the devotion Kofi and Ramzi shared.

Kofi nodded before looking back up at the camera. "It's no excuse for doing wrong, but I… felt like… I had nowhere to go. And everything that guy said just sounded so fuckin' good. I told him we had to both be together, but I'd watch out for Ramzi. So he gave me an address and a time to meet the next day. We showed up and met a man who said that he only took highly recommended people to work for him. He said we'd get a percentage of everything we earned, and we'd share a house that he and his wife lived in. He said there'd be food to eat."

"That must've sounded like an amazing offer," Charity said.

Kofi looked at her and swallowed deeply. "We agreed and showed up, and I thought at first we'd found a jackpot. I thought that way for a while until I eventually learned we'd made a deal that was too good to be true."

Charity looked at the defeated expression on Kofi's face, and the fear in Ramzi's eyes and her rage grew. Now, she wanted to take on the fight for these two.

23

Oliver glanced over to see the hard set of Leo's jaw. His brother always had such a serious countenance, even when they were kids. He was suddenly flooded with memories of the times Leo stood up for him and watched over him. He readily acknowledged he had a great brother but had often focused on the way he'd sometimes felt as though he didn't quite measure up. Which of them could run faster? Which one could bench-press more weight? Which one had the toughest career in the military?

The reality was that those were stupid comparisons, not worth wasting time on. And Leo had never made him feel that way— just typical second son bullshit. All that really mattered was that Leo was there whenever he needed him. If Oliver had been hungry, with no place to sleep, Leo would've given anything to ensure Oliver's basic needs were taken care of.

And looking at the video feed of the expression

between Kofi and Ramzi, he recognized the same devotion in them that he and Leo shared.

Looking back at his brother, he now discovered Leo's gaze was pinned on him. He didn't have to wonder what Leo was thinking. The bond between brothers was strong, and they were witnessing in the younger boys what he and Leo shared.

Shooting his gaze around the table, he noted the rapt attention of each of the Keepers as they watched and listened to what Kofi was saying.

"What did they demand you do?" Charity prompted.

"At first, they taught us how to steal. We'd go hang out at the food trucks where vacationers were ordering food for kids. They'd juggle their money and the food, be all distracted, and make it easy to swipe their wallets. We would also learn how to recognize and lift designer bags. They taught us to work in pairs so that one is always on the lookout. Once we'd proven ourselves, then they taught us new shit to do."

He rubbed his forehead, then continued. "When we were sleeping at the park, we saw kids who were selling themselves, selling drugs, hell… everything. The people we were staying with weren't into that kind of shit." He swallowed deeply, then continued. "I guess I convinced myself what we were doing wasn't really too bad. I knew it was, but it didn't seem like it was that wrong. When you're hungry, stealing from someone who has a lot makes it easy to convince yourself that it's okay."

"And the people you stay with?" Oliver asked. "How did they treat you?"

Kofi hesitated, looking over at Ramzi. "It didn't take

long to learn that everything had a price. They would give us a percentage of what we brought in. At first, just having some money in our pockets was way more than anything we've had."

Oliver noticed that Ramzi grinned for the first time since they had to come into Charity's office. "Remember when we ate at that restaurant? We ate so much, we both got sick!"

Kofi smiled indulgently toward Ramzi and nodded. "Yeah, and that was the first time I really thought about the money. We ate at a restaurant and spent most of the money that we'd gotten from the couple. But I knew that was no way to live. If we were ever going to have our own place and be our own bosses, then we needed to save money. None of the other kids in the house did, but I was determined that's what we needed to do. I couldn't open a bank account, but I started hiding the money we got so that if Eliza ever went looking, she wouldn't find it. They always encouraged everyone to spend and buy. I think that's how they kept all of us in line."

"You just mentioned a name—Eliza," Oliver said.

Kofi's eyes jerked open wide. "Shit, I shouldn't have done that."

"Kofi." Charity gained his attention. "I know that you asked for Oliver and the others to listen as you talked. That tells me that you don't want any more secrets, but maybe I'm wrong. Tell me what you want from Oliver."

Shoulders slumping, Kofi nodded. "I brought us here to stay. And I know that's the first step to getting safe.

But I can't right the wrong I've done if I don't do something to try to stop them."

"I'm scared," Ramzi confessed, his face scrunched as he stared up at his brother.

"I know," Kofi said. "But you don't just have me watching out for you anymore. We've now got this home and Charity. And if Oliver agrees, we have him, too."

"What else did they have you do?" Charity asked.

"Once we proved to be useful and resourceful and got to a place where they trusted us, they taught us how to put skimmers on ATM machines. I don't understand how all of it works, but once we do that, they can take the information from someone's bank card and start making withdrawals. We were told that these were people who could afford to go to the bank and get more money, so it didn't seem like it was bad."

Oliver turned his wide-eyed gaze over to Carson, whose brows had lifted. This was exactly what Landon had mentioned an FBI agent was working on.

"What kind of threat do they hold over you?" Oliver asked.

"If kids didn't meet their quota or didn't bring in enough merchandise, they'd put them in the cell."

Oliver was startled, and as his chin jerked back, he watched as Charity reacted the same way. "The cell?"

"They built wooden cells in the basement and would lock kids in with no food or light for a couple of days. Then they let them back out; believe me, they want to do anything after that. I managed to stay out…" His voice drifted off.

"Not me," Ramzi admitted, his chin quivering.

Oliver felt fury moving through his veins like molten lava.

"I was standing across the street and watched an old couple go to the ATM. You could tell they didn't have a lot of money, and I wanted to run across the street and beg them not to put their card into the machine. I later overheard Eliza complaining, saying she didn't get much money from a couple of old geezers' accounts. But she decided to wipe them out. That was right after I met you. And I knew I couldn't keep doing this and live with myself. And I couldn't teach my brother that this was the right thing to do. So here we are."

The Keepers were silent, and so were the brothers. Finally, it was Charity who leaned forward and asked, "Who are these people? I need to know who they are and what they look like so I can warn my staff to be on the lookout. I want to keep you safe, but I also want to keep everyone else here safe."

Without hesitation, Kofi sat up straight and looked first at Charity and then shifted his gaze to the camera. "Cory and Eliza Halston." He rattled off their address, a grimace etched on his face.

Carson gave him a nod, and Oliver said, "Kofi, I want you and Ramzi to get settled in tonight. Do everything that Charity tells you. Make sure you follow her rules and don't make any decisions alone. That might jeopardize your safety. You've made the right first step. Now, the group I work for is going to find out how to take down the Halstons. But don't worry about what we're doing. We will see you tomorrow."

"Is Oliver gonna come back here?"

"Absolutely. Once I settle things here, I'll be there."

"Oliver!" Kofi called out quickly.

"Yeah, right here."

"I... it doesn't matter what happens to me 'cause I'm the one who was doing wrong, but I don't want Ramzi to get in trouble—"

"No!" Ramzi called out, grabbing his brother's arm.

"Hold on," Oliver ordered. "Right now, don't worry about anything other than staying safe and letting Charity take care of you. Get a good night's sleep, and I'll be there in the morning."

Charity said, "Don't worry, Oliver, I'll take care of everything here."

"I'm driving to your place tonight."

"You don't have to do that—"

"I'll be there tonight," he reiterated. Gaining her assurance that they would stay locked up until he got there, they disconnected.

Jeb was already calling out, "Cory Halston. Forty-four years old. Born in the outskirts of LA to a mom with a coke habit. Looks like between her trips to rehab, he lived with his grandparents. At fourteen, he was in juvie. Small shit. Since then, no rap sheet. Eliza Richards Halston. Forty-six years old. Parents worked for several families in LA. Mom was a maid, and Dad was a gardener."

"Probably where she got a taste for the finer things in life," Natalie quipped.

"They met ten years ago," Jeb continued. "Well, guess where? Both were working at a bank in San Fransisco.

She was a teller, and he was working on installing ATM equipment, a trade he learned in electrical school."

At that, Tricia's brows lifted. "Damn, I guess if he knew how to install them, he knew how to manipulate them."

"She was fired after it was noted that she slipped a few hundreds into her purse. The bank didn't press charges, which makes no sense, but she was fired nonetheless."

"What about the location of their house?"

"Not a great neighborhood," Abbie said, looking at her computer screen. "In an area that probably wouldn't think twice about a bunch of kids coming and going. It's got old houses, and some look to be pretty crappy."

Oliver looked over at Carson. "This goes a lot deeper than just kids stealing from some tourists. Do you think this is the case Landon mentioned?"

Carson replied, "We need to get Landon back on this. Even if this isn't related to the case specifically mentioned, bank thefts are federal crimes."

Oliver's heart twitched in his chest. "What about the boys? Can they get offered a deal?"

"That'll be up to the FBI, but we'll find out first what we need to do from Landon."

While Carson put in the call, Oliver waited, both desperate to get law enforcement to take down the Halstons and terrified that the boys would be swept up in the attempt. His skin felt too tight until Carson finally got off the line with Landon.

"Landon is excited. He wants to talk to the boys tomorrow—"

"Not without me present," Oliver bit back.

Carson didn't hesitate, nodding instead. "He'll have no problem with that. Since the boys are unaccompanied minors, Charity needs to be a witness to their conversations anyway, and with you there, the boys' interests are protected."

Once he'd gathered the other Keepers' intel, Oliver headed to Leo's place to pack. As he turned into the driveway, he sat for a moment and looked at the house Leo and Natalie lived in. It was modest but had everything they wanted—the perfect home to welcome their baby and raise a family.

And he thought of what kind of home he wanted to buy. For once, he no longer thought of square feet, upgrades, or a view. Instead, he thought of simply a place to come to at the end of the day. A place filled with smiles and laughter. A place to sleep peacefully. A place to fix good meals. A place to host friends and family. And he thought of Charity... and wanted a home to be a place she would also like to be.

A knock on the window had him jerk his head around to see Leo standing next to his SUV.

"You okay, bro?"

He climbed down and stood next to his vehicle, nodding.

"I know you want to do right by those boys," Leo said.

Oliver swallowed deeply, then turned to hold the gaze that so often mirrored his own. "They're nothing like us as far as their background goes, yet I see us in them."

"The way they can talk to each other without having to say a word," Leo said, smiling.

Oliver chuckled. "The way Kofi looks out for Ramzi the way you used to."

"Hell, we were only eighteen months apart... I didn't have to do much looking out for you."

"You were always a tough act to follow." He snorted. "And I was a little shit of a younger brother."

Leo rolled his eyes. "What the hell makes you say that?"

"I don't know, bro. I guess I was always trying to keep up with you and one-up you. Just stupid shit."

"You didn't have to try to one-up me, Oliver. Hell, you are always smarter than me."

"You're full of it."

"No, I'm serious. I would always go slow and weigh the pros and cons before making a decision. It's one of the things that held me back sometimes as a Delta. But you'd rush balls to the wall to get something done. Not that you were rash, but you were willing to take more risks. I admired that... I still do."

Oliver snorted. "Yeah, jumping in without looking sometimes got me in trouble."

"I spent a lot of years in love with Natalie before I finally admitted it. I don't regret our friendship years, but I sometimes wonder what it would be like if we'd given in to our feelings earlier. I'm glad you've met Charity and aren't holding back going after what you want."

"Well, we're hardly ready to slap a label on what we are, but I spent a lot of years chasing a good time with women who were only looking for the same thing. Finding someone who makes me want to be a better man is nice."

"Then go for it. Ride it out as long as it lasts, and if I know you, you'll make it last."

Natalie walked outside and stood on the front porch. Her words held mirth, but her eyes were full of worry. "So did you two get your dose of brotherly love?"

"Smart-ass," Oliver and Leo said at the same time.

They laughed, and then Natalie grinned. "I've known both of you for almost twelve years. The best of brothers can fight, argue, and push each other to compete. But you also know what is really important… family. As I watched Kofi and Ramzi today, I was struck by how they were like you in that regard."

Leo walked to her and kissed her. "And that is why I'm in love with this woman."

As he walked into the house to pack for the night, it struck Oliver that he could see Charity with his brother and sister-in-law. He also couldn't wait for her to meet their parents. He just hoped he wasn't moving too fast for her because he knew, beyond a shadow of a doubt, that he wanted her in his life.

24

Charity sat on the small landing outside her apartment, her stomach clenching more with each minute. Finally, her phone vibrated, and she jumped, then looked down to see Oliver's text that he was there. She raced down the steps and threw open the door.

As soon as he walked through, she said, "You need to have the code to get in this door!"

Despite the seriousness of the situation, he smiled and lifted a brow, giving him the irrepressible expression she adored. "From a security standpoint, I'd advise against you giving out your code to random men."

She rolled her eyes and couldn't help but allow a little smile to curve her lips also. "I hadn't categorized you as a random man. So maybe on top of everything else we're dealing with, you and I might need to have a conversation."

He wrapped his arms around her and pulled her close. She rested her head against his chest and allowed his strength to seep into her.

"We can have any conversation you want, but if you're thinking about giving me easier access to you, then I'm all in, Charity." His words were mumbled against her hair, and she loved the feel of his lips as he kissed the top of her head.

Leaning back, she simply nodded as she looked up at him. She couldn't deny that her feelings for him had grown quickly. So quickly, that some might have claimed it was insta-love. But for her, it didn't feel instant. Maybe because ever since they first laid eyes on each other, life had thrown so much at them. She knew more about Oliver now than she had with any other man she'd dated. She knew how he responded when he was angry, frustrated, happy, uncertain. She'd met many of his coworkers and some of his family. She'd had the opportunity to see him in multiple situations, not just on a date.

And even in the short time she'd known him, she'd watched him grow in understanding of a situation he'd never considered before.

"I don't think we need to have a conversation about whether or not you should have the code to get into the lower door," she said, with her arms still wrapped around his waist. "I know the kind of man you are, and I know I want you in my life. As long as we're moving forward together, I trust you."

He bent as he pulled her closer, his lips sealing over hers, and she willingly gave herself over to the passion, handing her frazzled emotions to him.

He lifted her in his arms and walked over to the sofa,

sitting while gently settling her in his lap, somehow managing to keep their kiss intact.

The kiss held the same vibrating electricity that moved through her body just like every time they kissed. But this time, the emotion she felt the most was safe. Whatever was going on with the center, especially with Kofi and Ramzi, she felt more confident that everything would turn out okay with Oliver at her back.

As his tongue glided over hers, she felt the velvet tickle and gave herself to him. One of his hands gently rubbed up and down her back as the other cupped the back of her head, his fingers massaging her scalp. As she grew languid in his arms, he slowly ended the kiss.

Her eyes blinked open, and she stared at his face, unable to tell what he was thinking. She'd wondered if he would stand and carry her to the bedroom. Instead, he simply sat on the sofa with her in his lap, offering comfort.

"How are you doing?" he asked. "How are you really doing?"

She held his eyes, seeing the concern in their depth. "Nervous, anxious, wondering what tomorrow will bring, hoping tonight goes okay for them."

"Did the boys settle in?"

She nodded. "I've texted George each hour, and he assures me they're in their room and already asleep."

"They've probably slept with one eye open for so long that to be in a safe area is the first time they've truly been able to relax."

Having worked with homeless teens for years, she

knew that to be true but was surprised at how quickly Oliver understood.

"I don't want to keep texting George because he needs to get a good night's sleep, but it's hard for me to be here and not worry."

He glided his hand from the back of her head to her face, cupping her face as he gently rubbed his thumb over her cheek.

"Tell me about your dream home."

His sudden change of conversation topic startled her. "My what?" She glanced around at the living room before returning her gaze to him. "Dream home?"

"I guess that question came out of the blue, didn't it?" He smiled and shook his head. "You've told me where you grew up, and even though it was small, there was love there, so it was special to you. Now, you're in a small apartment, but you've also made this place special to you. I've never had a real home after I left my parents' house, but I'm in the market to buy and talked to a real estate agent the other day. His questions threw me, and I wanted another perspective." He leaned in and kissed her softly again. "I'm just curious about what would make a dream home for you."

Her brow furrowed, and she thought about his question. "I've never talked to a real estate agent. Staying here has allowed me to save money, but I need to work a couple more years to have enough for a down payment." She heaved her shoulders and tilted her head as she continued to hold his gaze. "What kind of questions was he asking?"

"Things like square footage, how many bedrooms,

how many bathrooms, how big I want the kitchen, how many floors, did I want the main bedroom on the first floor, how large a lot?" He shook his head, and she smiled at the befuddled expression on his face.

She scrunched her nose and hesitated as she thought about the answer to his question.

"What's that look for?" he asked.

"Well, to be honest, sometimes I look at realty websites and just browse to look at different homes."

"Perfect! Then you know more than me. So what would your dream home be like?"

"I don't dream of a large home. I just need at least three bedrooms and two bathrooms. If I'm lucky enough to have kids down the road, I'd like them each to have their own bedroom. And while the single me doesn't need more than one bathroom, having two is easier for a family or when guests are over."

He nodded, his face a mask of seriousness. "That makes sense."

"I know a lot of modern homes have the owners' bedroom on the first floor, and I think that's important for some people, especially if there are mobility issues. But if I have kids, I want to be close to them at night."

His brows lifted almost comically, and she wondered if he thought her reasons were foolish.

"Wow!" he enthused. "I never thought of that." Now, he tilted his head to the side as he peered at her. "I should take you with me when I start looking."

She knew he meant she'd be a person who could offer an opinion on the houses he was considering, but her heart ached just a little at the idea of helping him find his home, knowing she wasn't looking for herself. Wincing slightly, she pushed that selfish thought to the side. Clearing her throat, she continued, "The larger the lot, the more landscaping and mowing I'd have to do. I want room for flower beds, a small garden, and room for kids to play, but I don't want to be so far away from neighbors that I can't make friends." She snorted as she added, "Of course, not everybody who is a neighbor turns out to be a friend, so having a little space wouldn't be too bad."

He chuckled and agreed. "Good point. I think a fence to keep kids in and neighbors out when needed is a good thing."

They both laughed, and she breathed a little easier as the heaviness of their day eased. "I suppose, more than anything else, I'd like to have a house full of... um."

His brows lowered as it was now his turn to peer deeply into her eyes. "Full of what?"

She blew out a breath and admitted, "Full of love."

His face softened as his lips curved upward. "Yeah, me, too. A house full of love."

They sat for a long moment, neither speaking, as volumes passed between them through their gazes. Suddenly, her phone vibrated, and she leaped off his lap and turned to snag it off the coffee table. Looking down, she spied a text from George. Her heart pounded as she stabbed at her phone to pull it up. But when her eyes read the text, she released a long breath. Looking down at Oliver, still sitting on the sofa, she smiled. "George says he just checked on them one last time, and both boys are still sound asleep."

Oliver stood, pulled her into his embrace, and kissed the top of her head. "We've got a long day ahead of us tomorrow, so I suggest we do exactly what the boys are doing and head to bed."

Filled with gratitude, comfort, and even nervousness, she couldn't help but lean back and ask, "If I have trouble going to sleep, do you have a cure?"

His impish expression filled his face, and he nodded. "I plan on wearing you out with orgasms, so you'll have no choice except to sleep peacefully."

She slipped from his grasp and started toward the bedroom. "Sounds like the cure for insomnia!" With that, she hurried toward the bedroom with Oliver right on her heels.

25

Oliver accepted the cup of coffee that Charity placed on the kitchen counter. He laughed at the sight of their two mugs. One proclaimed **I'm Not Bossy... I Just Know What You Should Be Doing**. The other had a picture of a chicken and read, **I May Look Calm, but In My Head, I've Pecked You Three Times**.

She was dressed in slacks and a light pink sweater for work, and he spied a little makeup covering up the circles under her eyes. When they'd climbed into bed, he'd worked her body over, giving her as many orgasms as she could handle in as many different ways as he could. She'd been an eager participant, ensuring he'd also found his release several times. And what he knew for sure, is their acts weren't fucking... it was making love. He knew it and felt it from his perspective, and he was sure she felt the same way. A sliver of doubt crept in. *At least I hope she felt the same.*

"Poor George!" she said, shaking her head. "He would get up and check on the boys to be sure they were okay. And, of course, they settled right in and slept through the night. He knew I was worried and sent two more texts during the night. But you wore me out, and I slept right through his texts!"

Wrapping his arms around her, he touched his lips to hers. "Glad I could be of service, ma'am."

She hummed and lifted what appeared to be a starry-eyed gaze to him. "Did you sleep after wearing me out? I hope I gave as good as I got!"

"Oh, sweetheart, you can be my insomnia cure anytime you want." The quip slipped out effortlessly with the ease he felt in her presence, but in truth, he wanted to express more. "But you should know that what I feel for you is way more than just what I feel when we're making love."

Her top teeth landed on her bottom lip, and she sucked in a hissing breath. "Really?" Swallowing, she continued before he had a chance to reply. "Because I know it's early days, but I really like you, Oliver. I know we haven't even talked about exclusivity or what we are, but—"

"Oh, hell yeah, we're exclusive. My dick, my girl."

She blinked before barking out a laugh. "That sounded so cavemanish!"

"Sorry." He scrunched his nose, hoping she hadn't been offended. "I just mean that what we are is exclusive. I'm not looking for anything or anyone else."

"Me either."

A sigh of relief escaped, giving evidence he needed to hear her say the words. "Good. And for the record, I want to see where this feeling between us can go. It may seem sudden, but you make me feel things I've never felt before. You make me want to understand the world around me in a way I haven't before. You make me want to be a better man. And you sure as hell make me want to do what I can to make your world better. Too soon? Well, I'm old enough to know when something is right for me."

She lifted on her toes and kissed him lightly. "I agree, Oliver. I want to take us as far as we can go."

Her phone buzzed with another text from George. "Oh, the boys are up and in the shower." She let out a long breath, then turned and sat at her small table and inclined her head for him to take a seat with her. "I hate to end what we were discussing, but I need to talk to you this morning before we get downstairs and everything goes crazy." She leaned across the table and took his hand. "I'm so grateful for you, Oliver, for stepping up for them. It means so much to me, but more importantly, it really means a lot to them."

"You don't have to thank me, Charity. I'm only doing what anybody should do. Hell, I was the one who wasn't willing to give them a chance in the beginning."

"Well, they had just robbed a restaurant, so don't be too hard on yourself that you didn't give them a chance! It's only because of my work that I was able to recognize desperation when I saw it."

"They've been handed a shit hand, and I'd like to try to help them. But let's be honest, Charity, you're the real hero in their story."

"I'm just glad they came in, and we can offer them a

fresh start so that they can hopefully face an adulthood different from their childhood so far."

They finished their coffee, and she stood and walked to his chair, reaching for his empty cup. He pulled her onto his lap and kissed her. With his hand cupping her jaw and his finger sliding through her hair, he breathed her in. Angling his head, he took the kiss deeper. "Christ, I've missed you," he muttered against her lips.

As they ended the kiss, she nuzzled her nose against the side of his head and whispered, "This can give you a little taste of what you can have tonight when we finish with work."

"Oh hell, don't tell me that, or I'll rush through the day, and you'll never get rid of me."

She held his face for a moment, her lips curving upward into a soft smile. Tilting her head to the side, she asked, "Would that be so bad?"

"Absolutely not. Being with you is honestly all I think about now." He shook his head and barked out a chuckle. "I would say that I feel like a teenager who can't get the special girl off his mind, but then, when I was a teenager, I sure as hell never felt like this."

"Felt like what?"

Just then, his phone buzzed, and he dropped his chin to his chest. "Sorry, I have to take this."

She laughed and patted his chest. "Saved by the bell."

She turned to take their coffee cups to the sink when he grabbed her waist and gently turned her around to face him again, ignoring his phone. "I wasn't saved but just interrupted. Believe me, talking about what we are and where I'd like our relationship to go is not something I'm trying to get out of."

Her smile widened, and he leaned down to kiss her softly again. His phone continued to vibrate, and she laughed. "Let's get to work, and we'll save the relationship talk for later."

With that, she danced over to the sink, leaving him with no excuse not to answer his phone. A few minutes later, he shoved his phone into his pocket and said, "Looks like our day is getting started. I have two FBI agents who are going to meet us here."

Her inhalation was more of a gasp, but she remained quiet as she walked close to him and placed her hands on his waist, peering upward. "I'm scared for the boys."

"I'm gonna be there the whole time. I'll make sure they're protected."

"And I'll be there, too!"

"Then they get the best from both of us," he declared.

They quickly locked up and headed down the stairs, entering the center. He hoped that the day would go well, and the anticipation of his night with Charity was firmly on his mind. Hours later, all good thoughts had fled as he felt the weariness of being in a battle and unsure who won.

Landon Sommers exceeded his expectations in every regard. Calm. Assuring. Effortlessly connecting with the boys and assuming the role of advocate. He could see why Landon worked well with the Keepers—so much so that they considered him their indispensable FBI liaison.

However, when Randy Meckle, the FBI agent investigating the bank frauds, arrived, he epitomized every clichéd B-movie stereotype of an agent. Brash and overflowing with confidence. His demeanor was less of an investigator and more of a bulldozer, intent on plowing through obstacles with little regard for the leftover wreckage. It was evident Randy wanted to push the bank fraud case through, seeing it as a way to get his ticket punched to the next promotion. It was also evident he didn't give a fuck who he used to obtain his goal.

"Absolutely not!" Oliver vehemently argued as they sat in the room after the boys' interview. Charity vibrated with anger next to him, and he placed his hand over hers under the table, giving it a squeeze. He knew Randy's type... he wouldn't give a fuck about Charity's opinions. "You do not need to coerce Kofi into working for you to get your evidence. He's given you the information on which ATMs they've hit. You can trace that shit back to the Halstons."

"Without the evidence that I can get from these kids, the Halstons could weasel out. I need irrefutable proof."

"What more proof do you need?" Charity blurted, her words laced with anger and a dose of incredulity.

"Direct proof would be the best for a conviction," Randy sneered, his gaze barely looking at her. "Not just the word of another criminal who could be the one behind it all."

She gasped, but Oliver jumped in. "You've got to be shitting me! You've got a young man who's trying to do the right thing by handing you evidence, and you're going to piss that off and try to make him go back in and get more?"

"Don't make these boys into something they're not!" Randy bit out. "Remember, they're criminals, too. They may not be the masterminds, but they're no better than the people who sent them out to do their dirty work!"

"Agent Meckle!" Landon finally growled. "You have a case to investigate, and you're being handed prime evidence. Kofi and Ramzi Jackson are witnesses who have come forth of their own volition. Plus, don't forget the fact that they're minors."

"Minors!" Randy sneered. "The oldest is almost eighteen years old. Even now, I could have him arrested and tried as an adult."

"What the fuck is your problem, man?" Oliver barked. He looked over at Landon, now hating that they'd agreed to bring in the FBI.

Kofi and Ramzi had warmed easily to Landon, telling their story much like they had the previous night with the Keepers. While all understood Landon's need to bring in the agent who was actively working on the case, Randy's attitude and lack of caring about the boys' situation rankled.

"Look," Randy continued. "All I'm asking is for the oldest one to go back, make up some story about why they didn't come back last night, and where his brother is. Then he gets another ATM skimmer from the Halstons. We monitor him as he plants it, and then we follow the trail of money withdrawals to the Halstons. I have agents ready to monitor all his accounts."

"You've already got a trail now that Kofi has given

you the Halston's name. He's practically handed the whole case to you," Oliver argued.

Landon leaned forward with his forearms on the table and speared Randy with a hard stare. "You don't need to send him back in. You have the list of ATMs that already have skimmers in them."

"It would make the case rock solid, and you know it, Landon. You've become as much of a bleeding heart as those friends you hang out with."

Landon shook his head slowly. "I'm not even going to dignify that with an answer."

Oliver leaned back in his seat, hating the way the meeting was going. He'd mistakenly had Kofi and Ramzi inside the conference room when Randy arrived. They had already met Landon and felt comfortable with him. Ramzi was wide-eyed while talking with an FBI agent, but Kofi was appropriately cautious. Kofi wanted to ensure Ramzi would be taken care of, but Oliver didn't like how Kofi wasn't also advocating for himself. He was grateful when Landon spoke to both boys, advising them of their safety.

Randy came in, took notes as they gave their story again, and immediately went into the tough guy role. He threw out words like accomplice, equally culpable, interfering with an investigation, and even jail time. Oliver could see Ramzi's eyes widen and hands shake, and Oliver jumped in to shut down Ramzi's possible meltdown.

"Charity, please take Ramzi and Kofi outside for now." He could see her argument forming on her lips but leaned closer. "It will give them a break." Emotions warred on her face before she nodded. At first, Kofi didn't want to leave, but Kofi reluctantly acquiesced when he saw how his brother was reacting to the meeting.

After they left, Oliver allowed the meeting to continue until it was evident that Randy would continue his belligerent rants.

Randy glanced toward the door and growled, "Those kids have probably bolted by now. I can't afford to lose them." He rose from his chair, his expression hard.

Landon ordered, "Keep your seat, Agent Meckle. Those boys need a chance to process what's going on."

When it looked as though Randy was going to argue again, Landon spoke, "You cannot tell me that with the cooperation the boys have given you, you can't lock your case up tight."

"And you know," Randy countered. "With those boys on the inside, this case can be wrapped up and airtight."

"Who's going to protect those boys while they're doing this for you?" Oliver asked, knowing Charity was worried.

"I'll have agents stationed around, and if you're so worried about him, then you two can tag along."

"Oh, we'll be there," Landon stated emphatically.

The three men remained quiet for a moment, wondering who would break first. Finally, Randy said, "Here's the deal, gentlemen. While I agree those boys have had a rough go of it, there's no denying that their actions have caused some people to lose a lot of money. In no way is that right. But I also agree that the boys are not who I want to put behind bars. I want the Halstons."

"And the houseful of kids that they hold? What of them?"

"Once the Halstons are arrested and we know their entire operation, I can have the kids they held at juvie—"

"Social services needs to be called," Oliver said. "And I don't want Ramzi and Kofi split up."

Randy snorted. "Can you honestly tell me that would be so bad? What kind of influence has Kofi had on Ramzi?"

"You can't sit here and make that judgment," Oliver argued. "Everything Kofi did was to put food on the table and a roof over his brother's head."

Landon interjected. "Randy, this will be a moot point if you even consider splitting them up. Kofi and Ramzi would head out of here and be in the wind before you can get them to do anything. And I will not allow you to coerce them by threatening them."

Randy grimaced, his jaw tight. "Fine," he conceded. "They stay together."

"And you won't prosecute them," Oliver pushed. When Randy nodded, Oliver continued to press. "And the decision is theirs. I'm not gonna allow you to threaten or coerce Kofi to do anything you want him to do. I want him to learn that coming forward and telling the truth is the right thing to do. I want him to know that standing up for his brother was the right thing to do."

Randy's face was set in a hard scowl, but he nodded. "Agreed."

Oliver stood and walked to the door, then turned

and looked over his shoulder. "Give me a minute to talk to them, and then I'll bring Kofi back in." He stepped outside and easily spied the two boys standing with Charity. On the surface, she appeared calm, but he was already familiar enough with her to know that it was a facade. He was sure underneath the woman who seemed on the outside to be handling everything, she was nervous. And from the looks of it, so was Ramzi.

"What's going on?" Kofi asked, barely waiting for them to walk over.

"We worked out a deal with the FBI. They will not prosecute you or Ramzi for anything you've done. But they want to ask you to do something for them. It's important for you to understand you do not have to do this. You are under no obligation to say yes—"

"No. Absolutely not."

Three males looked over as Charity shook her head. "Oliver, I don't want them to have to do anything!"

"I agree," he shot back, "but the FBI has a right to ask, and then Kofi has a right to say no for himself."

Her eyes narrowed, and her hands gripped tighter as she held them in front of her. Jerking her gaze from Oliver to Kofi, she said, "I don't think you should talk to him. You've already given your statement as a witness as to what happened."

Kofi and Ramzi shared a look before Kofi turned back to her. "Ms. Charity, I understand where you're coming from. But I need you to understand me. I may have been influenced to do shit that I shouldn't have to survive, but I still did it. Let me at least hear what it is they want me to do to get the Halstons off the streets, away from making other kids do shit."

Her lips were still pressed together, but she nodded. It didn't pass Oliver's notice that she didn't make eye contact with him. Sighing, he knew he had his work cut out for him to get past this hurdle. He had no doubt they would, although it might take a little groveling on his part. "Ramzi, you stay here with Charity and let Kofi talk to Agent Meckle again."

Ramzi opened his mouth, but after one look from Kofi, he snapped it shut. Oliver couldn't walk away without at least reaching over and placing his hand on Charity. Giving her arm a squeeze that he hoped was comforting, he turned and clapped his hand on Kofi's shoulder, escorting him back into the room.

26

Kofi's gaze swept the room, taking in the faces of the men who held his fate in their hands. Agent Meckle's countenance was unsmiling, but his eyes gleamed with a sharpness Kofi recognized as hunger. Not the gnawing hunger of a missed meal but the craving of having something just out of his reach that he desperately wanted.

On the other hand, Oliver's FBI agent, Landon, shared a similar intensity in his eyes, but it was laced with sympathy. Kofi had learned to recognize sympathy, having noticed it when he and Ramzi were on the streets and a kind-hearted person would offer them money.

He glanced to the side at Oliver, whose expression was the hardest to read. There was anger, but Kofi discerned it was anger for Kofi's situation, not directed at him. This was a new sensation. Something he couldn't remember ever having other than experiencing it with Charity. It was the feeling of not being alone anymore.

Returning his focus to Agent Meckle, Kofi felt the heavy weight of his situation bearing down on his shoulders. He wanted to make sure everything was said exactly right in front of Agent Sommers and Oliver.

"So if I go back to the Halstons' house, convince them that last night Ramzi and I were just hanging out with a friend and that I'm ready to put in a new skimmer and do so, then that's all I have to do? I won't be arrested, and neither will Ramzi. You'll leave my brother and me alone, and we're free to decide where to live. You won't try to take Ramzi away from me and put him in some foster home. Right?"

Agent Meckle's jaw clenched, and he nodded. "That's right."

Oliver interjected. "Kofi, you still don't have to do this."

Turning his attention to Oliver, he held the gaze of the man he'd come to respect. "I understand. But you have to understand that I want to do this. I want to put them away and not have the Halstons hanging over my head. It's time for me to man up and figure out ways to take care of my brother that don't involve something illegal. I know that you and Ms. Charity will help us, but until the Halstons are put away, the threat of them will always be around, dragging other kids to do their dirty work."

Oliver nodded slowly, but it was evident to Kofi that Oliver struggled with the decision. Swallowing past the lump in his throat, he once again realized it had been a long time since he and Ramzi had ever had anyone at their backs.

"I got this, Oliver. I can do it, and then it's done." Blowing out a long breath, Kofi leaned closer, abandoning his need for personal space, and held Oliver's gaze. "But if anything happens, I need your word that you'll take care of Ramzi."

Oliver's quick inhalation showed how hard Kofi's words had been to hear. Oliver's jaw was tight, and his eyes narrowed. "Not one fuckin' thing is gonna happen to you. But, no matter what, you have my promise."

With that, the four men in the room began to plan.

Hours later, Kofi bounded up the back steps into the house. He wasn't surprised to see Eliza sitting at the kitchen table. He began to wonder if she ever did anything but sit at the kitchen table and gripe about everyone and everything.

"Where the fuck were you last night, boy?" she bit out before beginning to hack the cigarette cough he'd grown used to.

"Ramzi and I were hanging out in the park."

Her overplucked brow lifted. "What the fuck are you doing at the park? And why the fuck did it take all night?"

"It was nothing," he protested. "We ran into someone we knew from school." He chuckled, adopting an easy attitude and shaking his head. "Course, that was years ago when we were in school.

Turns out this guy dropped out at the same time we did."

"In the park? He was probably selling drugs, right? Was he trying to convince you to do that? You know we're not putting up with that shit. One thing in this house, you don't use drugs. We need you clear-headed and sharp to be able to do shit for us. You're supposed to be here every night. Are you too stupid to remember that simple rule? So if that's what you think you're going to do, you can just—"

"We didn't do no drugs," he argued. "He was just someone to hang out with for a little while."

She stood, tapped her cigarette into the ashtray, and, with narrowed eyes, leaned forward. "Then why the hell didn't you come home last night?"

"Because some cop showed up at the other end of the park, so we got the hell out of there. The last thing I figured you wanted was for some cop to follow us back here." Throwing his arm out, he continued, "We spent the night in an abandoned house just so no one would follow us back here. Geez, fuck, I think you'd be grateful."

"Where's Ramzi?"

"He was still sleepin' in. We got to sleep late. I woke him up to tell him that I was gonna come here, grab a piece of toast, and see if Cory had another job for me. I'll get him when I finish, and then we'll be back in later."

"You got an answer for everything, boy," she sneered. "I can't tell if you're dumb as shit or smart enough to lie your way through life."

Before she had a chance to berate him further, Cory stomped into the room. "Wondered where you were. The skimmer on the ATM over on River Road is fuckin' up. I got a replacement I need to go in."

Kofi nodded. "I'll get it done."

"Get it done fast, and get it done right," Eliza warned sternly, her gaze piercing.

"Don't I always get it done?"

"Don't you get smart with me, boy. And you make sure you stop by to see that fuck of a brother gets home. I don't trust that boy to be out all night again."

"I'll get him to go with me so that he can do a lookout. Then we'll come back together," Kofi lied. He kept a straight face—if there was one skill Kofi could do well, it was lie when needed. And there was a second thing Kofi knew how to do—protect Ramzi.

Eliza continued to regard him with suspicion, ready to argue further, but Cory intervened. "Come on."

Following Cory down the hall, Kofi watched as Cory picked up the new skimmer. He looked around at the various computers Cory had set up in the room. He'd never paid close attention before because it wasn't important to him. But now, he realized Cory was the technical brains of the operation while Eliza was the enforcer who kept the kids in line with her dragon lady threats of the basement cells.

Cory turned to him. "I checked this one myself, so it should be good. Removing the bad one and putting it in might take an extra second. Don't fuck it up."

Kofi extended his palm and was thankful Cory simply dropped the thin skimmer into his hand. He walked out into the hall and, with a quick glance, could tell he was alone. Retrieving a small box from his pocket, he dropped the skimmer inside without smudging any of Cory's fingerprints that would have been left behind. Shoving the box in his coat pocket, he avoided the kitchen and Eliza and slipped out the front door.

Refusing to back out from fear that one of them would come racing after him, he walked casually to the corner of the street and then broke into a jog. With each step he moved away from their house, he breathed a little easier and felt the weight ease from his shoulders.

He glanced across the street and spied the black vehicle carrying Landon and Agent Meckle. Now, to get the job done and finally find freedom for him and Ramzi.

27

"How could you just let him go like that?" Charity asked, her frustration boiling over the calm she normally maintained. She kept her voice low as her eyes darted back and forth to see who else might be around. Ramzi was no longer in the area, having been taken to a classroom to work with one of their instructors. Charity hadn't wanted to take a chance on him becoming caught up in whatever was going on with Kofi and the FBI.

She turned to spear Oliver with her heated glare. Her fury might be unreasonable, but feeling the need to be angry with someone, Oliver happened to be the one standing in front of her.

When the meeting in the conference room had ended—a meeting that she now regretted leaving, she'd offered a searing glare to Agent Meckle, hoping it might incinerate him. But when he'd walked out of the room with a gleam in his eye and a smug expression that she was sure translated into a promotion for him, she knew her ability to turn someone into ashes with a glare was nil.

Next came Landon Sommers, a handsome agent with a kind face that was now twisted into a discomfited expression. He and Oliver had clasped hands to shake and tilted their heads in for a quiet conversation.

Kofi exited the room with Oliver and didn't rush up to her as she'd wished. Instead, he walked over with Oliver and Landon, shaking their hands and now being part of a private triad conversation. Then with only a nod toward her, Kofi left with Agent Meckle and Landon.

And when it was finally just Oliver approaching her with a tight-jawed yet somehow sheepish expression, she unleashed her pent-up fury.

"He's not an adult! It's like sending him back into the lion's den! How do we even know that the Halstons will believe that he is back to do work for them? Is anybody watching him, Oliver? This is ridiculous! How could you have gone along with this?"

Initially on the defensive, Oliver had his hands jammed into his front pockets, but he withdrew them and firmly but gently grasped her by the shoulders. "Charity, sweetheart, I couldn't stop it. The FBI had the right to make the offer, and Kofi had the right to agree or disagree. I did ensure his rights were protected, the choice was his, and that the FBI agreed that neither he nor Ramzi would be arrested or prosecuted for their part of the crimes."

She attempted to jerk away when he stepped closer,

bending slightly to stare into her eyes. "You think this doesn't make me crazy, too?"

She dragged her tongue over her bottom lip, torn between holding on to her anger and realizing it wasn't fair to direct it solely at Oliver. She exhaled a heavy sigh as her shoulders slumped. He gently brought her forward, his arms now sliding around her back, enveloping her.

"I've already talked to Carson, and he's sending Leo and a couple of the others down here. I'm heading out in a few minutes so that I'll be with Landon and Meckle. Once Kofi lets us know which ATM he's hitting, we'll be there. Kofi will meet with Meckle, and he'll get prints off the skimmer. We'll be nearby when Kofi plants the skimmer. Then the FBI will be in charge after that, monitoring what the Halstons do with the information. As soon as they pull money, they'll be arrested. And Kofi and Ramzi will be free. They can testify if it goes to trial, but that's all. With the evidence that Meckle gets, I can guarantee you that the last thing the Halstons will want is for this to go to trial."

She listened to every word he said, even though her lips remained tightly pressed together. "You've got this all figured out, don't you?"

A scoff erupted. "I don't have anything figured out, sweetheart. I just know that I want to protect the boys while allowing them to make good decisions."

With her cheek pressed against his chest, she nodded and felt the air leaving his lungs in a long sigh. Finally leaning her head back, she peered up. "I know you need to leave. I'll take care of Ramzi until you and Kofi come back safely."

He lifted his hand and cupped her cheek, and she pressed against the warmth of his palm. Her eyes were still on him as he bent closer, and his breath whispered over her face.

"I'll be back and plan on spending the night with you."

"If you keep this up, I might get used to spending the night with you." She spoke half in jest but was curious as to what his reaction would be.

His eyes danced between hers, and he smiled. "If that's the threat, I'll take you up on it. And if it's a promise, I'll hold you to it."

With a silent nod, their lips met in a fleeting kiss. As always, the air became electrified between them. She felt his reluctance as he broke away, and he headed out the center's front door with a gentle smile aimed in her direction. She stood for a long moment, a solitary statue in the middle of the lobby with others moving around. Finally, she offered a tremulous smile toward Paula and hurried into her office. For once, she welcomed the mundane tasks that occupied her before checking to see how Ramzi performed on his evaluations.

After staring at the same report and grant proposal for almost an hour, she finally acknowledged her slipping focus. She headed to the multipurpose room, spied the afternoon school bus pulling up, and hurried to the door. She greeted each student before accompanying them inside, giving them her full enthusiasm while her insides were tight with worry.

The teens knew what they needed to do and quickly dispersed. She walked to the classroom but didn't see Ramzi. Poking her head into the next room, she spied the teacher. "Hey, did Ramzi finish his evaluation?"

Betty's smile radiated reassurance. "He's a very bright young man, as I'm sure you know. Once I do a few more evaluations in the next couple of days, we can sit down and talk to him about his options."

"Thanks. He really is special, isn't he?"

Betty laughed and nodded. "As you always say, they all are."

She smiled as the tension eased just a tiny bit. "Do you know if he's back in his room?"

"I'm not sure, but he seemed anxious to find out about his brother. He said when he left here that he was going to find Kofi. I assumed he meant he was heading up to your office."

Charity scrunched her nose and waved goodbye to Betty. She hated that Ramzi was worried, but the only thing that would make him feel better was when Kofi walked back through the door. She had no idea how long it would take for the FBI to have the evidence to arrest the Halstons, but she was determined that the boys would be finished with their risks today.

She walked back through the multipurpose room and started into the boys' dorm area when she ran into Helen. "Have you seen Ramzi?"

"Not since this morning."

She continued and popped her head into the room that he and Kofi shared, but it was empty. Turning, she walked back down the hall, each step becoming a little more determined as a snake of unease began to slither through her gut.

She hurried to the lounge and other rooms but still didn't see him. Now running into her office, she grabbed her laptop and pulled up the camera views Poole and Tricia had shown her how to work. "Dammit!" She continued cursing under her breath as she fiddled with the program, finally figuring out how to back it up and view the digital feed from the outside cameras.

She gasped as she watched Ramzi dart through the front door and quickly looked at the time stamp. Almost twenty minutes had passed, and she wondered if she could catch up to him. Grabbing her purse and shoving her phone into it, she ran through the lobby and out the front door.

Dialing Oliver, she jumped into her car and pulled out of the parking space. "Oliver! Where are you?"

"Across town with Landon, keeping an eye on Kofi. What's wrong?"

"Ramzi's gone. I saw him on the camera leave about twenty minutes ago. I'm heading after him."

"Wait, you don't even know where you're going. We're bringing Kofi back to the center when everything's finished today."

"Ramzi was left out of all of Kofi's plans. I'm afraid Ramzi has gone back to the Halstons. He probably thinks that's where Kofi has gone back to."

"We're near the ATM that Kofi was at... the one that Cory sent him to. He's placed the skimmer in after Meckle got the prints. I'll get to the Halstons as soon as I can, but stay put. Don't do anything until I get there."

"Oliver, there's no way in hell I'm going to wait for you to get Kofi and drive back here in late afternoon traffic. Anything could happen to Ramzi by that time! I'm gonna find him, pick him up, get him back to the center."

"Don't do anything in haste. You don't know what you're walking into!"

"I don't act rashly!" She turned the steering wheel sharply, hoping Oliver didn't hear her tires squealing.

"Oh, like you didn't slam into me while trying to keep me from chasing the boys when we first met them? Or you racing down a dark alley after them?"

"I mean that I'm not *usually* rash!"

She heard him telling someone that he needed to get to the Halston's house and assumed it was Landon. "Oliver! I'm close to where they said the house was. I don't see Ramzi, so I'm going to park down the road and just look. It's not like I'm going into the house! I'm just trying to catch him before he gets there."

Suddenly, she spied a young teenager in a dark blue hoodie darting around an alley behind some houses. "I see him! I'll get him back to the center with me." She dropped her phone into her purse. Parking next to the curb, she hopped out of her car, pulling her purse crossways over her shoulders as she darted after him. Racing into the alley that ran behind the row of houses, she maneuvered between the trash cans. "Ramzi!"

He didn't hear her, and by the time she made it to the back fence, he'd disappeared into the back door, the screen just closing behind him. "Dammit," she muttered. The house was two stories, and she remembered what Kofi said about the basement. She looked around, wondering what to do, when she heard a woman talking in a loud voice. Sneaking through the backyard, she stayed near the fence edge, partially hidden by overgrown hedges, and stood below a window close to the door Ramzi disappeared through.

"You and your fuckin' brother—more trouble than you're worth!"

The hoarse voice growled, causing Charity's heart to beat faster while she worked to keep her breathing steady.

"I told you, I was just out last night. Me and Kofi—"

"What about you and Kofi? Huh? Tell me where you were, boy, because I'll bet your stories won't match."

Charity's eyes widened in fear. Kofi had been here and talked to the Halstons. She couldn't see Ramzi but could imagine the fear racing through him. There was no way Ramzi would know what Kofi had told her. A flash of anger bolted through her at how Agent Meckle wanted Kofi to hustle to do one more job and never thought about Ramzi back at the center.

Her hands shook so badly that she could barely pull her phone from her purse. Firing off a text to Oliver, she hit send. **At Halstons. Danger. Hurry.**

Her heart pounded even harder, and she placed her hand flat against the bricks, both to hold her up and a desire to connect with him. With danger for Ramzi filling her mind, she eavesdropped on the conversation, thankful it was taking place in the kitchen and terrified that Oliver wouldn't arrive in time.

28

Ramzi had walked into the kitchen, willing to be around the Halstons for a little bit longer if it meant he would be with Kofi. But now, he wasn't sure Kofi was there. Eliza's talons clutched his arm, her cigarette still in her fingers close to his skin.

"What about you and Kofi? Huh? Tell me where you were, boy, because I'll bet your stories won't match."

He wished he'd first checked to be sure Kofi was here before coming inside. There was silence for a moment, followed by a horrid cackle.

Eliza nodded slowly. "You didn't know that, did you? He was here. Told me about last night."

"He's still here?"

"Boy, how stupid do you think I am? I knew that fuck was lying when he stood right where you are." A hacking cough erupted, and then the woman continued. "So you tell me where you were and what you were doing. I want to hear your story without big brother to lie for you."

He wanted to tell her to piss off, but a smart-ass comment would simply get the back of her hand across his face. And considering the ring she wore, he'd rather not get her angrier. Trying to think of the best lie he could offer, his mind blanked, and he stammered, "I... we..."

"That's what I thought," Eliza sneered.

Suddenly, Cory's booming voice entered the conversation. "What the fuck is going on here?"

"I'm talking to you, boy," she growled, shaking Ramzi. "What the fuck were you doing last night? Where were you and Kofi?"

When Cory stepped into the room, Ramzi hated having to lean his head back to look up at the man. All he could think of was that if he was a few years older, a few pounds heavier, and a few inches taller, he could take the man. He swallowed, knowing Kofi would play it smart and play it cool.

He looked Cory in the eye and then turned his gaze to Eliza. "We were just hanging out, that's all."

"I think Kofi was lying to us about where he and Ramzi were last night," Eliza said, glancing over at Cory. "If you ask me, they were up to no good."

"Is that right?" Cory growled. "Well, you don't worry about Kofi. I have him right where I want him, doing just what I need him to do—"

"Where is he? What have you done with him?" Ramzi asked, desperation filling his voice.

"Deal with this little shit!" she ordered, as her glare moved from Ramzi to Cory. "You don't got no control of Kofi unless you take care of this one here! Hell, you ain't got no control of either of them."

"No, I'll—" Ramzi began.

"Don't think for one second that I'm fooled!" Eliza said, her focus back on him. "It's gonna take Kofi a long time to work you out of the basement cell. Finally, that might teach you not to be such an idiot!"

Cory stepped closer to Ramzi. "What's going on? I thought you were with your brother."

"Why would you think that?" Eliza asked.

"Because that's what Kofi said when I sent him out on the job."

"Then you're just as dumb as them if you believe a word that comes out of his mouth," she sneered.

"Shut up, woman," Cory groused and shook a beefy fist at her.

"Did Kofi get the job done?" Eliza asked.

Cory's demeanor changed instantly. "You bet! I could tell when he popped that new skimmer in. I've been downloading money for the past ten minutes and have a program set up to keep it going."

"Well, at least one of these boys has a brain. This one is a dumb shit."

Cory looked at Ramzi, his gaze assessing as he rubbed his chin. "What have you been doing? You run away from Kofi?"

Ramzi stared, no longer knowing what to say. He was scared, but at least he knew Kofi was safely away from the house.

"I asked you a question," Cory barked again, taking a menacing step forward. "Why aren't you with Kofi?"

"He said he didn't need me," Ramzi replied.

"Then one of you is lying. Kofi said you were with him, and you said he didn't need you. Which one should I believe? The one who's actually doing a fucking good job for me or the little prick standing in front of me?"

"I'll tell you where he was," Eliza interjected. "I think they were off selling drugs somewhere." She tried to laugh, but it came out as a cough as she took another drag of her cigarette. "They act like they don't get enough from us."

"I'll get him downstairs, but when Kofi comes in, you keep your mouth shut, woman!" Cory ordered. "I'm already getting money out of the last skimmer that got placed. And I can see where Kofi just made his hit. I'll deal with both of them when he gets back here."

"Let's go." Cory grabbed Ramzi's arm in a vise grip and started to pull him toward the basement door.

"No!" he screamed, digging his heels in but simply slid on the floor.

"You fight me, boy, and I'll make you wish you'd never lived. Then I'll do the same to that lying fuck of a brother of yours when he gets back."

Ramzi cried out in pain, but as soon as Cory threatened Kofi, Ramzi began to scream loudly, hoping someone might hear.

"I'll break your other goddamn arm if you don't shut up!" Cory roared.

This time, Eliza grabbed Ramzi from the other side, the burning cigarette clutched in her fingers, touching his arm. He yelled out in pain and tried to get out of their grip, but Cory just held on tighter as he dragged Ramzi to the top of the basement stairs.

29

Ramzi's anguished cry echoed through the air, catapulting Charity into action. Instinct had her gaze darting around, searching for anything to use as a weapon, but she saw nothing. If the Halstons had hit Ramzi, there was no time to lose and waiting for Oliver wasn't possible. She raced to the back screen door, her fingers gripping the handle with a mixture of fear and determination. A sigh of relief escaped her lips as the handle turned, and she pulled the door open.

Rushing into a cluttered kitchen, she zeroed her attention in on a large man and a thin woman grappling with Ramzi between them as they moved toward an open door on the other side of the room.

Her world was painted crimson as rage surged through her. Shoving a chair to the side, she propelled herself forward and then jumped, landing on the closest person to her, regardless of it being a man much larger than she. With a banshee cry at the top of her lungs, she screamed, "No!"

"What the fuck?" he roared, releasing Ramzi while struggling to turn to see who was on him.

Charity clung tenaciously, her arms locked around his neck and her nails clawing at his face. Her relentless scream continued, filling the room. "No! Leave him alone!" Never having been in a physical fight, she was unprepared for him to whirl and slam her back forcefully against the wall. The impact stole the air from her lungs. Grunting in pain, she dug her nails even deeper into his neck and face.

"You bitch!" Eliza yelled, letting go of Ramzi's arm and turning toward the intruder. Before she could make a move, she stumbled over the chair that had overturned, and Charity glanced to see Ramzi had pushed Eliza down onto the floor.

Cory stepped forward and then repeated the action of slamming her back into the wall, this time with such force that her head also hit the solid surface. She grunted as the pain slammed into her ribs and her head at the same time. Her grip loosened, allowing him to break free from her grasp and whirl around, his rage brightly burning in his eyes.

"Who the fuck are you?" he demanded, wiping the blood from his cheek as he stared down at her.

Charity looked up at him, fear now gripping her body. Her legs trembled with the pain in her ribs, and spots appeared before her eyes. His arm cocked back, and she pushed off from the wall, but her legs gave way.

In a swift and unexpected move, Ramzi grabbed the wooden kitchen chair next to him and swung it with force, hitting Cory in the back of the head. Cory's mouth dropped open as his body crumpled to the floor. Ramzi held part of the broken chair, daring Cory to rise. "Come on, you fucker!" he roared, his expression contorted with rage.

"What the fuck are you doing, boy?" Eliza screamed, jumping up from where she'd been pushed to the floor. Her gaze was pinned on Cory before shifting back to Ramzi. Eliza's face twisted into a grimace as ugly as her soul. "You fucking shit!" With her hands raised and her long fingernails extended like talons, she stepped toward him.

Ramzi raised the chair again, daring her to come close, but Charity scrambled forward, forcing her legs to move despite their shaking. She managed to tackle Eliza to the floor. "You stay away from him!" Charity cried out, pressing down on the woman still trying to claw whoever she could reach. Shifting to kneel on Eliza's back, Charity pressed her hands down on Eliza's arms to keep her from using her long nails to cause damage.

The rapidly approaching footsteps sent her gaze beyond Ramzi. Several of the kids from upstairs rushed down the hall and stood looking at the entrance to the kitchen, wide-eyed at the chaotic scene.

"Stay back!" Ramzi yelled in a surprisingly authoritative tone. "I'm warning you, stay where you are!" He climbed over the chair in the way and leaned down to Charity. "Are you okay?"

Before she could answer, Cory groaned and pushed up from his prone position on the floor. He reached out and grabbed Ramzi's leg. As the young man tried to kick out, Cory stood, now grabbing Ramzi's arms.

"Get off her, you bitch," Cory growled, his face twisted with anger, dragging Ramzi to the open door in the hall. Before she could move, he turned and shoved Ramzi through the doorway before charging toward her. She heard the sickening sound of his body thumping down the stairs.

"No!" she screamed, scrambling to get off Eliza.

Her movements were halted by the noise of the front door being kicked open with shouts of "police." Cory darted through the basement doorway, slamming the door behind him. The kids in the front hall screamed, some dropping to the floor while others plastered their backs against the wall. Orders were shouted as police officers rushed in, their guns raised. The back door flew open, and Oliver and Landon rushed through.

"Oliver!" Charity cried, her voice joining the cacophony. She watched as Oliver's gaze found hers amid the chaos. He rushed over and lifted her off Eliza's back, swinging her to safety.

Eliza leaped up, her claws out again, but Landon quickly subdued her. She continued to spew threats as he cuffed her and shoved her toward one of the police officers.

"Ramzi! We have to get to Ramzi!" she cried. "Cory threw him into the basement!"

It was impossible to hear anything from the basement with the noise around them, but she flew out of Oliver's arms and rushed to the door. Grateful the knob turned, she threw open the door. At the bottom of the stairs, Cory stood with his arm wrapped around Ramzi's chest.

"No!" she cried, starting down the stairs. Oliver stopped her, pulling her back as he peered downward.

"I'll snap his neck," Cory growled, his voice shaking.

"Oh God, Oliver," she whispered as he released his hold on her.

"Stay here, babe," he whispered in return. "Do not go down there."

He slipped away, and she heard the back screen door open again. But she didn't watch Oliver leave... she wasn't about to take her eyes off Ramzi as he stared up at her. His face held fear as well as anger, much the same as hers.

Only a few minutes had passed, but they felt like hours. Suddenly, a loud shot was heard, and she watched as Cory's body jerked, his grip slipping from Ramzi, who fell forward as Cory slumped against the wall, blood covering his shoulder.

No longer heeding Oliver's words, she raced down the wooden steps, dropping to the dirt floor next to Ramzi. She glanced over to ensure that Cory was incapacitated, satisfied when he cried out as blood oozed through his fingers where he held his shoulder.

Oliver threw open the outer cellar door and bolted down the steps while several police officers followed her downstairs. She looked over to see a small window at the upper wall of the basement, near the outer steps. The window was opened slightly, and realization dawned that Oliver had shot Cory through the small opening.

Her attention swung back to Ramzi as he called out, "This is Cory Halston." One of the police officers knelt over Cory as he cuffed his hands behind his back.

Oliver reached her and Ramzi, wrapping his arms around both of them. "Are you hurt?"

Charity shook her head. "Not me, but Ramzi—"

"Help! Help!" The voice came from behind a wooden door on the other side of the basement.

"Shit!" Ramzi cursed as he leaped to his feet, wincing at the pain. "Someone is in the cell!" When he ran to the cell door, he looked over his shoulder at Oliver. "Cory has the key!"

Oliver obtained the key from the police officer searching Cory and stalked over to the door, quickly unlocking it. Throwing it open, he stepped in and then called out, "Charity!"

She raced to him with Ramzi next to her and spied a thin teenage girl with tears streaming down her face. Horrified, she reached out to the girl, hating when she flinched.

"It's okay, Marcie," Ramzi assured, reaching out to take the girl's hand. He led her out, where she allowed Charity to wrap her arms around her.

Leo came down the outer cellar steps, and Charity watched as his gaze darted around the room. "Need another ambulance?" he asked, gaining Oliver's attention.

Oliver looked at her, and she nodded. He came over

and said, "Come on, sweetheart. Let's get everyone upstairs."

The kitchen was filled with police, paramedics, a few kids, and a still screaming Eliza being held by Landon.

Agent Meckle walked in, FBI printed boldly on his jacket. He looked around and began barking orders, and Charity couldn't help but wonder why he hadn't been the first to rush into danger.

"Ramzi!" another voice yelled from the back door. Charity looked over in time to see Kofi standing in the doorway.

Kofi made his way through the crowd of people crammed into the small kitchen over to Ramzi, who flung himself into his brother's arms.

"Are you okay?" Kofi demanded, his voice trembling with emotion.

"Yeah, just bruised, I think."

"What the fuck were you doing here?" Kofi continued.

"I thought you were here, Kofi. I thought you'd come back, and maybe they would put you in the basement. I had to see you and make sure you were okay."

"But why, man?" Kofi pushed, anguish lining his expression.

"You've always been there for me. You've always taken care of me. Always." He ignored a tear that rolled down his cheek. "You would help me be good so that Mom would be happy, and her boyfriend of the month might think we were worth having around and want to be a daddy to us. You made sure I had something to eat. Made sure I took a bath and got my homework done. At school, you made sure no one picked on me." More tears fell, and he swiped at his eyes with the sleeve of his hoodie.

Charity's heart ached, and she felt tears well in her eyes as she listened and watched the emotions play across the two brothers' faces.

But Ramzi wasn't finished. "It was never enough for Mom. She kept dating losers, and eventually, we realized that none of them wanted to be saddled with two boys. Some weren't so bad, but some of them... well, you protected me then."

He turned his anguished eyes toward the others in the room before settling on Charity. "I hated to realize Kofi walked out of the center today, knowing he was coming back into this. I know the FBI said they'd keep him safe, but don't you see? Kofi has always been there for me. I need to be there for him. He's my brother. Then I saw you, Ms. Charity, and I couldn't let them hurt you either."

Kofi shushed him but held him tight. A rush of emotions crashed through Charity as she watched Ramzi cling to his brother. The adrenaline pumped through her blood as she gave in to relief and gratitude.

Oliver cupped her face, dragging her attention to him as his gaze roamed over her.

"I'm fine, I'm fine," she assured, seeing fear in the depths of his eyes. "Really, I am." She erased the distance and kissed him, giving him her entire soul in the touch of their lips. Finally, separating, she spied the relief in his eyes now, and she smiled.

Turning her smile toward the brothers, she said,

"Thank you, Ramzi. Thank you." She then swung her gaze over to the other kids, who were still wide-eyed and stunned as they stood in a group, surrounded by the police officers. She stepped out of Oliver's arms and summoned her strength even as her legs still shook. "We need to call social services."

Agent Meckled intervened. "I want statements from all of them. We'll take them into custody and—"

Charity shook her head. "You'll do no such thing. At least not until social services have been called, their identities and ages have been determined, and they have legal representation." She walked over to the other kids and said, "My name is Charity. I'm going to make sure that your rights are protected as the police take a look to see what has been going on here. I promise that nobody's going to haul you off to jail or do anything to you."

The police escorted Eliza in handcuffs under the direction of Agent Meckle as a handcuffed Cory was taken to the hospital. Another policeman called for forensics to come in. Another officer was shown the room where Cory kept his computer equipment. Another one went upstairs with one of the other boys to see the rooms where the kids were kept. Slowly, the kitchen became less crowded.

Oliver walked over, clapped Kofi on the shoulder, then grabbed Ramzi by the back of the neck and pulled him in for a hug.

"We'll talk later, but know this..." Oliver said, bending to hold Ramzi's gaze. "You just proved to be the kind of man you're going to be. I'm fucking proud of you."

Ramzi blinked back tears and nodded. His lips curved slightly.

Landon walked over to Oliver once he'd arrived back at Charity's side.

"Boys? Let's get out of here. We can get your statements where you feel safe."

Kofi nodded and grinned. Ramzi sucked in a deep breath and looked at Charity, Oliver, and then Agent Sommers. "I want to go back to Bright Futures. Please, take us home."

30

Oliver stood outside the dorm door as Charity said good night to Ramzi and Kofi. The day had been exhausting, and he wanted to get her tucked in as much as she wanted to ensure the boys were all right. Oliver had seen the way Ramzi and Kofi handled themselves as they gave their statements to Agent Meckle and the police. He'd also witnessed how they'd been attentive to the needs of the other kids taken from the Halstons' house before social services assumed responsibility for those who were underage. He'd already let both boys know how proud he was of them.

He and Leo had reported back to Carson, and he was glad to let the Keepers know that the boys and Charity were fine other than some bruises. He was shocked when Ramzi told him that Charity had leaped on Cory's back and clawed him. In truth, the emotion he felt then was a whirl of pride, fear, and the need to wrap her up and keep her safe.

As Charity joined him in the hall, George patted her arm. "Helen and I will keep a close eye on them, but I think they'll sleep just fine. Now, you go do the same."

Nodding, Oliver led her through the center and up to her apartment.

"I'm not sure I can sleep," she moaned as he nudged her into the shower.

"Then I'll just have to make sure you do," he promised, gaining a smile from her as he stepped into the small shower with her.

As he washed her off, he clocked every bruise, wishing he could shoot Cory all over again. Holding in his anger, he focused on lathering her body and hair. Once rinsed off, she was yawning. They lay together, and he pulled the covers over them.

She rolled toward him, her eyes barely open. "I really want you to make sure I sleep well."

"Babe, you're exhausted—"

"Not too exhausted," she protested.

Holding her gaze in the moonlight, he grinned. "Well, okay. Looks like I have a job to do." He rolled over, settling his hips between her open thighs. Kissing her deeply, he shifted upward, his body reacting to hers. They moved as one until they came simultaneously, their bodies and minds in sync. And it felt like he'd found home.

Three Months Later

Oliver carried the last box from the U-Haul into the house, setting it down in the living room. At least it will be a living room once all the boxes are unpacked so that he can actually sit on the furniture. Looking around, he grinned. *Oh, yeah... sit on the furniture... feet on the coffee table... eyes on the TV.* He heard Charity's and Natalie's laughter coming from the kitchen and shook his head as his grin widened. *Sit on the furniture with Charity... her head on my shoulder and her feet resting over my legs propped on the coffee table. The TV on but our eyes on each other.* He liked that image much better.

Leo walked back into the house and clapped Oliver on the shoulder. "Did you hear about Landon?"

Oliver shook his head.

"He told Carson he's taking time off from the FBI."

Tilting his head to the side, Oliver asked, "What's he going to do?"

"Carson told him to take a vacation. Get away. Spend some time out in nature and get his career re-centered. Someplace like Montana."

Oliver stared at his brother, knowing more was being said than the actual words. And he figured he would find out when the time was right. "Well then, I hope he finds what he needs to."

Leo nodded and looked out at the now empty trailer in the driveway. "Don't worry about this. I'll take care of it."

"You don't have to take it back to the rental place," Oliver protested.

"No worries," Leo said, then grinned. "Plus, I'll use it as a chance to go to that dumpling restaurant that Natalie loves, so I get brownie points for taking her there."

Laughing, Oliver asked, "Is that her new craving?"

"Bro, I can't keep up with her cravings!"

"I heard that!" Natalie called from the kitchen.

The two brothers lifted their eyebrows as they glanced at each other. The expression mimicked the same one they'd often shared as kids when their mom called from the kitchen, having overheard their conversations.

"Come on, babe," Leo called out. "We gotta take the trailer back and get you some dumplings!"

Oliver smiled as his sister-in-law entered the living room, her arm looped through Charity's. He couldn't deny that Natalie glowed, something he teased her about. But right now, in truth, Charity held his gaze captive by walking toward him through *their* house.

She slipped underneath his arm and smiled up at him. "Why do you have such a smile on your face?"

"What's not to smile about? Bought a house. Moved in. Ready for all the good things in life to keep happening."

"That's a really good answer." She laughed.

He bent to kiss her smiling lips before they walked Leo and Natalie outside. After hugs and goodbyes that seemed almost overkill, considering they would see each other often, they waved as Leo and Natalie drove down the street.

Standing on the front porch with Charity still

tucked underneath his arm, he glanced around the older neighborhood. A neighborhood that was familiar to him.

Three months ago, when Charity was safe in his arms after he'd heard her screams as he raced toward the Halstons' house, he vowed not to waste another moment. Some people would call it hasty. But he knew what he felt. Home, to him, was going to be wherever Charity was. When he asked if she would consider moving in together, she simply smiled and replied, "I want home to be with you."

As they looked for a house to buy, he spent almost every night at her apartment, occasionally crashing at Leo's. They had get-togethers with his parents, who adored her, parties with the Keepers, and lots of times just cuddled up in her little living room. He'd spent weekends at the center, getting closer to Ramzi and Kofi, and getting to know some other youth staying there.

One evening, when he and Charity sat in Leo's backyard, Natalie looked over and said, "In case you're interested, I have a real estate lead for you."

He'd bemoaned not being able to find exactly what they were looking for, so he was willing to take any lead his sister-in-law thought was good.

Three months later, he and Charity stood on the front porch of the house they bought. A modest two-story brick colonial with a white picket fence.

As he looked across the street and down three houses, Leo and Natalie's house stood, ready to welcome their baby. He couldn't think of a better home or neighborhood for him and Charity to live in, one day raise kids in, and he hoped, to grow old in.

While Charity now had to drive thirty minutes to work instead of just walking down the steps, she found a young couple, both social workers, who were thrilled to take over her apartment at the center. She now used her commute to listen to audiobooks and sip her coffee out of a new collection of travel mugs with ridiculous sayings.

Months ago, when he left the Army, if someone had asked him to describe home, he would've snorted, rolled his eyes, and given a lame description. But now, as he walked inside with Charity under his arm, Blessings words still remained in his mind.

"...good food and warmth, the touch of a friendly hand, and a talk beside the fire. It is the time for home."

Three Years Later

Oliver parked outside Bright Future's Home, barely having time to appreciate the changes. Charity was able to increase the number of youth she could assist when the city donated the neighboring building. Bright Futures now included medical services and drug counseling.

The front door opened, and he watched as his wife pushed through the doors, her beautiful face made even more beautiful by the wide smile on her lips as her gaze met his.

They'd married two years ago in a small ceremony. Since his mom had been thrilled to plan Leo and Natalie's wedding, she was also excited to step in to assist in planning for his wedding. He and Charity had exchanged vows in a simple ceremony at the base of the lighthouse, with the sun setting over the water crashing against the rocks below.

Now, he hopped out and hurried around the front of his SUV to open her door. She immediately moved into his arms, and he bent to kiss her before assisting her into the passenger seat. He chuckled as her body vibrated and knew it was with excitement for where they were having their anniversary dinner.

It didn't take long to drive to their destination. Parking, he helped her out of their SUV and walked her up the steps. Standing outside the door, he lifted his hand to knock, but the door swung open almost instantly. The scent of roasted meat and homemade bread wafted past, tickling his senses and causing Charity's stomach to growl.

Laughing, he glanced down and squeezed her shoulders. "Skipped lunch?"

She crinkled her nose as she nodded, and then, as the door opened, she hurried inside the apartment. Oliver grinned as she threw her arms around the much larger man, offering a heartfelt hug.

"Kofi!" she cried. Then seeing the other young man move out of the kitchen, she hurried to him. "Ramzi!"

Oliver stepped in, following with heartfelt handshakes. Kofi was still wearing his uniform, Burrows Electrical emblazoned over the chest pocket. "I just got home, but Ramzi has everything under control. Give me a couple of minutes, and I'll be right back. Make yourself at home." With a nod, he turned and headed toward the back of the apartment.

Turning back to Ramzi, Charity looped her arm through his, and they walked into the kitchen together.

Oliver took a moment to look around the apartment. It was small but had two bedrooms, and the rent was affordable, even being in a decent part of town. That was the one thing Oliver had insisted on when he helped the two find a place to live. The last thing he wanted was for them to be taken advantage of again. But he should've known both boys had their heads on straight when it came to what they wanted for their future.

Kofi and Ramzi stayed at the center until Kofi completed his GED, then completed his electricity certification and interned with Tricia. She hired him immediately, and he continued his electrical studies while earning money.

As soon as he'd obtained his GED, Kofi had lived in an efficiency apartment near the center, and Ramzi had moved in with him. Charity had fears for them, but both boys had said they didn't want to take up a spot at the center that someone else could use. With close supervision, they made it work.

Having moved into the larger apartment a few months ago, Ramzi was almost ready to graduate from high school, including the culinary arts certification he'd received at vocational classes. He worked part-time in a restaurant and was planning on attending a culinary school after graduation.

As Oliver's gaze shifted around the room, he noted there weren't a lot of decorations in the apartment, but on the wall close to their television was a framed photo—a beautiful picture of him and Charity, flanked by Kofi and Ramzi with the sunset in the background. The boys had been thrilled to be invited to their wedding, and Charity had insisted on the photographer taking their picture.

Deciding to follow his nose, he walked over to the kitchen counter to see Charity bending over one of the pots on the stove, tasting Ramzi's sauce. The young chef's face was bright, and she had a wide smile as she declared it the best she had ever had. Hearing footsteps behind him, he turned as Kofi, freshly showered and wearing jeans and a T-shirt, walked up behind him. A satisfied smile settled on his lips as Kofi gazed at Charity and Ramzi.

"Life treating you good?" Oliver asked.

"Couldn't be better," he said. "I have my brother, we've got a place to live, I have a girl I'm asking out for the weekend, and I have the best friends a man could ever want in you and Charity."

Soon, the four of them were seated at the table, sharing a meal, stories, and laughter. Once again, he found himself at home. It wasn't just where he and Charity lived—it was in his friends' houses, with his parents, at the center, and even with coworkers in the compound under the lighthouse.

As he lay in bed that night, his mind was filled with the blessings he'd been given.

"Hey, you okay?" Charity whispered, drawing his attention back to the biggest blessing he'd received.

He grinned as he rolled closer and kissed her, finding home was even in her lips. "Oh, yeah. Life with you, good friends, and great jobs… damn near perfect."

"Hmm," she murmured against his lips. "Just near perfect? I'll bet I can make it more perfect."

Waggling his eyebrows, he pulled her closer. "Yeah?"

"Oh, yeah. In about eight months."

He blinked, staring down at her smile that had grown wider. Suddenly, understanding hit him. "Shit." He rolled off her quickly. "You're pregnant? Really?"

She laughed and pulled him back to her. "Don't worry. You can't squish the little bean just yet."

As their lips melded in celebration, he knew that home would now include wherever their family was together.

Lots to check out!
The next books in the Long Road Home Series 4
Home Team Advantage by Abbie Zanders
Home Town by Cat Johnson
Dreaming of Home by Caitlyn O'Leary
Finally Home by Kris Michaels

Lighthouse Security Investigations Series
By Maryann Jordan
All in KU

Lighthouse Security Investigations West Coast Series
By Maryann Jordan
All in KU
(Oliver joined this security group!)

Are you ready to start the Lighthouse Security Investigations Montana series?
Click here for Logan

ALSO BY MARYANN JORDAN

Don't miss other Maryann Jordan books!

Baytown Boys (small town, military romantic suspense)

Coming Home

Just One More Chance

Clues of the Heart

Finding Peace

Picking Up the Pieces

Sunset Flames

Waiting for Sunrise

Hear My Heart

Guarding Your Heart

Sweet Rose

Our Time

Count On Me

Shielding You

To Love Someone

Sea Glass Hearts

Protecting Her Heart

Sunset Kiss

Baytown Heroes - A Baytown Boys subseries

A Hero's Chance

Finding a Hero

A Hero for Her

Needing A Hero

Hopeful Hero

Always a Hero

For all of Miss Ethel's boys:

Heroes at Heart (Military Romance)

Zander

Rafe

Cael

Jaxon

Jayden

Asher

Zeke

Cas

Lighthouse Security Investigations

Mace

Rank

Walker

Drew

Blake

Tate

Levi

Clay

Cobb

Bray

Josh

Knox

Lighthouse Security Investigations West Coast

Carson

Leo

Rick

Hop

Dolby

Bennett

Poole

Adam

Jeb

Chris's story: Home Port (an LSI West Coast crossover novel)

Ian's story: Thinking of Home (LSIWC crossover novel)

Oliver's story: Time for Home (LSIWC crossover novel)

Hope City (romantic suspense series co-developed with Kris Michaels

Brock book 1

Sean book 2

Carter book 3

Brody book 4

Kyle book 5

Ryker book 6

Rory book 7

Killian book 8

Torin book 9

Blayze book 10

Griffin book 11

Saints Protection & Investigations

(an elite group, assigned to the cases no one else wants…or can solve)

Serial Love

Healing Love

Revealing Love

Seeing Love

Honor Love

Sacrifice Love

Protecting Love

Remember Love

Discover Love

Surviving Love

Celebrating Love

Searching Love

Follow the exciting spin-off series:

Alvarez Security (military romantic suspense)

Gabe

Tony

Vinny

Jobe

SEALs

SEAL Together (Silver SEAL)

Undercover Groom (Hot SEAL)

Also for a Hope City Crossover Novel / Hot SEAL…

A Forever Dad

Long Road Home
Military Romantic Suspense

Home to Stay (a Lighthouse Security Investigation crossover novel)

Home Port (an LSI West Coast crossover novel)

Thinking of Home (LSIWC crossover novel)

Time for Home (LSIWC crossover novel)

Letters From Home (military romance)

Class of Love

Freedom of Love

Bond of Love

The Love's Series (detectives)

Love's Taming

Love's Tempting

Love's Trusting

The Fairfield Series (small town detectives)

Emma's Home

Laurie's Time

Carol's Image

Fireworks Over Fairfield

Please take the time to leave a review of this book. Feel free to contact me, especially if you enjoyed my book. I love to hear from readers!

Facebook

Email

Website

Made in United States
Troutdale, OR
08/16/2024